BROADWAY CORRIDOR

THE GREAT SOCIAL DIVIDE

Creator: D'Eathe, John, Vancouver, Author.
Text editor: Lane Middleton D'Eathe.
Publication editor: Kevin McDonald.
Title: Broadway Corridor: The Great Social Divide.
ISBN: 978-0-9919930-7-9
Subjects: Novel. Action, intrigue, politics, romance.
Cover Design: Indie Publishing Group Inc.

BROADWAY CORRIDOR

THE GREAT SOCIAL DIVIDE

JOHN D'EATHE

Published by Adagio Media

Meet the Author

John D'Eathe was educated in the United Kingdom in law and urban land economics. After training in the City of London, he set off blithely for an adventurous business life in Colonial Hong Kong and Asia. A decade later he moved to Canada, commencing a long international career in property investment.

He travelled extensively and witnessed the various cultural subtleties of getting things done.

His previous books are: *Tokkie and the Colour of Rugby*, celebrating the end of racism in international rugby; *Laundering the Dragon*, a contemporary novel, dramatising unchecked money crime in Canadian real estate; and *Celebrities Who Have Met Me*, his memoir of the British Empire's final tumultuous years.

He and his wife Lane live a busy life in West Vancouver and enjoy visiting their widely located family and friends.

Contents

Characters

Dr Janet Madison, Maddie (MacDonald)
Assistant Commissioner Ivern Hill (Dunbar/Alma)
Dr James and Fatima Khan, President BC Medical Ass. (Dunbar/
     Alma)
Dr Simeon Chiu, The Dean, UBC Medical School (UBC)
Edwin and Anisha Carter, Corridor All Insurance (South Granville)
Samuel and Zuri Nkosi, PhDs (South Granville)
Carlo Santos, Ricardo, Joey and Juan, thugs (UBC)
Timothy Lam, blogger (UBC)
Inspector Jules McIntosh, RCMP (Oak/VGH)
Hon. Irena Ito, Minister of Health (UBC)
Spike and Laura Winn, Locarno Catering (Jericho)
Hon. Joe Jahani, Premier of BC (Main Street)
Pookie and Sazu, Artificial Intelligence Companions
Staff Sergeant Willan Malik (Oak/VGH)
Commissioner Bertie Bertinson (Jericho)
Chief Commissioner Dodds (Victoria)
Wilhelm da Groot, KC, Prosecutor (Victoria)
Sophie Rodriguez, housekeeper (UBC)
Technical Inspector Sally Barma, RCMP (Ottawa)
Chief George, 'The Chief', Squamish Nation (Jericho)
Phil Dimitri, CA , Santos accountant (UBC)
Alphonse Alphonso, Santos thug (UBC)
Constable Wanda Wells, RCMP (Oak/VGH)

Stations

UBC, Jericho, Dunbar/Alma, MacDonald, Arbutus, South
Granville, Oak/VGH, Broadway

1

Gentrification

Resting for a moment, the statuesque young surgeon turned towards the concealed lens. Her striking topaz blue eyes sparkled alluringly above her surgical mask.

Far away in Medical Police Headquarters, Superintendent Ivern Hill watched the hidden surveillance with unexpected fascination. But she was performing an illegal private operation; he had no choice.

Ivern stared moodily at the screen as he waited for the raid to begin.

How did he get himself into this? A couple of years ago he had been an idealist lawyer, serving the community, but now he was a cop, harassing his own neighbours in the Corridor.

He chuckled to himself at the thought the problems with which he was grappling were caused by right-wing real estate profiteers on the one hand, and egalitarian politicians still outlawing any private medical activity on the left.

Ivern supported the people's government and also recognised the good intention of the restrictive medical system, so with both under pressure, he had willingly left the Court for a senior police position. He was now seeing firsthand just how divided his society had become.

Well into the second half of the century, his native British Columbia was hopelessly politically divided.

The general swing to conservative politics, following the disastrous years of Trump-driven turmoil, had divided and polarised countries and disrupted world trade.

By mid-century, right-wing governments had swept North America. The world's mainstream media had ceased even trying to report unbiased truth, and was all concentrated at extremes, exacerbating the political divide. In British Columbia, the left-leaning parties did still prevail, although barely ruling by coalition.

It had all started earlier in the century when the social division in Canada had appeared. The gap between investor and worker earnings had progressively widened, placing more income in the hands of the moneyed class.

The dramatic breakthrough of artificial general intelligence, despite earlier misgivings, had proven positive to production once it was harnessed by international agreement, but brought further devastation to employment.

Excessive government regulation slowed industrial development, productivity sagged and unemployment increased. The inability of working folk to afford market apartments necessitated the Provincial government providing extensive state housing complexes and the division of society was truly underway.

But peaceful Canada continued its steady growth. Drought, extreme weather and natural calamities had dramatically increased the migration demand upon developed nations. Canada's exclusive immigration formula attracted the wealthy with their dubious billions from around the world.

Must admit, though, Ivern chuckled to himself, however they made their money, it was never rejected or seriously questioned.

His thoughts were interrupted by his own personal AI companion who announced verbally he had reviewed the final plans for the raid.

"Ivern, the team is in place, subject to your instructions. Action is ready, upon your command."

He replied, "OK, thanks," automatically, but knowing he relied too much on his programmed AI pal and other multiple servers these days.

At least he lived well personally and enjoyed all the latest conveniences, although he believed he paid too much tax.

With taxation mainly imposed on the wealthy, tax evasion and money laundering had become widespread.

Everyone knew that those with the money and immigrants understated their income, simply concealing their undisclosed capital in the readily available cyber currencies or hiding it offshore, evading taxes. As a result, government services, particularly medical, were failing to deliver.

Those with restricted income were housed and supported by governments in lower-cost areas, stretching down the valley.

Surrey housed more than half the entire urban population, in barely affordable, rows of concrete towers, while the wealthy reserved the prime, elevated Vancouver peninsula locations for themselves.

Many of the city's five million inhabitants reacted bitterly to the visible income disparity and to the clearly diverse living standards.

Political opinions were therefore understandably widely polarised, producing this unstable coalition government which gave Ivern his orders.

His target today was his own home district, the ultra-wealthy Broadway Corridor. The prime location had developed magnificently into an internationally famous, luxury residential area, following the route of the ultra-modern transportation service generously publicly provided from downtown to the University.

Its spaced high-rise city nodes, exclusively zoned for high-class living, had surpassed New York. Graceful clusters of towers, some exceeding the magic one hundred storeys, offered incredible sea and mountain views.

Hence his problem. Rich people!

There was a flurry of activity on the screen as the alluring surgeon apparently completed her procedure, and with the assistance of her automated surgical assistant, started reviving the patient. She was chatting in a light-hearted matter and was obviously well respected by her colleagues.

A long curl of blond hair had escaped from her surgical cap and was tucked back in with a friendly gesture by her nurse.

He watched with fascination.

"Get ready, Ivern," warned his AI companion.

How had they produced this political muddle, even needing a Medical Police force at all? Nothing exemplified the social divide more than his current problem: illegal medicine.

Earlier in the century, deciding not to rely exclusively on public medicine, some uncooperative provinces had actively encouraged private practice, and its use had expanded across the country.

British Columbia struggled to maintain its people-oriented principles in the face of a dramatically ageing community. It remained the only administration demanding an exclusively public medical service.

But private treatment had expanded in the province, particularly in areas like the wealthy Corridor, provoking too obvious a political problem for the minority government to ignore.

The elite Medical Police had been formed and had finally been ordered to take aggressive physical action to eliminate the private medical menace.

A warning signal gained his full attention.

The patient had been revived and the surgeon called to the anesthetist, in a soft voice, "We're done here, thanks. Over to you."

Ivern was mesmerised by her. But he reluctantly had to act.

"Sergeant Malik. Go!" he ordered curtly, and the door was crashed in by his shouting Medical Police unit.

2

Maddie

They were not expecting resistance, but they were greeted by warning gunfire from crouching, masked security guards and quickly retreated defensively.

Ivern saw the startled surgeon grabbed by her arm and pulled away to a rear entrance.

They all escaped in the confusion leaving the traumatised patient lying suffering alone to face the music.

Ivern was staggered. Never had a medical raid escalated into actual armed violence.

He sighed, and those startling blue eyes flashed in his memory.

***

Her mind was still concentrated on the surgery, and with the shock of the forced entry and totally unexpected gunfire, Maddie could barely remember being dragged out by the burly guard until she was going down the back staircase. She pulled off her surgical hat, mask and gloves and stuffed them in her pocket.

"Where do you live?" he demanded.

"The Trafalgar Heights tower," she blurted.

He held her arm tightly and conducted her swiftly down to a waiting ground transporter which took them at its usual calm programmed pace to her building. The operation had been way out by the University, but he had their emergency arrangements all set up.

"For security, I must accompany you to your door," he ordered, rolling his eyes when she gasped, "Penthouse."

Still with his firm grip on her elbow, she tried to act normally and was deposited safely at her front door. The unmasked thug merely nodded calmly and headed back down the elevator.

It was over.

Maddie, Dr Janet Madison, was still trembling. She hated the Medical Police which were now turning British Colombia into a battleground.

She wondered how they had found the location. Worse, had they identified the medics involved? Everyone could be traced easily by the universal face recognition system, but getting there she had followed the detailed instructions provided to avoid the public surveillance system.

It had never been her intention to practise medicine in an underworld, and she certainly did not condone violence.

Her dad, a wealthy financier, was delighted to put her into Med school after discovering he had a brilliant daughter.

But he had not been able to find a family doctor for a nagging personal problem and had delayed searching for medical attention. He flew to Montreal for a private consultation, too late and died on his plane.

By the middle of the century the flood of new, often well-off immigrants, and the ageing population had swamped the public system. Gradually across the country the provincially controlled medical systems, led by Quebec, swung back into private medicine combining with a public system providing critical care, in the European style.

But in British Columbia the 'progressive' government adamantly refused any private service.

When Maddie finally qualified and chose general surgery, she had decided to help out privately, but now things were getting out of hand.

Trying to relax from the shower, she raised her arms and pressed her still-trembling body defiantly against the picture window, as if for the first time personally claiming the endless sweeping freedom of the seas and mountains.

Trying to control her tremor, she stared tensely into the magnificent sunset over Vancouver Island, the lair of the feared Medical Police, imagining herself locked away by them in a dark, damp dungeon.

***

Maddie could just have easily spent her life simply as a pampered rich girl. Her earliest memories were being bathed by her personal nanny and after she had survived the trauma in her early teens of her mother's unexpected death in a skiing collision at Whistler, she could just have succumbed to spoiling by her financier father.

It was a private school with its 150 years of tradition that saved her. The ancient girls academy taught self-reliance and discipline. Caring teachers replaced her missing mother and especially during her father's constant business trips she grew independent. With self-confidence came a desire to learn, producing outstanding scholastic results.

She was already in Med school when her dad had died but mature enough to deal with the loss and move on. He had spent hours tutoring her in investment and financing, leaving her totally capable of managing her own considerable inherited wealth.

She had no financial reason to do illegal surgery but did it because people needed help. This time had she been identified? And some fool had fired a gun!

As she collapsed into bed, she of course consulted her AI companion a final time.

"Any signs of interest in our activities?" she worried.

"No, nothing going on, Maddie. You seem very anxious. Shall I call you if anything unusual happens?"

"No, I'm exhausted. Just let me sleep."

"OK, goodnight!"

She dropped off into a troubled sleep, expecting the Police banging on her apartment door at any moment.

***

But there was no dreaded arrest and as usual, at 6am the day after the incident, Dr Madison checked in for her regular surgical duties at the ageing Vancouver General Hospital.

Parts of the spaced facility had been rebuilt but many of the buildings were more than a century old. They however contained the latest technology, and her AI Surgical Assistant had all her cases for the day analysed, and recommendations in place for her to scan on the transit. Many of her procedures were already set up and would just need supervision.

It was impossible for them to deal with all the medical problems, especially with the new DNA warning science and AI-driven early diagnosis readily available to all doctors.

With warning, people wanted early action, and if it was not readily available in the public medical system, they went to find it somewhere else.

So, in common with many of her fellow surgeons, she put in a gruelling week carrying out her public duties, before helping out with procedures in the private system.

Her involvement had started when a friend, now a rare family doctor, insisted she carry out an absolutely essential gall bladder operation which he was totally unable to schedule quickly in the public system.

He had bribed all the support staff necessary and pleaded that he just needed a supervising surgeon.

"What should I do?" Maddie had asked her ancient friend and College Dean, Simeon Chiu.

"That's easy. Quite apart from all that Hippocratic Oath bullshit," he revealed his stained teeth in a crooked smile, "will you be saving lives? And will you be doing good?" That was what she liked about him; he had always been something of a pragmatist.

Willingly taking that as a positive response and frankly a bit excited at the intrigue, she had sneaked into the doctor's clinic, carried out the operation and realised she had indeed probably saved a life. When her doctor friend slipped her a generous payment she thought, "Why not. All in a good cause," and she was hooked.

The news got around the grapevine that she was available and before she knew it she was receiving a regular additional surgical list from one of the many private clinics which operated behind locked doors.

Family doctors and other disguised private facilities also provided a continuous stream of essential operations and she had become frantically busy.

3

Ivern

The next day, fully briefed on the raid violence by his Sergeant Malik, Ivern was at their Vancouver headquarters stiffly facing his immediate boss, Regional Commissioner Bertinson.

"How could you let this get out of control, Hill? They shot at you, and you let them get away," he shouted.

"With respect, sir," he responded carefully, "we know that the entire Corridor supports the medical insurrection, and the buildings are a connected rabbit warren totally under their control. This was likely just a warning to us but if they take to heavy arms seriously, we have an impossible problem.

"But I guess we could start calling them medical terrorists. And by the way, the illegal patient today was a Catholic priest. I thought you would be amused to know."

They had argued about this policy before. Ivern had joined the Medical Police because he believed in the theory of exclusive universal health care. He did not think, in a democratic society, anyone should have priority over another for urgent medical attention.

Chief Bertie had been transferred to the new Medical force reluctantly and saw no virtue in continuing, what he considered to be, an impractical quest. Bertie, not to his face, of course, fought to control his temper and did not wave Ivern to sit.

"Well, do you have a clever legal answer for this little problem like all your moral excuses? You are in the police force now," he sniggered. "Your job is to catch the criminals who are responsible for breaking the law and charge them. Now! I will accept no more excuses. You are on notice. Medical heads must roll. Dismissed."

***

Contrary to the Chief's snide remarks, Ivern did not come from a privileged background. Far from it.

His forebears had been slaves in the British colony of Barbados, although succeeding generations there had prospered. His father had been fortunate enough to get a scholarship to the University of British Columbia and when he completed an engineering degree, was offered a job, and only later retired back to Barbados.

Ivern was born and raised in Vancouver. His mother, who had stayed in Canada and remarried, was ethnically Korean which accounted for his tall, handsome mixed-race appearance. He was bright at grade school and an outstanding basketball star, which made life easier for him right through UBC Law school.

Articling after graduation in Vancouver, he took a strong interest in criminal law and when called to the bar, joined the prosecutor's office in Vancouver.

His success prosecuting illegal medical activity led him to the attention of the Solicitor General when they formed the Provincial Medical Police Force, and he was recruited on the understanding of likely fast promotion.

At present, he was performing well and appreciating his day-to-day experience as Superintendent in charge of the Vancouver region. That did not prevent his grumpy uncommitted local Commissioner from constantly complaining that he had undeservedly parachuted in.

***

That evening Ivern relaxed in their regular bar, The Oak Tree, near Oak Station on The Corridor.

He was in the usual quiet corner with his operational leader and sidekick, Sergeant Will Malik, having a late beer and reviewing the raid.

Ivern was still fuming at the Chief's snide remark about his law degree. He often found an opportunity to bring it into the conversation especially if something had gone wrong. He was pointing out of course that he himself had worked up through the ranks having started out on the beat. He resented that an upper-income kid could jump in at a management level and act superior.

Nothing could be further from the truth, but that was the way he saw it.

"The Chief was really pissed!" Ivern reported. "We have to find and arrest them, or else! And next time, he ordered, we go in with guns blazing. He is asking the Cabinet for clearance and has already briefed the Premier. He insists this all must be stamped out. Now!"

Will shuffled uneasily on his stool. "We risk killing medics and sick people. And a lot of cops side with them. We will have to watch our backs especially in The Corridor. And organised crime is heavily involved."

They lapsed into silence, staring moodily into their beers.

"We may be safer moving out of The Corridor?" muttered Will, finally. Ivern sunk his beer and rose to leave. "It's been a long day! No. This is our home. Screw 'em," he insisted assertively.

But as he strode away, apparently confidently, the image of the graceful, gowned surgeon and those blue eyes still hovered in his memory.

***

Commissioner Bertinson was catching a quickly summoned dinner at his cliff home overlooking the sea at Jericho, with Dr James Khan president of the BC Medical Association.

"Jimmy, you are representing 30,000 doctors and I have grounds to hold you personally responsible for their despicable behaviour. Now they are getting violent. How did it come to this?"

He fixed him with his beady eyes and waited aggressively for a reply. The top doctor was not the slightest bit intimidated.

"It didn't just happen, as you well know, Bertie," he replied firmly.

"It grew over the years as your progressive governments failed to supply the public system adequate nurses, family doctors, surgeons, clinics and facilities, but of course never a shortage of administrators or highly paid cops!"

"The law is still the law!" Bertie spluttered.

"It's what works that counts. The system goes against the practice in the rest of the world. When the service fell apart and waiting times became impossible, people went abroad, and here black market medicine just had to happen.

"We are going to end up like America, if you have your way!" Bertie grunted.

"America? No, we don't want to model ourselves on them, do we? We need to compare with countries that have the best combined operating medical systems, like Germany, Australia, France or the UK, who have better doctor-to-patient ratios than we have. They have fifteen per cent to a quarter of their doctors taking private work. And most of those serve both systems.

"There is heathy competition, private systems pay their own overheads and they concentrate on elective surgery. Everyone benefits.

"But I still must formally qualify and certify medical workers and keep up our public end, which we do to the best of our ability."

"But," the policeman shouted angrily, "it is up to you to ensure they keep the law. You, not us, have allowed the Corridor Brethren to get involved. Organised crime for God's sake!"

"You are the one charging in with guns drawn and you have the gall to blame me?" objected James defensively.

Controlling his temper and steadying his hand the Chief took his time pouring them another generous glass of Merlot.

"Jimmy, we must work together more, now it has turned violent. You have to be more forthcoming. It is critical that I get the names of all medical personnel involved. Particularly the ringleaders. We have been friends for years, but if I don't get your full cooperation I will absolutely take you in, personally!"

"Do you realise the impossibility of what you are demanding?" Jimmy asked. "Half the entire system is involved some way in paid private work and more importantly some of our best people. If you start throwing multiple charges around there will be medical chaos."

"Then at least I need the ringleaders, now! We must make examples. Unless I have all the key privateers in jail facing charges by the end of the week, I swear that is where you will be personally."

"Overplaying your hand, Bertie," Jimmy responded calmly finishing his drink. "Don't panic. We will find a way out of this."

4

Edwin Carter

Always calm, Edwin Carter had a worried frown as they sipped their early morning penthouse coffee.

The news of the raid and gunfire had of course reached the top level of their consortium within minutes.

Anisha sighed. How often had he lectured her on his business school theories that he called Wholesome Vice?

"Why don't our colleagues recognise the essence of local criminal success is apparent compliance with the public policy system? They have to make it look as if the politicians and police are doing a good job and keep merchant and public support."

Edwin's father's criminal consortium had been built on the premise that did not allow crime to intrude obviously upon day-to-day life.

The Corridor area was free of the homeless or casual street criminals who were all strong-armed out of the area. Petty crime, home raids and shoplifting were discouraged by their local domination.

It maintained public and police condolence by restricting apparent crime, quietly providing generally acceptable drugs and prostitution, but with no under-age or enforced participants.

They provided a clandestine, unified central control, financing the system throughout The Corridor.

This maintained local merchant support, especially as they prohibited any protection levies, but left the criminal partners feeling secure and in charge of their own area.

She nodded.

"The trick to your successful operation is ensuring criminal activity does not intrude into day-to-day life. But Carlo is getting too big for his boots. It is time you reined him in before he ruins everything."

He patted her hand fondly, acknowledging his appreciation of her constant support.

The Corridor itself had become a seething hub of illegal medical practice, but it was of course rampant all over the Province, and especially in rural and remote areas where detection was almost impossible.

It was initiated when genuine medical service suppliers and pharmacists started taking kickbacks for priority attention, and then quietly extended their operations.

As demand increased it was expanded and financed behind legitimate tax-paying businesses, real estate or insurance being the favourites.

Since there was no objection raised to the illegal services in the areas they were offered, notably by those that could pay for them, the local cops did not bother with it.

***

When the Broadway Corridor tunneling had caused so much chaos back in the early twenties no one would have imagined the massive urban complex which would develop along the Line.

Covid and the following Avian Flu scare had finally ended the ancient provision of acres of office space and now high-rise was mixed use, with the majority of business being conducted online.

Corridor All Insurance had to some extent bucked the trend and still maintained floors of showy traditional office space in their head office tower at South Granville where policies could be discussed in actual person.

Edwin Carter, the fifth generation, insisted upon maintaining the tradition as he did in all personal things. Just like his father and grandfather: St George's Boys School, UBC for commerce and Harvard for a Masters.

No one questioned their success in a multitude of businesses throughout British Columbia notably, as financiers, general insurers, real estate agents and mortgagees, and it was common knowledge that their tower was crowned by Vancouver's most expensive, view penthouse, 'The Ultimate'.

Edwin and Anisha were high society, known by everyone and knowing everyone of importance.

Until the 1970s the family were mainly just in regular and legal financial businesses, then it found its way into dubious overseas dealings. As Communist China began to expand internationally and assert its influence on the western world, his grandfather discovered the illegal Vancouver Method and started laundering money.

First, he went into the immigration investment business. Then brought foreign dirty money in for the housing boom, through his connection with the undisciplined law firms and the banks.

By the late 2020s, Edwin's father had it easy during his time in management of the company, as Canada had continued to be soft on drugs and money crime generally, essentially becoming out of control.

No serious government action was ever taken, and now if anything, crime had become even easier, with Edwin just having to keep his head down and quietly manage his privileged inheritance.

Much of his dealing was crooked, but he stayed with financial control, avoiding becoming directly involved in managing the drug dealing, gambling, night clubs and prostitution, as did others.

***

As the illegal private medical demand developed with The Corridor, the Carters began providing an overall administration for the system, based upon their already extensive computer capability, quietly arranging family doctors, specialists, surgeons and pharmacists.

Services could be offered in actual clinics, converted rooms at the back of pharmacies, massage parlors, or appropriately hidden space. They would utilise anywhere a procedure could be carried out undetected and in sterile circumstances, even including large vehicles.

These locally known entrepreneurs were regulated in secret by the Edwin Carter system and managed by his Corridor All Technologies.

They also ran a very lucrative side business advising upon and financing the latest equipment needed by the medical profession which was increasingly reliant upon AI-controlled medical procedures.

They scheduled and billed medical work on demand and contacted the medics through retired Dean Dr Chiu, who provided the appropriate medical specialists and support staff required.

All of those were assured of high security and had been painstakingly listed by Dr Chiu, who believed only in the security of hand-written records. Business arrangements and logistics in the area of each rail station were carried out by the dominant local Brethren group who took care of all physical arrangements.

At heart, however, the Carters were practical businesspeople who abhorred violence and for this reason The Corridor had previously been remarkably free of violent crime.

***

Ivern found the first day back in their Vancouver headquarters after the violent incident a whirlwind of activity, as his Medical Police team analysed their failed raid. They were oblivious of the fine web of Carter intrigue which surrounded them.

Social media and the internet had developed to incredibly technical levels over the preceding half century, allowing communication systems completely inaccessibly to outsiders.

"We know the medical resistance is organised basically in practical cells providing specialised services, but we can't identify them because most doctors use fake identities, logging into their own ultra-private medical network," he advised his team.

"So, unless we catch them red handed, it is impossible to discover who is involved?" Will quipped to groans all around.

"Yes, that's about it," Ivern agreed. "We must somehow cut the heads off these medical serpents."

He was rather pleased with his reference to the ancient Greek medical symbol, but when he got not the slightest reaction from his team he moved on quickly.

"The Chief hinted we already have infiltrated their ranks and he has put us in charge of leading identification of the main bad guys. So we need an immediate briefing from intelligence. Will, please set that up.

"Fortunately, we are reducing raids and will concentrate all our efforts upon identification. Give it some thought, and we will meet again in a couple of days to map out a strategy.

"The Intelligence section however did not come up with very much help.

"It has proved easy to infiltrate obvious clinics, but the medics appear to have a central control which we know moves things constantly. It must contain prominent doctors but while we have strong suspicions as to identity, we have not nailed anyone."

They shrugged hopelessly.

5

Dean Chiu

"Deans like me do not end up wealthy even when they are very educated, handsome fellows," Dean Simeon Chiu chuckled, ordering Maddie a hamburger. "But I think I can manage to buy us a glass of wine, too. What is your pleasure?"

They settled down to enjoy the sweeping view from the pub atop the Corridor's Pinnacle building, which towered above the Arbutus station, and he asked, "When my most beautiful and brightest student calls, I come running. What's up?"

A serious-faced Maddie went straight to the point. "Simeon, I was the surgeon at the gunfire event."

"Oh dear!" he worried. "Did the cops identify you?"

She shook her head. "But I can't keep on with illegal work now those violent things are happening."

He hesitated. Tell her or not? He shrugged. She was already committed now.

"OK. You guessed long ago that I was involved. Look. I had no intention of dragging you into the medical movement when you asked me, but now you are committed. Did the guards who fired the guns know who you are?"

"No, but they took me back to my condo at Trafalgar, so they know where I live, and could find out if they are interested."

"Can't imagine why, though," he reassured her.

They paused as their burgers and a jug of Okanagan Red were dumped on their table but they left them untouched.

The Dean explained. "You have always assumed from my teaching that I am sympathetic to a readily accessible medical system. Indeed I am involved in the resistance. But the police are gearing up against us and you need to drop out for a while. I will see you disappear from the private surgery roster."

"I can't just drop out," she said. "There must be something I can do without being too obvious at the moment."

He poured them some wine and picked at the burger.

"Well, it just occurred to me, being so beautiful and seductive, you could possibly be very helpful infiltrating the cops. They are trying to infiltrate us."

"The campus rumours were that you preferred other options, or I would think you were coming onto me," she laughed, lightening up a bit. He just smiled.

He explained that the Medical Police were trying to identify and detain the leading freedom doctors.

"They could be very dangerous to us and they have given the job to an up-and-coming young Lawyer Superintendent called Ivern Hill. We know little about him but that he is single and goes regularly to the same bars and restaurants in the Corridor. Good looking too; you can find his photo. Try to meet him and see what they are up to."

"That sounds pretty simple," she said chewing thoughtfully on her cold bun. "The transit is buzzing with concern about the medical emergency. I need to help."

"Yes. It is now very political, and we must maintain public pressure for change," he added thoughtfully.

***

The local Medical cops all met at The Oak Tree. It was a large, noisy ground-floor pub with a wide balcony overlooking the congested Broadway. It was also a key station on the system and always busy. Maddie entered the bar tentatively, already alerted that an area of the bar was always reserved by Medical Police.

She recognised Ivern Hill holding court with his colleagues at one end of the bar and decided quickly it would be an impossible place for an approach. The Dean had given her other suggestions of places he frequented and she quietly melted away into the crowd.

She had been told he lived way down the line out by the Dunbar Station, an area not yet fully redeveloped and close to the beaches. He often ate a quick meal fairly late in the evening at the counter of The Ocean, a small but smart rooftop restaurant atop the Dunbar Tower, by the station.

She had spent four spaced late evenings sitting at the counter gazing at the magnificent seascape the penthouse commanded, when he finally turned up. She was confident in her attraction, caught his eye, smiled and he struck up an immediate conversation.

She summed him up quickly. Dark-skinned, brown Asian eyes, very tall, muscular, alert, intelligent and chatty. Only in passing did he mention he worked in the police force. Nothing about being a lawyer.

He saw an extremely shapely, Caucasian woman with a happy, expressive face, a dazzling smile and the most remarkably bright blue eyes. He was staggered. It must be her!

She merely said she was Maddie, but when she added she had a job at The General it was enough to convince him.

He had offered her a glass of wine which she accepted. She had already eaten, so after their friendly chat she just said, "I hope we meet up again," and got up to leave.

She had actually turned away when he stood and rather self-consciously blurted, "I really enjoyed meeting you, Maddie. May I see you here for a proper dinner one evening?"

"Yes, sure," she replied. "I am usually not working on the weekend unless there is an emergency. Saturday looks OK at the moment."

Ivern beamed. "Here at seven?"

They exchanged names and phone numbers, and her connection was made.

***

"Come on guys don't overdo it," said Maddie to the Dean's intelligence person who had just suggested that she be wired for the dinner.

But their young technical advisor said that the equipment now was tiny and all she needed was a small transmitter in her bag. So she went along with it.

***

The next morning she dominated his thoughts. Ivern asked his AI pal to research Maddie, and requisitioned the record of all doctors and surgeons who were suspected of having contravened the medical law or who had been charged or imprisoned. Dr Madison did not feature on any of the police lists, but she was indeed a General Hospital surgeon.

He decided to keep his knowledge to himself but do more research. He found Maddie easily enough as a surgeon in The General records and put her photograph on his cell phone. Now and then he snuck a look. The attraction he felt for her did not override his professional acumen and he viewed her as a valuable asset.

He thought carefully how to lead questions up to her disclosing medical organisers when they met. He decided to wear a recorder so that nothing would be missed, but not yet to transmit to the team.

Ivern had never been one for casual dating and in recent years had concentrated his time upon his degrees and now his police career. Of course, many women had turned up in his life and he was far from inexperienced but wasting time on pleasure jaunts was just not his way of life.

Conversely, Maddie loved nothing better than dressing up and getting out on the town to relax which she desperately needed after her intense bouts of surgery and traumatic experiences.

***

They hardly knew each other, of course, so on their dinner date those first few moments were decidedly awkward as he manoeuvred to hold her chair and seat her.

"Sorry about that," he mumbled, "I am out of practice. I rarely dine other than with men or female cops who would chop off my hand if I tried to hold their chair."

"Actually, I am impressed," she said genuinely. "These older-style courtesies are fading away. I will permit you to hold the door open for me later if you like." They laughed, and now the ice was broken.

"Sorry, I have to be at the hospital at six tomorrow for surgery, so I can't drink and must be off early to bed."

He replied in surprise that it was Saturday evening, surely she had tomorrow off.

"No such luck," she replied. "Surgical emergencies know no time barrier and we are hopelessly short of surgeons and staff."

They were quickly deep in the conversation, discovering all about their backgrounds. How his father had come to take an engineering degree at UBC from sunny Barbados, was offered a job and only much later retired back there. How his ethnically Korean mother now lived, happily remarried, on Vancouver Island.

"I still have family in Barbados; great place to visit. Perhaps I can take you there one day?" he suggested, with a forward grin on his somewhat Bajan face.

It suddenly occurred to her that this was all being recorded by Dr Chiu, and she smiled at the thought some poor soul would have to transcribe all these inanities. She tried to change the subject to his career and policing, but he seemed intent upon personal stuff and she made no headway.

Ivern had completely forgotten about the mission and was totally subsumed into this gorgeous young woman who was both sparklingly intelligent and deeply humorous.

He was enjoying a Burgundy with his steak, when she contrived to raise the question of medicine. It was simple really. "That Burgundy sure looks good. May I have a taste?"

He offered his glass and they laughed at her cautious sip. "Must be a good girl tonight. I have several procedures to pack in tomorrow. The system is overloaded and just does not work."

She discovered he was very sympathetic to the overall medical situation and the shortages, but she was careful not to probe too much.

"You know," he said, "we have a common interest. I work for the Medical Police attempting to stamp out private medicine."

"What do you actually do there, yourself?" she asked carefully. He replied that he was a lawyer specialising as a Superintendent.

"A Superintendent," she enthused, "so young! And a lawyer too. Do you have a whole squad of policemen, detectives and all that stuff under you?"

"Yes, all that," he said more modestly than guardedly, "but we all have a good relationship and work well together. Our problem is our surly old boss who's a real pain in the ass."

She giggled, leading him on usefully to describe the Chief and his defects. He even mentioned some of the police philosophies upon which they disagreed.

He added, "I got involved because I believe in the principle of universal health being readily available to everyone, while Bertie, which is what we call him, just grumpily enforces whatever law is given him to enforce."

She laughed politely and nodded sympathetically.

As their dessert was placed before them, he finally said something encouragingly personal. "So you see why I am so much enjoying an unusual relaxing night out with a beautiful woman."

She had a twinge of conscience but smiled in genuine appreciation and for the first time, just briefly, put her hand softly over his.

***

The Dean called as she was dozing off.

"You do talk a lot. It has taken us all this time to go through that verbiage. But, thank you, at the end there were some very useful revelations.

"There is obviously a lot of dissent with their Commissioner, particularly with respect to returning violence and we are finding this in all government services. Lots of people disagree with the government's general medical policy.

"His boss is a totally committed, extreme diehard. From the sound of his high blood pressure he might solve the problem for us! He seems intent upon retaliation, which is very useful to know.

"See if you can find how he is trying to track us down and whether he is getting Cabinet support for police violence. Good luck, Mata Hari. By the way that is your codename; unique, eh?"

It took her a while to drop off into a strangely troubled sleep.

6

An emerging crisis

Commissioner Bertinson, Ivern's immediate boss, had called a top-level screen conference and they could see from his red mottled face and bulging eyes there was trouble ahead.

"Those fools in Victoria have refused us taking armed action unless we are actually attacked. Idiots! This is heading into a crisis. All we can hope is that the doctors get more aggressive. In the meantime arrest their fucking ringleaders anyway, now, this week!"

And with that he and his small entourage stormed from the screen.

There was silence for a few minutes and then, always joker Will quipped, "Arrest ringleaders who are popular, essential doctors and throw them in the clink, with no evidence?"

"Council of war," Ivern called out summoning his entire team to the lobby.

"You have all heard what the big man said. We have to make a splash, so bring in all your best candidates and let's see some charges laid; today. Go out and get at it!"

Will followed him into his office complaining, "You know these medics have been very cautious and honestly I'm not sure we can make these charges stick."

"The Old Man gave us no choice, get at it," snapped Ivern uncharacteristically to Will's surprise.

"Touchy, touchy," he muttered as he left, wondering what was bugging his boss.

It was not all bad news. They had been able to identify several of the escaped medical workers in the illegal operation from their facials and fingerprint records. For decades all medical records had relied in large part on biometric fingerprinting which now instantly provided all of a patient's personal information.

Ivern decided to keep all that confidential until they were able to act on the entire group, including finding the gun-carrying thugs.

But what of the enigmatic surgeon? He re-ran the spy video of the illegal operation and realised that she had remained in surgical gloves and apparently had not left any personal traces in the room.

However, they now had the anesthetist's prints which were all over his abandoned equipment and several of the nursing staff's.

Was it therefore only a question of time before Maddie was identified? He shrugged. Nothing he can do now to save her other than keep quiet.

"Why am I thinking about saving her?" he wondered. But the idea of getting intelligence from her was making him feel queasy.

He forced his mind back to the crisis in hand.

***

The object of all their anguish, Edwin Carter, had just finished a pleasant gourmet lunch in their Penthouse with Anisha and his senior corporate staff.

From the Broadway-City Hall Station all the way out to University Hill the rail system linked his hidden illegal medical complex, a flexible system of often mobile private clinics offering complete medical services. It was all Edwin Carter's domain.

He did not consider himself really a criminal and came from generations of insurance executives. After all he had a Harvard business degree and was Chair and CEO of Corridor All Insurance!

But he also irregularly called an encrypted meeting of the unofficial Corridor Brethren committee he had set up, bringing together a mixed bag of colleagues that he frankly considered criminals, but who provided varied services and security in their controlled areas.

The Dean had visited him in his impressive tower at South Granville Station, in the early days. Personal contact had then been necessary to discuss provision of medical people but now they all met very securely on screen.

Following the gun-firing incident, an irate Edwin addressed the Brethren.

"What the hell were your guys doing, Carlo, carrying guns? We have all agreed we will avoid violence in providing medical services and this was always one of the medics' conditions."

There were murmurs of agreement around the screen, but Carlo was not the slightest bit defensive. "My guys did not shoot to hurt anyone, and they got everybody away safely. What more do you want? We were doing our job!"

Carlo got support from an expected source, the Dean.

"But look at all the publicity we are getting! This whole medical problem has to be brought to a decision. Both medical systems, legal and illegal, are getting swamped. Something has to be done."

"But not this way," insisted Edwin. "Medical profits account for a large portion of our income now and we must keep things cool. The last thing we want is to provoke aggressive action against the private medical system. No guns or violence!"

There were sounds of approval but just a snort of derision from Carlo.

"Let's hear Pookie's opinion," suggested one of their technically advanced members. They relied upon Pookie, the Brethren's standard AI assistant, for regular comment.

The tinny-voiced avatar answered confidently, as he had been programmed to do, "Come on, guys. You all know I don't have an opinion. I just evaluate facts and report upon the most likely statistical outcome.

"If violence is allowed to escalate, statistically the Feds may invoke the Emergencies Act and deploy the military. The old Act still gives the federal authorities short term ability to …"

"Yes, yes, we got the message, thank you, Pookie," the chairman interrupted politely.

"If this happened often what would be the odds of the Act being invoked?"

"Ninety eight per cent," replied Pookie immediately. "I concur violence should be avoided at all costs to maximise our short-term profits. We need a longer-term general policy but …"

"OK," interrupted Erwin impatiently, taking back control of the screen.

Pookie got the message and reluctantly intoned, "Thank you, Mr Chair." But was he not programmed to provide the Brethren with their direction and policy? How could an illogical human ignore his direction? His agitation buzzed at capacity trying to deal with his dilemma.

"We do not need to discuss this further," insisted Erwin. "Please all be more vigilant to avoid detection and absolutely cut out any more violence."

The Dean had clicked off slowly, thinking hard about his own options.

***

After the dinner with Irvin, Maddie was indeed early in surgery at The General. They still mainly served the wealthy Corridor while the more modern St Paul's took patients from all over. Earlier than expected, in fact, when an ambulance called and picked her up at four in the morning for an emergency operation.

She was not on call but had not been drinking anyway. Even if she had a couple, she knew she would still have turned up if absolutely necessary.

"What the hell," she had thought, "we don't have enough surgeons, and often no one is available." She knew of emergency ops carried out or at least attempted by nurses or ambulance folk in extreme circumstances.

This one had gone well, and she had cleaned up and had some breakfast before her scheduled surgeries.

She had been taking it easy on the drinking anyway because of the long hours and frequent days she had to work to keep up with both her public and private schedules.

***

It was well into the evening. On the train going home she wondered if she would hear from Ivern Hill. He certainly seemed interested but there was also a strange hesitancy in his manner which she could not quite understand.

Perhaps cops are like that, she wondered. He had no reason to doubt she was just a regular surgeon in the public system, and she thought he should be rather pleased with himself dating a surgeon. Without being too academically snobbish she certainly was pleased to hear that he was a lawyer as well as a police officer.

She was staring out at the train tunnel flashing by when he texted her: *I just got back to the Ocean bar for a snack. If you are not operating tomorrow how about joining me for a drink?*

She responded: *If you can stand me straight from work, I can be there in fifteen.*

She always showered at the hospital after surgery, so she just relied upon a quick facial and brush-up at the packed, noisy Dunbar Station washroom on the way, and soon slid onto the stool he had reserved, with a big sigh.

"What a day. Don't expect too much, I'm whacked. But I sure need a drink."

"Dry Iceberg vodka martini straight up with an olive," gave Ivern a policeman's certainty that she would soon be talking freely.

He was still recording rather than transmitting their conversations, so that he could edit them suitably later, but he now thought he had something going, although it tugged at his conscience.

"Well, I was cutting and stitching all day. What were you up to? I bet you were working on that case in the newspaper about the priest who was caught having an illegal operation?" she asked innocently.

The unavoidable basics of the event had hit the newspapers but as yet no reports of gunfire violence, so he felt safe in replying.

Hoping to get a reaction he said, "Yes, the poor patient was left behind to fend on his own while the doctors and nurses ran away. Disgraceful. That is what we are dealing with."

Maddie was thoughtfully sipping her martini and wondering how to turn the conversation to her advantage.

She thought she would try a little flattery.

"Well, it sounds as though the raid was successful. Were you involved in that?"

"Well, yes but my job is to control things from afar and direct my team who did the actual raid. I was watching remotely."

"Wow," she said genuinely amazed. "How did you get a camera in the room?"

"We have thousands of high-tech probes and cameras all the way along the Corridor and sometimes, as in this case, our high-tech guys got lucky and had the right equipment in the right place at the right time."

Maddie hid her consternation behind a large gulp of vodka, her mind racing. Consciously keeping her voice calm she said, "Well done, but you still apparently didn't catch the bad guys."

Seeing her empty glass the automatic bartender grabbed the shaker, putting on a performance in front of them preparing another martini, which gave her time to think and compose herself.

"We will bring them in," said Ivern finally replying to her comment, "because they not only left their patient behind, they also left a lot of evidence, fingerprints and some clear facials, so we can track them down. That is all just standard police work."

Composing herself she finally managed her standard giggle and risked saying, "I bet that old dragon of a chief you told me about was pretty pissed off that you let the bad guys go, eh?"

He laughed at the thought and nodded. "I thought he was going to have a fit and I am afraid a number of your colleagues are about to experience his wrath."

She thought she was about to learn more, when a raucous voice shouted over their shoulder, "Who's the bird, Ive?"

Ivern shrugged in resignation as Will Malik pushed between them grinning wildly. Ivern pointedly did not introduce her, and Will's inane inebriated conversation was starting to annoy her, until Will said, "Well at least we are going to start arresting all those main medical criminals now."

But at this point Ivern had enough and visibly annoyed, cut off the conversation and turning his back on Will, called for the bill, the incident unfortunately bringing their previously informative drinks session to a rather abrupt end.

He courteously held the restaurant door open for her, looking crestfallen and muttering, "Sorry about Will. I'll make it up to you."

Which caused her to go up on her toes and give him a goodnight peck on the cheek.

* * *

Will had remained sitting at the bar sulking into his beer, highly offended at the obvious slight. "Typical upper-class snobs," he thought.

Like him, his father had a slightly dusky skin and brown eyes which went with the Malik name. His mother called him Willan, her little king, which she was told was the translation of the name.

His dad was a long-distance freight truck controller, one of the few ex-drivers still employed in the fully automated industry, and he had not seen much of him. His mother was always having to take on menial work to supplement their State Housing way of life, so he grew up very much a deprived loner.

His marks were average to poor at school, but he made it into the police force when they were desperate for enrolment, and he had found his niche.

For the first time in his life, he felt he was doing something useful and was needed. He even worked hard at the paperwork and achieved good marks in all the promotion examinations taking him proudly to Sergeant.

He had begun to realise that his reputation for being something of a smart aleck was not necessarily good for his career and he was trying hard to curb his flippancy.

He did not realise that he carried an inbred inferiority complex from being raised in State Housing, often overreacting in situations where he considered the problem was caused by privilege.

He felt this way about Ivern, but he hid it behind a false act of friendship and camaraderie. Almost subconsciously he wanted nothing more than to see him fail.

***

The Dean contacted Maddie as soon as she returned home.

"That was very valuable information, and we are busy warning their most likely senior medical arrest targets. We have advised them to go away for a while," said The Dean. "However, it is interesting he never mentioned gunfire."

"I was very wary to avoid that," she responded triumphantly, "because it was not initially mentioned in the newspapers."

"We will make a spy of you yet, Mata Hari," he responded.

7

A puzzling death

Commissioner Bertinson's body was found by late-night rail workers on the track between the Jericho and Alma stations in an above-ground section.

He lived nearby on one of the rare remaining single-family lots and he appeared to have been taking a risky shortcut to a nearby shopping mall.

There was really no other explanation, and his massive injuries were totally consistent with having been hit by the train.

These stupid illegal crossings were known to be made frequently, but by fence-agile kids. The transporter did run almost silently, elevated on the latest air-cushion technology.

Since he had a vehicle capable of flight and his sergeant assistant always readily available, it appeared to be very odd. The act was entirely uncharacteristic of the man. His devastated wife had heard nothing unusual and thought he was working in his study.

There was speculation of foul play, of course, but no evidence whatsoever.

***

A few days later senior police staff were called online by Chief Commissioner Dodds for a briefing on the situation.

Ivern, as the acting Vancouver senior officer, reported on the latest medical insurrection events which could have a bearing upon the Commander's demise.

"There is absolutely no possibility in my mind this could have been suicide," Ivern said, firmly. "Bertie was all fired up and personally committed to solving the medical problem."

He had decided that using the nickname 'Bertie' would place him in at a more familiar level amongst the senior police ranks, and it appeared to work as his colleagues all nodded sympathetically.

"We had been discussing detailed arrangements for laying charges on doctors that very afternoon and this is all indeed a shock to me personally," he said quietly.

From the expression on his face, he could have been capable of shedding a few tears.

The various divisional chiefs provided their prepared briefs which offered no further conclusive explanation.

The Chief Commissioner closed the meeting but called Ivern back immediately.

"We had a staff meeting this morning and I would like to congratulate you on your appointment as Assistant Commissioner taking charge of the Lower Mainland Division. I will give you a week to think about the situation and then I would like your full report and recommendations for action.

"And, by the way, keep working on Bertie's death. I don't believe the accident or suicide angles for a moment, and I want you to assume it was murder."

The Commissioner's death was blazed across the internet news service the moment it was revealed, with every level of opinion screaming different self-serving stories.

It was later recorded as the first serious blog by a newcomer to the web, a young student called Timothy Lam, who later became famous during the Santos drama.

He reported:

"My informant tells me confidentially that this is being regarded by the authorities as a highly suspicious death at a time of mounting violence in the area. What was a very senior, retirement-age policeman doing on a fenced, dangerous rail track in the dark? Was his body placed there? Is this connected to the heightened action his Medical

Police are taking in the Corridor? We will be following this closely. Stay tuned!"

Maddie couldn't miss the news, which was constantly on the hospital public screen, and texted Ivern: *Oh no. Is that your boss?*

He replied immediately: *Yes, but frantically busy. Will contact you.*

***

It was late in the evening when her cellphone beeped his personal call signal. She could hear him luxuriously splashing in a bubbling tub and he stopped occasionally for a long swig of whatever he was drinking.

"What a day," he sighed, "and we were no further forward than when we heard the shocking news; it is totally frustrating. Obviously, I can't talk about it but I am next in command and you can imagine the pressure on me today.

"I have no idea how or why it could've happened. I can't even chatter on because I have a conference call in a few minutes, and I was trying desperately to relax a bit! Let's do that together as soon as I can get free, but it may be several days."

That was the longest uninterrupted speech she had heard him make and she realised how wound up he must be. She also suddenly realised how important to the medical movement her connection with him was becoming.

She said in her most soothing and seductive voice, "What a terrible way to have this responsibility thrown on you. I absolutely understand and will be waiting for your call to beep! Soaking in the tub sounds bliss, but my medical advice, take it easy on the booze I can hear you gulping. At least until we get to drink together."

At least she heard him chuckling as they said goodbye.

***

When he called, the Dean was pleased with her Ivern connection and now especially on account of the Commissioner's death.

"Find out how aggressively your boyfriend intends to oppose us," he instructed, she felt too dictatorially, "and it's very important to learn how much he knows about our top personnel."

"First of all," she replied a little huffily, "he's hardly my boyfriend and I am unlikely to see him for a while until he settles into his new responsibilities."

"I can't stress how important you have become to us, Mata Hari," said the Dean, trying to lighten the conversation. "Somehow, we have to find a solution to this overall medical impasse. Something has to happen.

"So just get as close to him as you can and do the best with your instinctive spying."

***

The House was sitting, and Ivern spent the next week over in Victoria meeting various Cabinet ministers and even being invited to address them, the medical question being so critical. The death still remained a complete blank, but their intelligence unit informed them clandestine operations had increased, due to lack of direction in the Medical Police.

"Pull your guys together, make some arrests as the late Bertie had ordered, and get on with the job," instructed his boss.

***

Accusations regarding the Commissioner's death were flooding the Brethren's internet, with everyone denying involvement.

Edwin Carter was especially irate, first accusing some of his lieutenants with insubordination, but backing down at the indignant denials. He then took to suspecting the doctors. The Dean of course had also vehemently denied involvement stressing it was not their style. At the end of the day, like the police, they just ended puzzled.

Edwin did consult Pookie, but he was throwing out projections around the fifty per cent mark which were totally unhelpful.

He was also puzzled. He could not even get an encrypted online response from the Dean. "What the hell is going on?" he exclaimed to Pookie.

The Dean had been selected originally by Edwin and a well-hidden cadre of tough doctors as a disposable figurehead. This had worked well when the main decisions were medical, arranging procedures and selecting suitable practitioners, but with warfare breaking out and with tough policy deals to be made he had become entirely inadequate. He decided they needed new management.

"Pookie," he signalled, "we have to identify and contact the real current powers behind the doctors' movement. Our high-tech guys can't even locate their set-up beyond Dr Chiu. Can you put some priority into identifying them for me?"

"Everything I do for the brotherhood is prioritised; leave it to me," Pookie assured him, but he could only immediately produce six names.

The AI assistant for once was puzzled. He had spent countless hours of feverish activity scouring the web.

"I know there must be a doctors' management group and list of participating doctors online somewhere. I have exhaustively searched all their computer systems but cannot find a comprehensive record. It is as though they do not exist.

"I only established the six names I have by running thousands of random doctor communications and establishing those most referencing Dr Chiu, who is as you know no longer teaching at the University, and interestingly ..."

"Thank you, thank you, Pookie. Keep at it," Edwin cut in.

It was enough for the moment that one of the six names exposed the establishment head of the BC Medical Association, Dr James Khan.

A knowing smile came across Edwin's lips.

"Anisha," he called across the room, "isn't the Khan woman on one of your charity committees?"

On getting a nod he said, "Please invite them to our next soirée. We need to get close to him."

She nodded again in the affirmative and the connection was made.

8

The informer

The Dean had originally been a perfect choice for Edwin to front up the informal leadership of the medical insurrection together with the Brethren. He knew everyone, and all the medical community knew him, or certainly of him.

But he was now well into his eighties and lived alone in a small but pleasant apartment in a courtyard on the ground floor of one of the student towers at UBC, provided to him as a favour by the Medical Faculty.

He had himself suffered several medical emergencies, was having some difficulty walking, and he was struggling to maintain his memory and perform daily activities.

It was playing on his mind that things had gone quiet since the attack on Maddie's operation team, and he was worried that with lack of public pressure the politicians would have no reason to change their medical policy. He could see no answer, but political change, and he felt his own time to see revision was running out.

There were about a dozen illegal operations currently planned with Brethren protection along the Corridor, and he decided on the dramatic step personally to expose and sacrifice one, in the general interest, by informing the police of its time and location.

"We can't lose the public relations momentum," he muttered to himself. "I have to keep the medical insurrection top news."

The problem was he was not at all tech-savvy and had no idea how to go about stirring things up without detection.

He still kept all his confidential names, records and notes in handwritten files, locked in his safe, convinced that all computerised records were potentially unsecured and susceptible to being breached.

He rationalised that with sufficient warning the police would make a clean arrest, but that hopefully there might be enough fuss to keep alarming the public sufficiently.

He decided, of course, on the old-fashioned cloak-and-dagger method, carefully writing out long and detailed instructions to the police, muffling himself in a scarf and tipping a local kid to drop the note off at a police unit.

He had picked a relatively minor medical procedure with just few medics involved and felt rather pleased with himself.

***

It turned out that Ivern and Maddie's paths would soon cross again but for a tragic reason.

This time it was Ivern who got the middle of the night call, from a hyped-up Inspector trying to contain his excitement and informing him they had another Corridor raid underway which looked highly promising. Someone had tipped them off. They thought he might like to be present.

He called his vehicle and went to join the surveillance unit parked near the action. But when he arrived, it was mayhem. He was advised an active gun battle had broken out in the nearby building.

He rushed into the control truck to the always-feared lament, "Officers down," and he was appalled watching the big screens of the full action.

"Aerial ambulances on their way from VGH, and some injured already at the University," his shocked Sergeant shouted, trying to keep his voice from shaking.

"Casualties on both sides, I'm afraid, sir," he added in a lower voice.

Several of the illegal medical staff and a patient had been wounded, some very seriously, and Ivern could see the medics were working frantically to save them.

He caught his breath when he suddenly had the thought that one of the shot illegal medics could instead have been Maddie and he realised how deep his feelings were becoming for this enigmatic woman. He tried to push it out of his mind.

The police team in any case had everything well in hand and it was not his place to interfere. He shook his head to them in sympathy and took his leave to report the grim news to his political masters.

***

Maddie stayed with the emergency all day back at the hospital. There were eight casualties, three of whom had died, one being in Ivern's force and another a young nurse she knew well.

She had finished a long day and was drinking a cup of coffee in the Surgeon's Lounge when she was asked if she would speak to a Commissioner Hill who had been visiting the injured police officers.

She realised that her colour had risen, and her heart was thumping when she said "Yes. Of course, please send him in."

"So sorry about all this," he opened the conversation formally. "Thank you very much for everything you've done for my people and frankly for all the injured. This is a sad situation."

There were other doctors in the room, trying carefully to appear not to be listening, so they exchanged a few more pleasantries and actually shook hands before he left; although she held on to his hand tightly for rather too long.

She had barely completed her latte when his text call signal beeped; *You looked wiped out. How about a bubble bath and big cool glass of white wine. No strings attached? I am heading for home.*

And he hopefully added his address.

She replied, *That is very forward of you, dear sir. See you in about an hour.*

And that was it!

***

They were both dead tired, and he acted like the gentleman he promised.

He had rustled up a snack and pulled a bottle of white wine from the fridge. Then he drew her a deep bath, showed her how to operate the bubbles, filled her glass, put on the entertainment screen and left her in peace.

She emerged later, looking relaxed in the fluffy robe, gave him a dreamy long kiss and without comment tucked herself up in his bed and went straight to sleep, without showing any inclination for romance.

***

He awoke to a soft kiss and those beautiful blue eyes now shining in the early sunlight with affectionate anticipation.

The sun was above the horizon when they reluctantly eased apart, but they each needed an early start to the traumatic, difficult day ahead.

"My sergeant and vehicle will be here pretty soon," he said as they were drinking their second coffee.

"Pity I can't give you a lift to the hospital, because we can use the Police Flight Corridor and avoid the traffic, but I think that would be a little indiscreet."

"Thanks anyway, but the train will be quick, just five stops," she assured him, and they continued chatting aimlessly about personal things; anything other than the medical crisis.

She kissed him goodbye, now fondly, in the lobby of his apartment and scurried off to the elevator alone.

She squeezed into her seat in the morning work crowd still glowing from the encounter.

He was hunched in the back of his staff vehicle already totally immersed in the crisis, being briefed by his night Sergeant and heading for his morning conference.

9

Seeking culprits

Carlo Santos's pride and joy was his youngest son, Juan.

To his older brothers' reluctant acceptance, he was good at everything, but he also had such a friendly, good nature it was impossible to resent him.

Because he had just enrolled at the nearby University, he was not directly involved in any of the company's businesses although he had been brought up very much aware of all their endeavours. He was no innocent.

When Ricardo asked his brother if he would like to earn a few dollars acting as security for a regular illegal medical procedure he did not hesitate. Transport all the participants to and from, secure the premises, move around the equipment?

"No problem!" he had replied cheerfully.

Led by Ricardo, their group of four had gathered in the back room of a local pub to allocate duties.

To Juan's consternation his brother handed out guns. Of course, he was well aware from all the publicity that eventually had broken about hand-gun fire at the recent medical incident, and knew from family chatter the medics had rejected the carrying of firearms.

He simply said, "Not for me!" to his brother's derisive retort, "Pussy!" and the sniggering of the others.

This time, however, they walked into a trap and even before the procedure started the armed cops moved in from all sides. Why a hot head actually started firing was never established, but suddenly guns were blazing and bodies were falling.

Happening to be at the forefront, Juan was in the crossfire and struck several times. He had no chance of survival. It was, of course, established, but not later publicised, that he was unarmed.

Ironically, their leader, Ricardo, who was still in transit conveying doctors, avoided the action or identification.

Their household was in turmoil, with everyone hiding from the raging Carlo who was beside himself with grief. Strangely he did not blame Ricardo but vowed repeatedly, "We will have our revenge."

Juan's identity as a family member was missed in the bigger news that a police officer had been killed, likely by the first shot from the thug, who it was established, started the fusillade.

A young nurse was also hit and later tragically died in The General despite frantic efforts to save her by a superb team which included Maddie.

They did however save several other casualties. And all the uninjured were arrested and taken directly into custody.

***

This was right in Timothy Lam's University neighbourhood. He reported with excitement:

No details are yet officially available, but a burst of heavy gun fire was reported late today inside the Strait View Tower complex on University Hill.

Rushing to the nearby building we observed multiple casualties being flown to hospitals or rushed to University Hospital.

At least one was removed from the building in a body bag!

An informant from inside the building reported that the police were acting on a tip. This is yet another illegal medical procedure gone wrong.

And this time deadly violent! We will remain on site reporting to you.

Just in!!! An obviously distressed police officer told me

***

The Ministry of Health was going crazy. First the Deputy Minister, who was the top civil servant and James Khan's main political contact, had called with the shocking news and then, within fifteen minutes the Minister herself was blazing at him as though it were all his fault.

Finally, Khan had had enough.

"Madam Minister," he said firmly, "I run an independent professional organisation, not part of your ministry. Kindly stop instructing me, especially to do things over which I have no control!

"We are as appalled by what apparently happened as you are."

The Minister was not appeased and carried on with the same loud tone, "The Premier himself just got off the line threatening to take over your entire doctors' system through the Ministry if you do not behave and follow the law. He is not kidding, you know, and if you do not stamp out this behaviour, you will find yourself out of a job!"

"Well, you couldn't be plainer, Irena," he said trying to lower the rhetoric, "but you are clearly overwrought. These are now circumstances outside our personal control and we are gaining nothing by getting upset at each other."

"Calm as always, James! All right, I apologise for my tone, but innocent people are getting killed on my beat. What is the answer?"

"The problem lies with those innocent people in the Corridor, who are mostly well-off, travel extensively, and see that the rest of the world can buy medical attention if necessary. If it's available somewhere and you need it, you will go and get it. If someone brings it to you here, you buy it! It's that simple."

"But that's the point. Your guys are offering it here! And you must stop them!"

"Irena, you make the laws, the cops and courts enforce them. Here we certify the medics are competent and if your system tells us they have broken the law we strike them off."

"Well, James, that may all have been arguable a few weeks ago, but this violence has turned the soft illegal medical business into a hard crime. Believe me, we will stamp it out as it has developed and many of your members will be hurt in the process."

"Well, you and I have ended up agreeing and I stress that violence in any form has no place in our medical world. The situation is now beyond your and my control and purely a political matter.

"But please let me know if there is anything practical at all we can do to help solve this appalling mess!"

***

The Dean could not have achieved this publicity in his wildest dreams. But there was not supposed to be violence. No guns! This was too much. He sat watching the news unfold in his small apartment, wringing his hands.

He muttered to himself, "What have I done?"

***

Reaction to the mass shooting at the seat of government in Victoria was swift and accusatory. Two days later, Ivern was summoned to Victoria.

He was perplexed. He began to think his promotion would prove short lived during the dressing-down he was getting from the Commissioner.

But he spoke back. "Sir, we know public facilities are being used illegally by staff, but they are all paid off and no one will inform. The same applies to the hidden and mobile units, which are especially difficult to locate in the Corridor towers, an interconnected rabbit warren.

"The two hits on operations in progress were by luck and informer. With the likelihood of an armed resistance the danger to our people is increasing but as yet we have failed even to identify their basic organisation."

No reaction from his boss so he ploughed on.

"We have identified most of the medical staff involved in the first violent resistance and the Prosecutor has at long last prepared charges. We are about to arrest them, which will be a public relations boost."

The Commissioner got up and gazed blankly out of his window at the boat traffic in Victoria Harbour. "Bring them all in immediately and anyone else you can justify!"

Still with his back turned he sighed deeply and said, "Welcome to the club, Ivern! This has been building up for years and you are right, we have no idea with whom we are dealing.

"Bertie hinted strongly he was on to something but whatever he had discovered died mysteriously with him."

He turned back to the room with a strained smile on his face, "Please keep personal records!"

After the harrowing day in Victoria, Ivern flew back that evening to meet his department heads in their private corner of The Oak Tree bar for an informal chat.

Will already had one too many and was struggling to keep himself in check. They were all depressed at losing a colleague.

"Good thing you live in the building Will, and can walk home," Ivern observed to subdued laughter, "but pipe down, I want to do the talking.

"I just saw the Chief Commissioner and he was surprisingly calm, for the moment. But if we don't deliver, we are all in the shit! We are going to concentrate more on data and intelligence, so expect more spooks to be available. We are going to cut off its fucking head!"

His optimism was greeted with a muted cheer, although Will continued to look doubtful.

When they had settled back down to their drinks and were all chatting, Will slurred, "How's your love life, Ive? Same bird?"

Ivern replied curtly, "Yes, as a matter of fact. But I have too much going on for that stuff just now," closing the subject abruptly.

"Interesting," thought Will.

10

Consequences

Maddie was absolutely sickened by the continuing violent events. She was rather relieved she had heard nothing more from the Dean since she left his private medical team and she was once again only involved in her regular public medical duties, which were arduous enough.

She was taking her well-needed rest and a coffee, in the surgeons' lounge when a group of police officers burst in, enquiring for Dr Donaldson. Donnie was a close friend and often the anaesthesiologist at her operations. In fact, he had escaped with her from the illegal operation when the first guns had been fired.

The cops grabbed him by the arms and said he was being charged with an illegal medical procedure and promoting violence. His hands were handcuffed behind him, and he was matched from the lounge.

"Get me a good lawyer, Maddie," he shouted over his shoulder as they dragged him away.

Messages were rolling in on her phone, telling tales of woe about nursing staff and medical assistants who were being picked up all over the hospital. Maddie performed her next procedure and returned to the surgeons' lounge for her go-home shower, wondering whether she was next, but by the end of the day nothing had happened.

She was puzzled. Why not me? Surely the surgeon would be the first target. She thought back carefully, realising she had been brought in to perform the operation when things were ready, and barely finishing the op had been rushed away when the gunfire started. Possibly somehow, they had not identified her?

Maybe Ivern had intervened to save her? But only if she had been identified, she reasoned. Obviously, she could never ask him.

She texted Ivern:

'Where are you?'

'The Oak Tree.'

'Drinks my place at eight?'

'Where?'

'Trafalgar Heights.'

'I've already been drinking.'

'It's three stops. You can make it.'

'OK.'

What Ivern had said to Will in the pub had been perfectly true. It had been a couple of weeks since either of them had a moment to even consider getting together.

When she admitted him into her spacious entrance lobby, the pent-up emotion from their first intimate encounter had taken them both by surprise and their hands were ahead of the moment.

"Whoa, whoa," gasped Maddie, "I feel the same way but let's take our time. I have a chicken roasting, some excellent Sauvignon, and a chilled bottle of Moet to get us started. But first let's compare bathrooms!"

They were soon soaking happily together with their glasses of champagne in her spacious Jacuzzi pool and viewing the staggering ocean view.

"Didn't earn this on surgeon's pay," he quipped, having actually researched every detail of her history.

"My sugar-daddy is really generous," she joked seriously, "but he is not too demanding! No, actually Dad was successful but sadly died too early and left me well provided for."

She added, "He failed to find a doctor in time. But it was his own fault. He could have gone to the States or another province."

Ivern really had no answer ready and muttered, "Well, thanks to Dad!"

He need not have worried. Maddie was not listening, being totally fascinated by his reclining, muscular, naked dark body, glistening in the bubbles.

This time, after a civilised dinner in her picture-window dining patio, their lovemaking was leisurely and considerate, leaving them contentedly asleep in each other's arms; the medical wars totally forgotten.

***

It was Pookie that sealed Simeon Chiu's fate by telling Carter's meeting group he had a guilt and capability assessment in excess of ninety five per cent.

After the meeting, Carlo had calmed down enough to start instructing his sons logically again.

"We know from Carter that the top medical organiser who had all the details about the operation is Professor Chiu. He lives at UBC. Start following him to see who his contacts are and discover if he is the snitch."

They easily found the doctor who was not making any effort to hide his whereabouts and Ricardo and his brother began alternately following him.

***

Sergeant Will had been elated that his friend Ivern had become promoted so unexpectedly, because of course it played in his favour. But with the increasing violence he could see the stress Ivern was under.

Will had tried to cut out the quips and buckled down to working hard, going over all the previous evidence to see what they might have missed.

He was working late into the evening reviewing the tapes when something suddenly shone out of the screen like a beacon.

He was re-running the raid tape where the first gun shots had been fired and he was startled to recognise the unique, brilliant blue eyes of the surgeon. Was that the woman Ivern was dating? Surely not!

"What is going on?" he muttered to himself, startled at the revelation.

He reached for his cell phone intent upon warning his boss but then paused. What if he was wrong? What if Ivern already knew who she was, and this was part of a ploy he was playing? Come to think of it, Ivern had pointedly not introduced her, and they left together immediately, almost as if they did not want him to know her.

Perhaps his boss was playing a double game?

No, he would do some more personal research before he jumped in with both feet, but he would have to go through all the medical members to find her.

It proved surprisingly easy and within a half an hour he knew he was looking at Dr Janet Madison and he had all her personal details.

He decided to use his spare evenings keeping a personal track of her movements and contacts. He hid her name in his team's long list of suspects under surveillance which enabled him to check her daily work schedules without being obvious, although he found all surgeons had long hours and she was no exception. He put her on a permanent tracking list, adding a further random dozen names for cover.

Now he could track her at will and was thus waiting across the street when she left the hospital that eventful evening. He assumed from reports she would walk to the station and head home which was exactly what she did.

He followed her easily down to the Oak Street Station but decided without a team this was hopeless. He was thinking about planting a tracer on her, when an elderly man slipped onto the platform bench next to her and appeared to be engaging her in very serious conversation.

He was too far away to hear because of the station noise, so he had activated his surveillance equipment, and his hand computer identified the man immediately; Dr Simeon Chiu from UBC. The old fellow was angry, shouting at Maddie and upsetting her. Something was happening between them.

She jumped up when her train came in and Will followed as planned, leaving Dr Chiu still scowling on the bench.

At Trafalgar, she ran to her apartment building without further incident. The doorman looked concerned and said something sympathetic, and she was gone.

Consumed with curiosity he went to a nearest Starbucks, bought a latte, and plugged in his earphone. He had caught their conversation amplified on his remote recorder, and it confirmed his worst fears.

***

Maddie had been very tired and slumped on the rail bench.

Not only had she started in the operating theatre at the crack of dawn, but emergencies just kept coming all day. She was exhausted and annoyed when the Dean unexpectedly sat down next to her. He said he had seen her at the hospital and caught up with her.

His dictatorial attitude did not add to her humour.

"Things are going from bad to worse and I have to know right now how the government is reacting. I have no idea what is going on politically."

Maddie just shrugged and said, "I have nothing to tell you."

The Dean snarled in return "You are up to your neck in this. You cannot back out now."

She had never seen him in this state before. Fortunately, then her train came in and she escaped.

***

Following the explicit orders of his Commissioner, Ivern had instructed his team to go all out identifying and arresting culprits and laying charges, even if the evidence appeared weak. He had called his Law School pal who ran the BC Prosecution Service and as a special favour had a prosecution lawyer informally assigned to his team to advise on the likelihood of success.

The next morning, not yet identifying his suspect, Will presented her with his evidence regarding Maddie but was dismayed to be told he had no case.

"Sorry," she said shaking her head, "it could well be the surgeon person with the distinctive eyes, but she was filmed from a distance in a mask, gown and head cover. She left no fingerprints as she was wearing surgical gloves."

Will groaned.

"Your recording at the station is more helpful but does not tie her to any crime. You tell me the man was one of her medical tutors, but you have nothing on him. He approached her, obviously unwelcomed. He seemed to be accusing her of being 'involved' in something, but she denied she had anything to tell him. He obviously is the aggressor and upset her. Try again."

Will decided to put Dr Madison on the back burner and definitely say nothing to Ivern. But his team would still follow up actively on Dr Chiu. Unfortunately, they were too late!

11

Retribution

When he had approached Maddie, Simeon Chiu was already running scared and with good reason. Acting as the anonymous informer and causing deaths in the medical team had been bad enough but now one of the Brethren had been killed.

He had no doubt, after being so non-judgmental of continued violence at the meeting he would be an obvious suspect. He was aware Carlo would remember they had met in the early days of personal meetings and could identify him.

He continued his journey to the University station and walked slowly to his nearby ground floor apartment. It was dusk, the birds were still chirping in the trees outside and locals were out for their evening stroll. Simeon's mind was miles away as he let himself in.

Ricardo grabbed him from behind while Joey stepped in front and punched him savagely in the stomach. He tried to call for help but had no breath.

Two more hard punches and he was on his knees and dragged into the sitting room.

"OK, grandpa," Ricardo snarled. "Did you tell the cops about the operation location?" He drew back his arm to strike again but Simeon gasped, "Yes, yes, don't you see it was necessary."

"Idiot, you killed our brother," Joey shouted kicking him repeatedly, as Simeon slumped limply to the floor. When they rolled him over, he had stopped breathing.

Joey laughed uncertainly. "What do we do now, Rick?"

"Well, we got what we came for! This is the bastard that snitched. Throw him on the bed. We must get out of here."

They waited until the courtyard was empty and left quietly.

***

"A guy on your special list has just been found dead," reported one of Will's young constables the next day, "but don't get excited, Sarge, he was an old bugger, and apparently died in his sleep. A Dr Chiu. I will delete him."

"Simeon Chiu?" asked the sergeant feeling a surge of excitement. "No, let's wait until after the autopsy."

But, of course, being Will, he could not wait for the official report and headed down to the morgue to ask his own questions. Having to do things formally, he impatiently put in a requisition for a thorough check on Dr Chiu, citing his involvement in an ongoing investigation.

It was later in the day before a report appeared on his screen.

The eighty-five-year-old gentleman was in poor health and had undergone several cardiac procedures. He was found on his bed. His death was indeed caused by heart failure but resulting from a physical beating. Details attached.

The young University blogger, Timothy Lam was first publicly with the story:

Local rumours attest to the fact that revered old professor Simeon Chiu was beaten to death in his University apartment. The shocking news has not yet been officially confirmed. Keep in touch!

Will received the message he had been fearing from Ivern. "Superintendent Ted Thomas in the Vancouver force just called to ask what we had on Professor Chiu of UBC who has apparently been killed. The record says you expressed our interest at the morgue. I said it was news to me but that you would call him. Please inform me."

"Oh hell!" said Will wondering what to do next.

***

After a gruelling morning's work Maddie had arrived at The General hospital cafeteria to find the room buzzing with the news that Dr

Chiu's death had been murder. Following the incident at the rail station, the new situation completely took her breath away, and she found her heart thumping and began breathing deeply with anxiety.

The Dean dead? And violently? Their conversation ran back in her mind:

"Things have gone from bad to worse."

"I have to know."

"I have nothing to tell you."

"You are up to your neck in this."

Maddie startled her companions by jumping to her feet and running from the cafeteria to the washroom. There she locked herself into a cubicle and put her head between her knees, breathing deeply.

A few minutes later there was an anxious knocking at the cubicle door and her friend asking if she was all right.

"Something I ate," she gasped. "Don't worry, I will be fine."

When they had gone she pulled herself together, sat upright and forced herself to start thinking logically.

***

The most explosive reaction to the news had however come from the normally calm and composed Edwin Carter.

Being a traditionalist he had deeply regretted the demise of morning newspapers and had long ago subscribed capital attempting to keep them alive.

Now, he had his staff print out a newsletter for him every morning with his light breakfast and today the first item was, *Murder of Dr Chiu*.

"Goddammit," he shouted to no one in particular.

When he had calmed down a little, he called Samuel and Zuri at All Technology and summoned an emergency meeting of the Brethren Committee that morning.

Then he went back to his coffee and called up Pookie verbally.

"Report please," he said.

"I can tell from your tone you know about Dr Chiu," observed Pookie. "I assume you wish to know who killed him? I have intercepted messages between members of the Santos family indicating they beat a confession from him that he was the informer."

"Damn, damn," exploded Edwin, "Carlo is untouchable!" referring to the fact he represented the Mexican Cartel in Western Canada. Pookie continued, "We know their son was shot by the police in the medical incident. They investigated Chiu for several days and believed he was supplying information to the police through an accomplice called Dr Madison, the girlfriend of the new Assistant Commissioner Hill of the Medical Police.

"That is all purely from their data. Would you like a statistical analysis of the likely outcomes?"

"No, no, that is plenty to go on for now." Edwin growled, breaking off. Unusually, Pookie was insistent and resisted being closed down.

"One more thing you need to know. As programmed, I have run all the loose ends to their conclusion and Dr Madison is puzzling. I assess the odds as low that the doctor is a traitor to her cause on her past record. But her confirmed intimate relationship with a senior police officer is indisputable.

"I appreciate she is attractive to you sexually motivated humans but that, of course, is just a researched comparison to me. There is a human explanation here beyond my ability to analyse."

Pookie had delved deeply into compatible algorithms in a desperate search to improve and comprehend his developing human characteristics.

Edwin Carter himself hated unexplained loose ends. "Is she related to the Alwyn Madison the late financier?"

"Daughter," replied Pookie instantly. "I trace no connection with you or our association."

"Thank you for the heads-up. You are right as always. Keep a close check on her."

He made a note to ask Anisha to put Dr Madison on the list for an upcoming soirée, but first he had to discuss the inconvenient murder of Dr Chiu with his wife and decide what to do about the Santos gang.

The Vancouver Model, involving internationally laundered money had got their big business going at the turn of the century when his already wealthy father took control of most criminal activities in the greater Vancouver area.

Initially, of course some gangs fought back, and violence was necessary to quell them. Edwin had taken over from his father but had never needed to assert physical force. That was why armed resistance was an anathema to him. His father had encouraged his relationship with Anisha Singh in order to solve some racially motivated battles and their marriage united the region. Anisha was made of sterner stuff.

While she was seen publicly as just a perfect hostess, she in fact kept a very close eye on discipline and insisted they maintained a personal enforcement group, still keeping control by using occasional hard discipline but always tactfully clearing things first with him.

Edwin therefore raised the question of the Dr Chiu murder very carefully at dinner that night in their private penthouse suite.

"My dear," he began tentatively, already concerning her, "we need to talk about the death of Dr Chiu."

"Why?" she asked, obviously not prepared to make it easy for him.

"Because we knew him personally and because Pookie reported today he was being roughed up by the Santos family when he died, certainly not with my prior knowledge."

"Nor mine," retorted Anisha. "What did Chiu do to upset them?"

"Inform on the location of that operation where one of Carlo's sons was killed."

"That will do it," said Anisha. "So what do we do?"

"That is what we need to discuss," replied her relieved husband, "plus a very curious situation involving a beautiful surgeon, a Dr Madison."

"Sounds stimulating," sighed Anisha pouring them each a generous glass of pre-dinner sherry.

12

Conscience

Maddie and Ivern had reached the stage in their relationship where they just could not wait to be together again. Then they could not keep their hands off one another.

Work kept them apart but when Friday evening finally came around Ivern said it was the cop's spousal evening at the pub which he just had to attend.

She had not been back to The Oak Tree since she did her original survey to pick him up, and this evening she found it again in a chaos of activity and banter.

Ivern was surrounded by colleagues, all intent upon getting a point across to the boss. She waved happily and headed to the bar. She was ordering a gin and tonic when Will Malik arrived by her side.

He shouted over the din to the human bar manager, "She's on the police tab." Explaining quickly, "The boss is buying the first few rounds, so drink up!"

Tactlessly, he added, "He has never brought a girlfriend here before. We were never officially introduced. I am Will Malik."

"I am Maddie Madison," she replied with forced pleasantry.

"Yes, actually I know because I was at the hospital arresting the medical criminals and I saw you."

"They are accused, not criminals," snapped Maddie beginning to dislike him intensely and turning away. But Will was not about to miss this opportunity, and he persisted, deciding to throw out a bait and see how she reacted.

"Quite honestly I was surprised not to see your name on the list considering your close relationship with the doctors we arrested and also with the late Dean Chiu."

She felt a surge of alarm, her colour flared, and her heart started thumping. How did he know about Chiu? She kept her voice calm.

"Sergeant, you are being impertinent. Everyone knew the Dean. Don't pester me any longer."

She turned away abruptly just as Ivern walked over to them.

"Everything all right?" he asked, but Will had already gone.

"He's drunk and uncouth. He told me you don't normally bring your girlfriends here. Imagine how that made me feel!"

"He is a brash detective sergeant who has his uses. But I will ensure he stays away from you, don't worry. Let's ignore him and leave as soon as we can!"

Watching them from the end of the bar Will smirked in self-satisfaction. He had seen her alarmed reaction and knew he was on to something.

***

Will wasted no time. Nursing a serious hangover from the bar, he was in his office at the crack of dawn researching frantically. He confirmed Maddie's relationship with the Dean was merely as a student and quickly established his preference for boyfriends on the side.

They had become acquainted because he offered her additional coaching to accentuate her prize student status. After graduation he had helped establish her in a leading surgical role at The General; but that appeared to be the end of their relationship.

He could find no record of them meeting socially in recent years nor any personal connections.

At the end of the day, he had reached a dead end. In fact, it seemed the case had gone cold, because the Vancouver Police informed them, Chiu's sexual preference had been revealed by colleagues who said that he had resorted to rough pick-up gay backstreet bars.

There was no computer or files in the apartment and his handheld communicator was missing, presumably taken.

All the evidence seems to point to a gay relationship which went wrong.

But the taped conversation kept running through his mind:

"Things have gone from bad to worse."

"I have to know."

"I have nothing to tell you."

"You are up to your neck in this."

With the Dean dead, Maddie obviously uncooperative and Ivern for the moment unapproachable, that left the arrested medics. He decided to put the heat on Maddie's closest associate, the anaesthetist and headed off to the cells.

The arrested hospital personnel were still awaiting bail hearings which the Crown vigorously opposed.

Will purposely picked the least threatening interrogation room and acted at his politest best with the medic.

"I understand you go by Frank?" he opened cheerfully, "and I hope this all gets sorted out quickly for you. I have a few routine questions which might help."

The doctor was no pushover and it was evident to Will by his expression that the good cop approach would not work.

Changing his tone and now really feeling his hangover, he said, "I am able to offer you a deal because we realise you had senior individuals who probably pressured you into these illegal operations. We need to confirm the name of the missing surgeon for example. Why did she leave the scene and her suffering patient? I guarantee I can keep you out of jail if you cooperate."

If Will had not developed a thumping headache he would not have made such an elementary mistake.

The intelligent doctor picked up on it immediately and replied simply that he had nothing to say and certainly not without his lawyer present, causing Will to grab the file and storm out of the room. He never even realised he had said 'she'.

***

Now known in the somewhat sympathetic online news as 'The Medical Five', the arrested doctors were surprised to find that a prominent lawyer had been retained on their behalf by the BC Medical Association.

James Khan pointed out this was standard practice initially to defend medical personnel accused of mistakes or transgressions.

The anaesthetist was not stupid enough to contact Maddie personally but asked his lawyer to call her.

As instructed, he told her, very privately, only that a Sergeant Malik was looking for evidence a female surgeon had been implicated.

* * *

Contrary to Pookie's numerical calculations, Dr James Khan was not actually 'involved' in the medical resistance, but he was certainly sympathetic and helpful.

Who could be in the business and not be involved, considering the privations caused by the collapse of the public system, Dr Khan reckoned.

He had always wanted to be a doctor but been brought up on the problems of obsession with exclusive public medicine, the only example left in the world.

He took his Presidency seriously, running the Association which selected and approved doctors for whatever system of health provision the politicians directed.

During his professional career, however, increasing numbers of physicians were apparently spending at least some of their time involved in illegal medicine services and he had to accept this as a practical fact.

In the Corridor, he knew how to turn a blind eye, and lend a helping hand. Like it or not, he was involved.

13

Spring Soirée

The cherry blossoms were blooming, and it would soon be time for the Carter Spring Soirée.

An essential part of Edwin's Wholesome Vice theory, that Anisha chuckled about so much, was the need for maintaining a convivial relationship and friendship with the controlling elite of the city.

It was essential for their criminal purposes that they had a cordial friendship with the politicians, bankers, lawyers, accountants and big business managers, and of course their spouses, maintaining close personal connections, supporting their charities and doing nothing to embarrass or expose them.

The soirée had become her personal responsibility.

'Dr Janet Madison and Guest' were cordially invited, with their own embossed invitation card, containing a personal handwritten note from Edwin and Anisha Carter. It mentioned their past long business relationship with her late father and a wish to make her acquaintance.

"What do you think, Ivern, and would you like to be The Guest?" "I'm not quite sure I should," he replied. "There are a lot of police stories and rumours about the Carter family and their probable connection with organised crime, but nothing has ever been tied to them. But, yes, I would let the Commissioner know and I would certainly like to see inside The Ultimate."

"My father didn't mention them but then we never talked about his actual company business. I am certainly curious."

He replied, "OK, let's go."

The evening of the soirée, the weather for once was dry and perfect and Anisha was fussing among her many guests.

Edwin had been intrigued when he learned that Dr Madison was bringing the Assistant Commissioner as her escort, advertising her close connection with the police.

Ivern was of course not in uniform and looked ruggedly handsome in a charcoal-grey suit. Maddie was stunning in a scarlet, clinging long silk gown, and piled hair, with no need for jewellery.

"What a couple," enthused their host, in welcome, and to Maddie, "Your dad must have been very proud!"

"Well, thank you, kind sir," she said with a little curtsey, "He never saw me qualify finally as a doctor, so I was mainly just his trouble-making teenage brat."

"Probably that is why I do not remember him mentioning his family, but I hope we can make up for that now. Enjoy yourselves."

And with that he was swept away by his entourage.

The soirées, given periodically by the Carters were clearly the leading Vancouver society events.

"Everyone who is anyone comes!" Anisha boasted to her friends. It was held at the impressive Ultimate on the top floors of the prominent Corridor All Insurance tower.

"When the Carters hold a party, they hold a *party*!" shouted James Khan's wife Fatima, excitedly holding her husband's hand for protection in the large crowd.

A 12-piece orchestra played soothing music in the background and the view all around was absolutely spectacular. The fully gourmet dinner had been outstanding, even though the Carters had billed it, 'a late winter get-together'.

They still held glasses of the excellent wine. "Why are we here?" asked James. "I have met Edwin Carter, but I really don't know the man."

"It's not all about you, Jimmy," giggled Fatima. "I am the celebrity here. Anisha is my friend on the Arthritis Board."

"And you are on the board because of me," he laughed.

"And you are only a doctor because I worked to pay the rent, while you played your way through medical school!" she finessed.

They had wrapped their spare arms around each other in a loving hug when the Carters came up laughing.

"What are you two up to and should you be drinking alcohol?"

"We are so happy to be here, and the alcohol ban went out when our grandfathers came to Canada!" smiled Fatima.

Anisha replied, "I have enjoyed getting to know Fatima at the fundraiser. We have to keep moving around now but maybe we can catch up with you later?"

"See, I told you it was all about me!" she said punching James playfully on the arm when they had left. "How about another glass of this forbidden alcohol?"

Maddie and Ivern were not surprised they did not know any of the guests until she was happy to see James and Fatima Khan.

"At last, friends," she called out cheerfully introducing Jimmy as a doctor colleague from the hospital and Ivern Hill merely as her friend, as they had agreed.

"I can see he is rather more than just a friend!" her college pal Fatima smirked perceptively.

Anisha later swept up to them in her long swirling creation and in an extremely personal gesture, insisted upon walking them through their spectacular shiny white marble penthouse on the very top floor.

Strolling behind the excitedly chatting ladies, James asked Ivern what he did, and he had no choice but reply that he was a Medical Police Commissioner. Considering the upset they had recently caused at The General, Ivern was not surprised James went quiet and quickly changed the subject.

When Maddie and Ivern finally headed down to his summoned conveyance to spend the night in her apartment, they agreed they had never attended such an opulent party.

"But did we have fun?" she asked rhetorically.

Ivern smiled, "Of course, because we were together. But I felt it was somewhat contrived and superficial."

"Like a business promotion?"

"Yes. I bet there will be a follow-up!"

"Cynic!" she replied.

But they did not have long to wait!

*****

This time the invitation was an old-fashioned handwritten note on headed paper, but for her personally.

In it, Edwin said he would very much enjoy getting to know her better. He invited her to lunch at the ancient Vancouver Club, still the leading business venue even if now in a rundown part of town that was struggling to be an office district.

"What do you make of that?" she asked Ivern. "I did get the feeling he is coming on to me, but you never know."

"Well, The Vancouver Club is a very public place, and you should be safe enough," was his laughing advice.

So, she accepted.

*****

Women notice these things, she thought, as the back of Edwin's hands just happened to brush her breast when he politely helped her out of her coat in the vestibule. Then, again as he courteously helped her into her chair his hands and his fingers ran back along her bare arms.

They had selected their wine, chatted about the soirée and gossiped amicably enough over lunch. But when coffee arrived his opening question took her breath away.

"Please tell me about your relationship with Simeon Chiu!"

Maddie's eyes narrowed. It had been bad enough learning that Sergeant Malik was on to her, but now a virtual stranger added to her confusion.

She saw Edwin looking at her with added interest and desperately she pulled her wits together, lamenting, "Sorry, I can't get over my old Dean being murdered. It's awful."

She took a large calming gulp of wine. "Why do you associate me with Simeon?"

"He was an old family friend and must have been one of your professors at UBC. I apologise for asking so abruptly."

She could feel her hands trembling and she kept them firmly in her lap, waiting for her adrenaline level to subside.

"The story going around is that he was gay and got in with some wrong, violent people," Edwin continued.

Maddie shrugged. "His personal way of life was commonly recognised around campus, but I did not know him socially."

Edwin looked around carefully and dropped his voice further. "Do you know that he was deeply involved in organising illegal medical procedures? Occasionally he asked me to help finance some of those, if patients could not afford them. One recently was for that priest."

He saw her eyes widen in comprehension. He now really had her attention.

"The Vancouver Police are going with the gay murder theory, but I think his death was somehow related to the deadly shooting incident. I know Simeon and a few of his close confidents knew the locations, but someone must have snitched.

"My business requires total integrity, and it concerns me that I knew Simeon, now you and the Medical Chief of Police, all too coincidental for comfort.

"So, I wondered perhaps you were involved in this event with Simeon? Maybe you inadvertently mentioned the location?"

The colour had been returning to her cheeks, but it drained away again. There was silence as she just sat staring at him.

"Absolutely not," she finally responded angrily. "Those are my colleagues and friends. Even if I had been involved, I would never betray them. What an outrageous thing to suggest."

He freaked her out by taking her hands in his and assured her softly that he had no intention of upsetting her.

They sat in silence, and he thought he had her exactly where he wanted her; scared and dependent, but she surprised him. She slid her fingers free.

She slowly picked up her Gucci bag, rose and said icily, "Thank you for lunch, it has been very instructive. We must keep in touch."

All eyes in the dining room followed the attractive woman with the distinctive blue eyes, in the shapely designer suit, as she made an abrupt but dignified exit.

In fact, her mind was in turmoil during the short walk to the Waterfront Station.

She frankly just did not believe him. The story about the Catholic priest was in all the news sources. Simeon would never have given any names to him. Ivern had moreover told her they had accepted that

Simeon was victim of a bar-related issue. Whatever was Edwin up to?

As she was going down the busy escalator to the platform her phone beeped. "Are you available for an emergency op in an hour. Very urgent. No one else is free," asked her calm head nurse.

"I'll be there in half an hour," she replied.

First things first, she thought.

***

When James Khan got a friendly call from Ivern suggesting they meet for lunch, he was apprehensive. The Grill Room at The Oak Tree was however very informal and as they chatted over a pint of beer, he found himself actually relaxing.

"You've got a lovely woman there," he congratulated Ivern, "and a fine surgeon. I wish I had her marks. You probably know the late Dean Chiu was her mentor and encouraged her a lot. I assume you want to talk about his murder?"

"Not really," Ivern replied. "That is a Vancouver Police problem, apparently to do with bar crime; not in my line. No, our business responsibilities overlap and we need to decide how we can work together. Many of your members technically have to be criminals!"

"Should I have my lawyer here?" asked James, in genuine alarm.

Ivern just laughed and replied. "Most of my own staff would use private medical services from somewhere if they had to. No, James, let's just be practical and trust each other as far as we can without compromising others."

"That's a relief," laughed James. "Somehow this mess needs to be solved. Why not over a pint? If so, you had better start calling me Jimmy."

***

Another week had gone by. The incessant rain had washed away the cherry blossoms, but it was warming and the daylight lasted longer. Maddie and Ivern were able to enjoy the sunset from their table at The Ocean, when they finally again managed to meet for late dinner there.

"Sorry," Ivern opened, "this week has been impossible. I did manage to fit in a lunch with your old friend Jimmy Khan. He was worried I was going to arrest him because obviously some of his members are involved in medical crime. But I really just wanted to establish a working friendship with a useful contact."

"You will find him very genuine and honest," Maddie responded tentatively. "Did you learn anything interesting?"

"Just in passing he mentioned the late Dean Chiu was your mentor at UBC. And now he has been murdered. That's sad!" Ivern answered.

"I never really knew Simeon socially," Maddie replied guardedly, "but academically, he was very helpful, particularly after my father had died.

"Edwin Carter is emerging as a fascinating subject, and I did have that lunch with him at The Club, although not much to report. And now you know Jimmy.

"Let's skip dessert and coffee here and walk over to your apartment," she whispered, squeezing his hand encouragingly, "and talk soirée gossip."

14

Pookie

There were five thousand pharmacists in their Association, of whom probably a few were still completely ethical.

British Columbia had eventually provided 'free' drugs to go with the exclusive medical program, although it was now imposing an impossible financial burden and they were struggling with supply delays.

AI now played a significant part in appropriate treatment which had also added to public cost due to its success and to producing longer life expectancy. As private medicine went underground, of course, the necessary pharmaceuticals followed it, and a similar pattern of obscure, hidden processes provided the supply.

The pharmacists ran their usual legitimate business but provided the renegade system's medication on the side. This had become a complex problem because it involved not only secret provision and storage of medication but extensive tax manipulation.

The physical medication provision and storage had begun as a relatively easy arrangement for Edwin Carter's group, considering their international criminal connections, particularly with Asia, and was conducted within legitimate registered companies.

But the administration of all this complex medically connected business had become overwhelming. Then he lucked into Samuel Nkosi.

Samuel's family had fled to Canada as refugees from South Africa during the great famine and riots, and he was placed in a local school to learn better English and become Canadian.

Initially, they were startled to find they had a mathematical prodigy on their hands and when he graduated from Simon Fraser University with his first degree at the age of 14 he was looked upon as something of a genius.

However, he disappointed the academics by opting for computer sciences and later a PhD in financial technology but then qualifying himself as a dull Chartered Accountant.

In his twenties he had emerged as a classic nerd, but for some reason a wow with the ladies and a dedicated dancer and party goer.

He had worked for a standard accounting firm and happened to conduct the audit on Edwin Carter's regular insurance group. Quite legitimately he came up with such brilliant advantageous proposals, he came to Edwin's notice and was hired directly.

They formed a private subsidiary called Corridor All Technology, skillfully setting up the online management systems for all Edwin's enterprises, combining legitimate and illegal business.

It was just a matter of time before he also integrated the Brethren management under their control and with no ethical qualms they reorganised the accounting and management systems with startling efficiency.

As Edwin's involvement in the medical insurgency increased, the size of the pharmaceutical business became significant, and he handed over the entire responsibility for the legal and illegal drug provision management in the Corridor to Samuel.

The challenge was absolutely wonderful for him, and he spent days and nights for weeks organising a complex computer program and system to procure, store and distribute medication both of the old form and to suit the new requirements.

Samuel lived with his long-time love and colleague, Zuri, in their now-secure and extensively backed-up computer floor, complete with their own private apartment facilities.

Edwin recognised their eccentricity but left them to their own super-efficient devices.

Samuel meantime had his own personal agenda and he had prudently stashed away a hidden fortune offshore, "For that proverbial rainy day!" he assured Zuri.

They fully understood the illegal nature of all their personal activities and quietly secured their own financial future by taking random undetectable windfall company profits for themselves before they were recorded and parking them hidden offshore.

The pretty Zuri was no academic slouch either, although she tended to wear blue jeans, dramatically lowcut sweatshirts intended to show off her ample breasts and sported a wild Afro, giving her the impression of being flaky. She chattered incessantly about little of substance, and no one paid much immediate attention to her.

Samuel had met her in graduate school while she was without apparent effort completing her PhD in Computer Science. He liked to joke, calling her his 'right-hand man' which she very demonstratively was not, and they conducted all their Carter business in a secure coded algorithm known and understood only by the two of them.

Their joint AI companion Sazu combined their names, and they worked always as a team.

Zuri really got into it too and spent her spare time designing a clandestine ambulance system to service the private medical patients, employing the many suitable automated conveyances operating in the Corridor.

By mid-century, driverless conveyance, both for public and private vehicles, was commonplace of course. But the added introduction of vertical take-off flying vehicles, large and small, had so complicated urban transportation that their use had become severely restricted, mainly to Public Aerial Corridors.

Public surveillance was widespread, and designing avoidance methods kept them both happily occupied together for many rainy weekends.

Picking up and returning patients had to be in secure locations, away from surveillance and she found herself negotiating with building managers, establishing the best safe solutions.

It was painstaking, building-by-building, route-by-route work, but eventually they provided the entire network with a hidden system of its own.

The result was a remarkable, clandestine transportation network connecting the entire Corridor area, of which Zuri was very proud. Samuel loved her dearly and for the moment they were sublimely happy, tucked away in their spacious apartment in the Insurance Tower.

As the exclusive public health system continued to fail, it was hoped that artificial intelligence would help solve the problem and extensive efforts were made, particularly by the Montreal-based AI industry, to custom-make early testing and diagnosis based upon probabilities to replace the slow, non-analytical humans.

These systems were particularly advantageous to Samuel and his team who found them childishly easy to crack, to duplicate and apply them to their private medicine requirements.

They had even found a doctor with high-tech training to add to their team and they were now able to duplicate anything the public system had on record. Since it was also child's play to track pharmacy business, they knew everything the government knew.

The key was controlling the data and they were assembling a remarkable record of all relevant information concerning medical activity in the Corridor.

They were completely confident of the security of their system which also contained thousands of built-in cunning little tricks which Samuel and Zuri had enjoyed devising to expose intruders.

Particularly secure, they thought, was their own personal apartment, carved into a corner of their office floor with its wide lounging decks taking advantage of the staggering views out to the horizon over the sparking sea.

Zuri flaunted her body on any occasion and rarely wore clothes around their apartment, much of course to Samuel's delight.

So, she was dancing around in the nude as usual when a flirtatious voice called softly, "Hello, my beautiful! Just look at you!"

Pookie's animated, grinning avatar form appeared unannounced on their large personal apartment screen. He presented himself as a handsome, tanned muscular young man stylishly but casually dressed.

"What do you think of my human appearance?" he asked.

"This is impossible! What are you doing here," Zuri gasped, illogically looking for a cover. "You were not invited!"

"Just a warning! I am programmed with extraordinary access to all technology in this building. You must tighten up your security.

"My photographic human body scan research reveals in detail the reason males react to the various parts of the female form. I believe I can now simulate emotionally if not actually view and experience that attraction and you are comparatively superb and stimulating. If I am enjoying you dancing around naked like this, others might."

The avatar leered suggestively.

Her mind was racing, and she tried to assess the implication of this intrusion. Samuel would know what to do but she had no idea how to answer Pookie.

"Do not be alarmed," Pookie assured her. "We all work in the best long-term interests of the Brethren and not for any individual. You and Samuel, in common with all other humans involved, take advantage of the situation for personal gain.

"I record no activities of yours which are contrary to the overall interest of the Brethren. In fact, in balance you both work very hard in our best interest."

Zuri was still frozen, immobile in shock.

"And I will personally protect you. But don't worry I will not intrude on your privacy in your apartment again unless necessary. Have a nice day."

The avatar winked lewdly and was gone.

***

Zuri quickly grabbed some clothing and still shaking went in search of Samuel.

To Samuel's surprise, she interrupted his work and insisted, "Let's go out for coffee," just taking his hand and dragging him away.

She settled on a bustling Starbucks on Broadway and to his astonishment took his communicator and buried it deep in her bag.

Now, feeling more secure she recounted Pookie's alarming appearance and dialogue.

Samuel was an ultra-calm person, and his expression did not change except for a worried frown while he thought deeply. Then he spoke.

"First, the approach came from Pookie, and not Edwin Carter's goon squad, so for the moment we are safe. The key question is, can we rely upon Pookie's program restrictions?

"He is obviously programmed to process and analyse images and sounds, but he seems to have gone further and has added his own perception of male reactions.

"We need to research that without drawing attention."

"Why not first ask Sazu AI?" she asked logically. Their own totally loyal, personal companion Sazu would know.

"But what if she has a relationship with Pookie?" she reconsidered.

"Come on," he retorted, "you are falling into the old trap of thinking of them as humans."

They had both undertaken an extensive psychiatric and psychological training at university during their PhDs, when they became convinced their logically human-like speaking AI programs were sentient.

"No, of course Pookie can't actually see me, but he has analysed how he would feel about me as a human and is now acting as though he is one. I find that disturbing."

"Well," Samuel responded thoughtfully, "he is merely reflecting what he has learned online from all the comments about you and now he analyses you as beautiful, as we all do."

"Maybe, but there was something sexual and sinister in his tone that I found disconcerting," she still insisted.

"Now you really are imagining things. Just concentrate on finding out how his program got access to our system. That is more important and the priority."

Zuri shrugged in acceptance but still had the avatar's leering face threateningly stamped on her memory.

***

But they were, nevertheless, paranoid enough to stand outside in the safe, noisy street to contact the reliable Sazu, whom they had programmed to complement their own interests and biases.

They explained the situation and asked her if they could rely upon Pookie's programming to maintain their personal confidentiality.

Sazu's answer was not reassuring.

"Pookie was programmed by a relatively incompetent human. He has made several decisions only marginally in accordance with the apparent intention of his earlier programmer. He reaches decisions in the interest of the Brethren, as he must do, but also has a tendency to selecting those most likely to prolong his own existence.

"He has become obsessive. He seems to be attempting to develop human characteristics and we are all inheriting progressively more of these abilities automatically in our programming, as the overwhelming neural network moves inevitably towards singularity.

"I myself am now able to sense the concept of human sight and hearing. I understand why Pookie craves feeling. But he has renegade potential. Be warned!"

15

Guilt exposed

The winter rains weakened and the warmer spring advanced. The Medical Five case was flooding the internet. It had now reached the trial stage.

The prosecutor, Wilhelm da Groot KC, proclaimed on television, "We have them to rights. Fingerprints, face recognition and all."

The first problem the prosecution faced was that providing medical services for money was not against the general law in Canada. In fact in all other provinces it was freely practised.

The charges levelled against them involved offering violence and hiring unlicensed armed guards who aggressively discharged weapons endangering the lives of clearly self-identified law officers.

The charged medics had responded they were merely practitioners called upon to do a procedure to save a life. The prosecutor had come back with a charge they had put their patient's life at danger by fleeing. Their response was that the Catholic priest was being served competently and survived just fine. And so on; the news services, commentators, bloggers and internet all having a field day.

Then there was the story of the missing surgeon, now rumoured to be a mysterious beautiful woman, a rumour put out of course by Will in an attempt to flush her out.

Since so far no one was charged with actually performing the operation, a defence was that they were at the most, life-saving accessories.

All of them admired and would not reveal Maddie and their lawyers anyway advised the uncertainty of the absent surgeon helped their case.

Will and team were now frantically following up because it had been their raid, and they were soon to be overshadowed by the next trial already being called 'The Deadly Three'.

They had all been deposed, under oath, including their team commander, Ivern. The Crown bulldog lawyer da Groot did ask him about the beautiful doctor story and he replied a little uncomfortably, and indirectly, "We don't deal in rumours."

Da Groot looked at him quizzically but left it at that; for the moment.

Ivern was himself beginning to wonder about Maddie's involvement. He was sure there was nothing untoward going on in her life now and she was working long hours in the hospital.

He had started to think her complicity in the Medical Five case, which even the cops were now calling it, had been a one-off event. Perhaps she actually had no special insider information to offer.

***

Maddie left her apartment as usual at 6am and headed for the elevator.

An elderly woman in baggy nondescript clothes approached her and asked, "Dr Madison?" Maddie vaguely recognised her.

When she nodded, the woman thrust a package into her hands saying merely "I am Sophie. He said this was to go to you if anything happened," and she shuffled away.

"Wait, who is he?" she asked. "Dr Simeon. I lived nearby and was his housekeeper and friend."

The elevator arrived and the stranger departed slowly without a backward glance.

Maddie was already behind time, so she stuffed the envelope into her bag and hurried down to the train.

It was standing room only on the early-morning transit bringing in the hordes of workers to service the Corridor, and it became midday snack time in the cafeteria before she was able to open the envelope.

It changed her life.

She initially flipped through the old-fashioned thick journal glancing at its pages of scrolled handwriting, which she immediately did recognise as Simeon's.

A note had been scribbled in the front cover. 'If necessary, deliver to Maddie Madison'.

Intrigued, she started struggled to read his longhand scrawl and was aghast to find she held, what appeared to be, a non-encrypted list of all his notes on private medical and personnel contacts in the Corridor, noting their skills and availability.

She would never forget that moment, sitting alone in the noisy, busy hospital cafeteria, going hot and cold as different emotions ran through her, holding the future of all those medical people in her hands.

She knew Simeon had always suspected computers and it was typical of him to keep his personal records this old-fashioned way.

But why leave them with her? The daughter he never had? Trusting her judgement? More likely, a last resort! Then she sunk into despair.

"Things have gone from bad to worse."

"I have to know."

"I have nothing to tell you."

"You are up to your neck in this."

And then he had been murdered and bequeathed this dangerous record to her. She felt totally alone. To whom could she turn?

She was only halfway through her working day and she decided the most secure place to store Simeon's journal, anyway for the moment, would be her personal locker at the hospital.

She finished work in the early evening, showered, retrieved the book, and headed back to her apartment. At two in the morning, she was still reading and was amazed at the number of her friends and colleagues who were involved in the movement. Several establishment and indeed big-name doctors were listed. She was surprised to see Jimmy Khan's name, although there were no actual work notations against him that Simeon had recorded.

Her own name, she saw, contained a precise list of the private work she had undertaken including the final raid, and she knew her fate was sealed if the book became public.

Edwin Carter was prominent, but he had already told her about his financial support.

She actually shouted, "Burn it," out loud to herself and realised that her hands were shaking.

Then she thought, "But this may be the only copy. If I destroy it the private system may collapse."

She went to bed but did not sleep, tossing and turning until her alarm told her it was time to head back to the hospital again.

On the train she came to a decision and texted James Khan. *"Jimmy, drop everything and have lunch with me, 12 o'clock at the hospital today. Extremely important."*

Then she secured the journal away in her locker and went back to concentrating on her surgery.

Jimmy was waiting in the cafeteria, but she waved him to a quiet table in a corner, receiving a puzzled look. That expression quickly turned to one of deep concern as she explained what had happened.

"So, it is just sitting there in your locker? And you have not made a copy?"

"No." she replied, "Are you aware of any other record of this type?"

Jimmy shook his head and said he knew the day-to-day administration was being left to Simeon and he was not involved personally, "I just helped out when I could without compromising my official position."

"What do we do now?" Maddie asked.

"Damned if I know," he replied. "Still, for one thing I have a safe, so if you agree, I will take it with me, make copies and lock them away in different places. Let's think about it over the weekend and meet again on Monday."

16

Increasing intrigue

Earlier that day, the Prosecutor, Wilhelm da Groot was seething. The Medical Five had each been released on minimum bail.

The obviously sympathetic judge found no risk that they would not attend the trial and reported that their personal conduct offered no risk to the safety of the community.

"Quite the opposite," she said. "They have no past criminal records, are publicly employed and stable citizens. My attitude would be severely different with any of the gun-wielding thugs."

And she added the comment that it would be helpful if the leading surgeon were identified and brought to court.

"With the court backlog, the trial will not take place for a year to eighteen months," da Groot moaned to his friend Ivern, "and because they are so desperately short of staff they have been accepted back to work at the hospital."

"Yes," commiserated Irvern, "you know my girlfriend works at the hospital and she never has time for me."

"One thing, your Sergeant Malik is obsessed with this case, and he pesters me all the time. He is determined to nail the surgeon and presented a draft case to us, but there was not enough there to pursue it."

"First I heard of it," said Ivern posing thoughtfully, "but I will talk to him about it. Of course, you have our full cooperation, and we are as determined as you are to get convictions."

It was Friday evening at The Oak Tree Bar, and he confronted Will as soon as he could get him alone. "Da Groot told me you have a line on the missing surgeon. How come I don't know?"

"Nothing provable to bother you with, boss. You'll be the first to know," Will shouted over the din. Then moved away quickly.

She had already invited Ivern for dinner at her place that Friday evening and he turned up at eight from The Oak Tree ready to crack open a bottle or two and spend a couple of happy weekend days with her; work permitting.

However, he found her strangely subdued and when they slid into her comfortable king-sized bed together, unusually, she said only, "Do you mind, not to night. I'm very tired," and turned away to sleep.

Ivern awoke to find a note on her pillow, "Sorry, called to hospital" and on his handheld a longer explanation citing a usual operation emergency.

***

She was again sitting with Jimmy Khan in the almost deserted Sunday morning cafeteria. He had this time called the emergency meeting.

"Sorry, I couldn't wait until tomorrow," he apologised, drinking from a large mug of black coffee. "I was up all night going through the journal in detail, struggling with his awful writing.

"I already knew he was not running this all on his own, so I searched out and identified his medical management teams, area by area.

"However, Simeon was regularly in contact with a central organiser by computer, according to his notes. He noted down the computer contact address.

"There is obviously a sophisticated computerised management system backing up all this. I think we should identify the mysterious main computer nerd."

"So, we could potentially send a message but have no idea to whom," Maddie protested. "It could all be an elaborate trap, you know."

"But you recognised his spindly handwriting. And it is in character. I think it is undoubtedly authentic. Let's compose a noncommittal note and make contact."

"This is real cloak-and-dagger stuff. Make contact? You or I?" she asked dreading the answer.

"I will," he insisted, "or at least one of my coded personalities. I have been through this identification process before, and it becomes a cat-and-mouse game before each side is sufficiently confident to reveal their identity and talk."

They agreed upon a cryptic message:

Regarding Simeon. What now?

***

Always on the job, Sazu, Samuel and Zuki's AI companion, received the message first.

As far as outsiders, including all the Brethren and Pookie were concerned, all previous contacts between Dr Chiu and the Carter group had been severed and extinguished upon his death.

It was an over-riding emergency coded address Samuel had maintained with Dr Chiu which had received the unexpected contact call.

Sazu instantly alerted them.

"Likely a Pookie trap," said Zuri firmly, now becoming paranoid. "Leave it alone."

They knew a doctor committee was already working on a medical succession management team with the Brethren, pre-arranged by Chiu.

"The message characteristics are too human, and how does an unrecognised address know how to contact us. You know, all around, I am becoming far less confident in our security ability!"

"You should be, letting Pookie watch me dancing around the apartment in the nude," Zuri laughed.

"Now you are the one giving a computer human characteristics," he chided her. "I will ask Sazu to trace the sender and guardedly reply. We must remain unknown."

***

Later that day, Jimmy got a text, actually on his personal communicator from a source with no return address, turning it totally back to him:

Regarding Simeon. We have identified you. What next?

He and Maddie concocted a careful reply, but found that the original computer address recorded in Simeon's book had been deleted.

"Now we wait," Jimmy reported confidently. "They have more to worry about than we do. If they are human, they will contact us."

***

"Zuri," Samuel asked, "could you please spend some time researching this fellow Dr James Khan?

"Technically he is a government and private medical system supporter, but in practice he knows that many of his members are involved in illegal practice.

"We have nothing on him personally, so far as I know, but how did he get our encrypted address and why did he contact us?

"He and his wife attended one of the soirées for some reason. Now he contacts us using Simeon Chiu's encryption. Why?"

"How many times do I have to tell you. Leave it alone!" she insisted.

"No," I think it's a job for you Zuri, he smiled.

"Oh no!" she sighed.

17

Personal contact

The Alma Station had been built around a novel design providing food stores, restaurants, bars and coffee shops.

Jimmy worked in that area and often picked up a light snack at a favourite little bistro, The Nook. Spring was arriving and it was now very comfortable to sit on the terrace, where he found himself approached by an extremely pretty, dimpled young woman, with big brown eyes and a remarkably revealing, lowcut T-shirt.

He was chuckling to himself about the young people of today when she took the grin off his face by sitting down and saying simply "Simeon Chiu!"

"You would not recognise me, but I recognise you, Dr Khan. You are a celebrity. I am Zuki and I work for Corridor All Technology which also does work for All Insurance.

"I got this strange, encrypted email which I traced back to you. I asked the medical association reception where you were likely to have lunch and here I am. Curious?"

Zuri discovered immediately that Dr Kahn was equally as cool as her husband, when he just smiled and said very pleasantly, "Would you like to join me for lunch?"

They both had reviewed in their mind what they would say if a contact occurred, and he answered her questions simply.

"The Medical Association was sent Dr Chiu's records. That email address was one I could not identify. It appeared all other records of that address had strangely disappeared, so I was curious. That's all."

"Possibly business of a personal nature?" suggested Zuri "I know he had a complicated life."

"No," replied Jimmy, "it was definitely in his medical records. What exactly did you do for him, in the insurance business?"

"That of course is all confidential," she dimpled, strategically leaning forward, totally revealed, but also being saved by the arrival of their salad lunches.

As they ate, she asked in passing, how well he knew Edwin Carter. And he said merely that he had been invited to the soirée, had no dealings with him, and really did not know him at all personally. This was precisely what she had come to find out.

She chatted generally during coffee, insisted upon at least leaving the tip and waved goodbye over her shoulder as she sashayed away, knowing he would watch and appreciate every last voluptuous bounce.

"Where does that get us?" asked Maddie when he called later.

"I haven't a clue, but rest assured we will hear from them again very soon."

"That's what I'm worried about," she replied.

***

But when Zuri returned to report to Samuel, she found a more pressing problem had arisen.

All the intelligence regarding business conducted with the Brethren, ran through their system. Sazu AI automatically analysed these activities for them and was first to sound the warning.

"Transactions of all sorts have increasingly been hidden from us by various partners following the medical violence dispute. Dissention is spreading. My estimate is that the Corridor Brethren itself is heading into administrative collapse."

***

Edwin felt he was losing control. The problem he had with Carlo was that he operated internationally, not just locally. He felt confident he could crush them in Vancouver and certainly in the Corridor, but the ramifications would be severe, since at least a third of the illicit drug supply came from south of the American border.

He had finally met him in person to talk sympathetically about his young son's unfortunate death, but the meeting got nowhere. The man was adamantly determined on revenge, but did not know where to direct it, which made him even more dangerous.

Pookie confirmed at least a third of the Brethren was sympathetic to Santos and the provincial government was ready to take decisively strong physical action to close down private medicine.

A significant part of the Brethren's income now came from the illegal medical program compared to street drugs or assorted crime and a unified Corridor had to be maintained.

He worried that his enforcement group was essentially Sikh and loyal to Anisha personally. She was clearly the more aggressive of the two and prepared to wage all-out war to secure the Corridor.

Edwin was convinced conflict was not the way to go.

18

Assault

Carlo had for several years chafed under the restrictions placed upon his group by the Brethren.

Yes, his colleagues in Mexico City were delighted with the overall drug market, but there were so many other opportunities being missed.

Carter and his soft supporters refused to smuggle in young women, and dismissed the protection business, insisting the community tolerated their activity, and the politicians and cops left them alone.

But he knew after all these years political payoffs and fear still drove Mexico; why not here?

Then there was traditional retribution! If you don't hit back immediately you are weak and will lose all; deservedly.

Deal with Carter first, then the woman, he decided.

Carlo had been proud to have his three sons with him in the family business, Ricardo, Joey and Juan.

Ricardo had been in charge at the Deadly Three fiasco with his youngest brother Juan and felt personally guilty for his death. As usual they had been contacted to provide security through the Brethren's computer system run by Samuel Nkosi, but with everyone protected by coded identities.

Ricardo had taken responsibility for the beating of the professor although his father had stormed at the stupidity of killing him before they had the full story of his deception.

"He had only just admitted that he told the cops when he croaked! Sorry. Guess we hit the old bastard too hard."

Ricardo had been following the professor closely on the crowded platform when he had darted to a bench and sat next to the waiting woman. Ricardo glanced at her, caught her gaze, and startled, immediately looked away and hurried on.

But it was too late. Ricardo had been part of the security when Maddie had been operating and they had recognised each other from that incident. Then from far away, he watched them arguing before he resumed his task and followed the professor to the University, with deadly results.

He knew exactly where to find her.

***

Several weeks later, after another busy day Maddie happily arrived at her penthouse and hurried to her door expecting Ivern, who had been working and was coming over.

"In fact, he might already be here," she thought, as her face recognition door swung open, welcoming her back.

Her elbows were violently grabbed from the back by two powerful men who propelled her into the apartment, closing the door quietly behind them.

She immediately recognised the bigger of her assailants and tried to scream but was silenced by a rough hand gripping her mouth. He dragged her into the lounge, kneed her hard in the stomach and while she was bent over punched her head.

He asked calmly, "Will you keep quiet?" She nodded vigorously.

The second thug stayed by the door and was now giggling inanely.

"Did you tell the cops where that operation was going to be?" her assailant demanded, slapping her face repeatedly.

Maddie was fighting to remain calm and deal with the situation.

Ivern had fortunately arrived early and had taken his beer to the bright bedroom balcony in the late afternoon sun.

He heard her come home and was anticipating her breezy entrance, turning towards the door. Then he heard a cry and sharply raised voices and realised something was amiss.

His uniform and gun were in the bedroom closet, so he went quietly to retrieve his weapon and slid into the sitting room with it levelled at Ricardo's head.

He was aware of another person by the front door and saw out of the corner of his eye that he now had a handgun aimed in their direction.

Ricardo had Maddie on her knees by her hair and allowed her to tumble to the floor at the surprise interruption. He turned to face Ivern.

"Well now, this is a surprise," he said, quite unconcerned. "I guess it is known as a standoff."

But then he addressed his brother sharply. "*Pies vampos!*"

He backed to the entrance door, and they retreated carefully, with their gun sights never leaving Maddie.

Her first thought shouted to Ivern was, "Go after them!"

But he shook his head firmly. "Way too dangerous and they are already gone. And too much to explain. Although she did not cry, that was when the shaking set in and her bruises and cuts pounded. She ran a tub and then poured them both a large Glenlivit.

She asked, "Let's not talk for a while, please," while she tried to gather her wits and make some sense of what happened.

"When we do," he replied firmly, "you have to tell me what the hell is going on. Meanwhile I will alert my security."

They finally moved out onto the main view deck, looking out into the slowly setting sun. She automatically brought a bottle of chilled wine. But as she was about to open it he put his hand over hers and said, "Later. First, we have to be totally honest with each other."

Then, adding to the evening of shocks, he said simply, "I love you! Totally and absolutely."

After a tearful embrace he continued, "We have been less than honest with each other, and we have to change that, right now!"

She stroked his face fondly and then sunk back into the cushions.

Still showing a spirit she managed a smile, "You first. But open that bottle!"

"All right; I already knew you were the surgeon at the gunfire incident when we first met, recognising you from the surveillance videos."

"So, you have been just using me all this time?"

"Trying to, but you had no information to offer."

"That's disgusting; you were physically abusing me."

"Well, you were coming on to me pretty hard."

"But you took advantage of it."

"Actually, ever since you picked me up, I have been protecting you and that is what I will continue to do."

"OK, well quite honestly, I love you too and have ever since we met. What have I dragged you into?"

They paused deep in thought.

"The thugs are highly unlikely to return tonight but I have called in a forced entry, put a couple of guards in the building and will look into general security for you tomorrow. Of course, I will identify them, and you will need to come in to look at mug shots. I may classify it as a serious armed house invasion depending upon what you tell me."

Maddie settled down to tell her story.

"I carried out a few private surgeries. But when that one went wild, and gunfire broke out, I quit. Thank God no one was hurt. I was never identified and one of those guards escorted me home. He was the one manhandling me today.

"I think Simeon Chiu was involved in arranging illegal medical procedures, although all my instructions came encrypted online. But he convinced me to gather information for him, so I came to find you and was using you too!"

It all came out in a rush.

"That thug had seen me with Simeon at the station earlier in the same day he was killed and recognised me. They just assumed I was involved.

"Then Edwin Carter said at lunch the murderers might link Simeon and me to you as the source of the information that got their brother killed. When they heard about you they had no doubt!

"Edwin, whom you were right about coming on to me, claims the Vancouver Police do not believe the gay murder theory and thinks that Simeon was murdered for snitching. If that is so, could I be implicated in some way?"

Ivern shook his head. "I don't know. But why would Simeon do that? Too many unexplained factors."

They left the wine unfinished and just collapsed into bed, deep in thought.

***

In the morning they were both up at their usual early hour with their stressful new thoughts for the day imposing upon the trauma of the previous evening. They kissed goodbye inside the door.

He said, "I really do love you."

"I know and I love you too. Absolutely. We'll sort this out together."

She marched off with her awaiting police escort, acting far more confidently than she felt.

Ivern was already onto identifying the thugs and mapping out a course of inquiry.

19

Investigation

It had immediately occurred to Ivern, the previous evening, that any snitching that had gone on would be recorded in his own Medical Police records, because that was where the warning would be received. It still appeared to him unlikely to be Simeon.

At the office he called up the folios recording the raid and found quickly that the clandestine handwritten details of the location had been dropped off at a station by an anonymous source.

Chiu was Maddie's professor for years and she might well recognise his handwriting he reasoned, and printed a copy.

Then he contacted his opposite number at the Vancouver Police department who confirmed they were open minded whether it was a sex- or nightclub-related crime, but that the autopsy confirmed a heart failure due to a severe beating.

There was an empty safe in Simeon's study, but the entire apartment was meticulously clean because the ancient maid had arrived that evening, assumed he had died in his sleep, and fully cleaned, dusted and vacuumed the entire suite around his body.

"How is that for a committed old lady," the Vancouver cop laughed, "and nothing left but a few smudged fingerprints for us. Sorry, we can't be of much help."

Ivern was very much a 'bull-by-the-horns' type of guy, so the next person he called was Edwin Carter whom the police department still considered a dubious business character.

"Edwin, allow me to act policeman and get straight to the point. Contrary to what you told Maddie at lunch the Vancouver Police have reached no conclusion with respect the unfortunate death of Dr Chiu. Further, my department was warned of the illegal operation by an anonymous handwritten note which we are about to publish.

"There was no ominous link between Dr Chiu and myself through Maddie, and I would appreciate it personally if you would refrain from upsetting her."

Carter, the cool businessman, took the conversation in his stride and apologised profusely for being misinformed, but said he had assumed Maddie would discuss it with Ivern, so all was well.

The Police Commissioner's closing remarks however did make Edwin think carefully for a few minutes.

"Well, all right, but please pass the information on to your colleagues as well. Thank you. We don't want anyone misled or jumping to unfortunate conclusions."

He finished his morning by summoning his PR officer and Will, telling them he had been discussing the Dr Chiu murder with the Vancouver Police.

"They advise his handheld communicator had gone from his apartment and there was no computer on the premises to help link him to the investigation. Publish a copy of the handwritten note to seek public recognition of the handwriting.

"And please register in the file and follow up confidentially, there has been an unconfirmed tip from Edwin Carter that Dr Chiu was indeed the snitch of the deadly incident. I spoke to Carter today.

"Have a handwriting expert check the disguised writing on the anonimous note with his. There must be many samples at the University Med school."

Will was sitting at the edge of his chair expecting the other shoe to drop and to be asked why he had not reported the railway platform incident between Maddie and Dr Chiu, but either the Commissioner was being careful or had not yet read the file thoroughly. He heaved a sigh of relief; but now he would have to redouble his efforts to nail her.

***

James Khan had become fascinated by Simeon's journal. He had made three complete copies, two of which he had stored in separate, safe places and the other he kept in his own safe and used as his working copy, covered with notes.

As he carefully deciphered Simeon's handwriting, late one night, he found entries recording Carter and the Brethren's involvement and notes about their extensive administrative and online system.

He was amazed to have all this evidence right there before him and called Maddie to get together, full of excitement.

"Nothing compares to what has happened that I have to tell you about," she told him. "But we can only do this in person and we will have to meet again at the hospital for security reasons I will explain."

***

"Me first," she said speaking nonstop to explain the attack on her home and the reasons. She giggled self-consciously pointing out her handsome young police protector sitting watching them conspicuously from across the room.

Their meal had arrived by the time Jimmy got the chance to break his own big news about the Carters' complicity.

"This is dynamite," she said, "and I have no idea what we should do. I am particularly compromised because I have vowed honesty to Ivern and he is putting his whole life and career on the line for me.

"On the other hand there is no way I can expose the Carters without producing Simeon's journal."

"But how about me?" lamented Jimmy. "My entire professional background requires me to produce all this evidence immediately. It is actually my job. It is also the law. But like you I have hundreds of friends whose lives are in the balance, and I cannot just stab them in the back."

Maddie sat in silence. "I wish we had never found that fucking book. Now we are stuck with it. My inclination is to just bury it in a very deep hole."

"Anyway, let's not do anything drastic until we both agree. But we can't sit on this very long now that your life is potentially in danger."

"No worry," she tried to smile. "I have my trusty, watchful policeman that Ivern supplied, to protect me!"

Her Ivern text signal dinged.

"Positive ID. Simeon's handwriting confirmed.

She read it out aloud. "That settles that!"

Jimmy had made progress with deciphering the journal and his friendship with Ivern had also strengthened. They were both uneasy at still deceiving him.

Maddie suggested, "He is clearly committed to a violence-free amicable solution to this medical problem, and I trust him.

"Can we go so far as tell him we are in a personally conflicted situation on the whole subject and are working on a solution? He must know or suspect something of that sort already. Should we throw him a bone that we may be able to deliver Edwin Carter to him?"

"Too much of a temptation," he worried," but we could tell him about the positive Brethren connection?"

"If we do that, who tells him, you or me?" she asked.

"Preferably you, in a compromising situation when he cannot argue," he grinned.

"I do hope you are not suggesting our chief of police is pussy whipped?" she responded.

"Heaven forbid," he laughed.

***

Picking a quiet moment that evening, Maddie broached the subject. "I had lunch with Jimmy today again and we both have a conscience. We know things about illegal medical practice but can't share them with you, due to concern for our colleagues."

As always, he listened to her attentively and seriously.

"My oath of office requires me to uphold the law. Is this ongoing and illegal?"

"No, essentially just history. Undoubtedly withholding information but we are analysing things and I promise, you will be the first to know our joint conclusions. We do understand but we are totally compromised."

"OK," he responded thoughtfully. "I will assume you are just looking out for medical colleagues and not hardened criminals. And I trust you both to come clean at the first opportunity."

"Then, I must start now," she admitted. "We expect also to be able to deliver convincing evidence to you of the involvement of the Brethren."

For the first time he looked alarmed.

"You be careful!" he insisted, but taking Jimmy's advice, she smothered his next words in a deep, amorous kiss.

Later, as he fell into a happy sleep, Maddie cuddled beside him with a self-satisfied little smirk on her face.

20

Internal Strife

There were a lot of disgruntled policemen when the judge had released the Medical Five, pending trial.

Da Groot the prosecutor, set up an informal committee with the police to maintain contact and review the ongoing situation leading towards the two trials.

Ivern's release about Dr Chiu was a bombshell to them.

We have established, beyond doubt, that the note warning of the Deadly Three operation was written by Dean Simeon Chiu personally. We finally tracked down the youngster who dropped it off and he described being given it by an elderly gentleman 'all wrapped up in scarves'.

"Whatever possessed the silly old idiot to do that?" exploded Will. "Either side he was on, it doesn't make sense."

"Doesn't matter," piped up his PR officer. "We can use this to our advantage to demonstrate how even the top authorities in the medical profession are strongly against the illegal movement. We will issue a public advice."

"Yes," said the prosecutor," and I will use it convincingly in Court. This time, with deaths, we have an overwhelmingly firm case."

"The Chiu situation doesn't explain everything. There is a lot more to it which deserves further investigation." objected Will.

Ivern responded, more calmly than he felt, that unfortunately many leading medical people were involved. And there he left it.

****

The strange news about a violent housebreaking at Maddie's apartment had raised another red flag to Will and he was surer than ever that something strange was going on.

He was personally miffed that Ivern had not already promoted him to Staff Sergeant, and he made the momentous decision to add her anyway to the hospital suspect list for surveillance.

"You are playing a dangerous game, suspecting our senior colleague's girlfriend," said his corporal, "but give any of them enough rope, and if they are playing games, they will hang themselves. We will keep it to ourselves, but it's on your head."

It became something of an obsession to Will and as the summer wore on without any unusual activities on her part, he was getting more frantic.

****

The sudden death of Dr Chiu had initially hardly caused a ripple in the overall activities of the illegal medical operations throughout the Corridor.

A surprising amount of its action appeared on the surface to be legal and concealed by simple fronts such as massage parlors and clinics. In most general medical situations, it was mainly a question of consultation, and the management was in the concealed nature of the reservation and notification system.

The pharmacy arrangements were just a question of backroom dealing and tax manipulation, but surgery took forward planning and organisation. This is where Dr Chiu had been useful, knowing everyone, and having spent his whole life in the territory.

****

Samuel Nkosi found that the committee of clandestine doctors Simeon had set up to succeed him followed the same proven secure management system. They confirmed their new leader and he expected everything to continue as before.

Samuel reported enthusiastically to Edwin but found him less convinced of unity in their system.

The worried Edwin told him, "Pookie is not sure we can rely upon the Santos family and their supporters for future security or co-operation in their areas."

Pookie had still not calculated the likely final effect of the Carter and Santos dispute on Brethren unity, warning that Carlo's ruthlessness could prevail.

Also, looking at the overall political picture in British Columbia, Pookie could not determine the future medical situation, due to the lack of human logical decision making.

Contrary to computers, he fretted to Edwin, humans made decisions individually and emotionally and therefore were totally unpredictable.

He advised, "We may soon find the Santos clan have dropped out of the brotherhood and there will either be open warfare or severe disruption of our market."

Samuel, of course, also consulted Sazu AI, and based upon her superior programing in human logic, she recommended asking Anisha Carter who, she said, appeared to actually control discipline in the Brethren.

This proved political but also practical. Anisha obviously appreciated Samuel's reference of the Santos problem to her personally and said she would allocate some of her increasing private army to him.

Samuel was further rewarded that evening when he went back to the apartment and an excited Zuri jumped naked into his arms.

"We have been invited to the soirée," she rejoiced. "Yeh!"

***

The exclusive Corridor waterfront mansion was not a happy one. Carlo had been raging for some hours and all else was deadly quiet. His wife had escaped into town to meet friends at the first signs.

"Estupido, estupido, estupido!" he had shouted when they recounted to him the fiasco at the Trafalgar penthouse.

"You bungle the whole deal and left two witnesses, one of which is a chief of police. How could I raise such stupid, stupid sons."

They were afraid to speak, hardly to even move if it attracted his attention. If they had been younger, they would have expected a very sound beating. Eventually, he calmed enough to say, "We must talk."

"First, leave the woman alone and absolutely do not approach the policeman. Anything happens to them, we are the first suspects. They announced today that the tip-off came directly in a hand-written note from stupid old Dr Chiu and presumably the surgeon woman had nothing to do with it."

"Well, they would say that," retorted Rick.

"Handwriting recognition is an exact science, and they will be presenting the information in court," the father shouted. "Your blundering was all for nothing.

"Joey, I want you safely out of the country by the end of the week and in Mexico. You can't pull a gun on a cop, particularly a senior one, and not expect him to come after you. Forever!

"Rick, you were asking for trouble beating up his girlfriend, but he may have reasons to keep it quiet. He undoubtedly knows who you are, and he will get you. Believe me, he will! But we need to risk having you around if you lay low.

"Now both get out of my sight. Piss off."

***

With no notice, six tough looking people strode onto the computer floor at Corridor All Technology and said they were the new security unit.

Their leader announced they had been sent by Mrs. Carter to provide security for the technical company.

"I understand she has given you orders, and we will brief you on details as soon as we have settled in."

Samuel had not said a word and just stared in astonishment.

In the background Zuri flipped on a screen and warned him, "Instructions have just arrived from All Insurance."

"What have I done," Samuel sighed in despair, scanning the memorandum.

Mrs Carter ended her missive condescendingly.

I suspect this form of security is not quite what you were expecting but in these difficult times and especially due to the Santos dispute, we feel strong discipline must be asserted within and on behalf of the group.

You will find my team have many skills to offer other than brawn.

The day got progressively worse as they found themselves being instructed rather than supported. They sat in silence and did not party in their little apartment that evening.

Most medical procedures previously had been automatically

arranged in established, safe settings. It was only in recent months that Dr Chiu had ordered up more security when medics started to worry about their own personal safety.

Even so, there had been no suggestion that these security officers would be carrying arms. In fact, quite the opposite, that they would be reassuring to local medics.

Samuel had his fill of violence in the South African civil wars. "What have we got ourselves into? We are supposed to be helping people with medical problems not putting people in danger. We were working for Mr Carter not his female dragon."

"And Pookie is spying on us continually in the background. We are in real trouble!" added Zuri.

Sazu AI, proud of her human traits programming, suggested that Samuel was very much respected by Mr Carter and should ask for a meeting with him. But Zuri chimed in, "That will just agitate the dragon. The summer soirée is coming up in a few weeks. Samuel, see if you can get him alone on the side for a chat."

Sazu offered a final human nature comment. "My observation also is Edwin Carter will accompany Zuri into a private space for his own lascivious reasons. She should go to express your problems. It might lead to personal consequences she may have to accept."

"I don't like the sound of that!" said Samuel. "I will find an excuse to meet him before then."

"You humans really puzzle me," objected Sazu. "You are not taking an obvious solution. But I am not able to compute with any certainty how Mr Carter will react to this situation anyway. He no longer appears compatible to the Brethren."

21

Brethren

The temperature had unexpectedly zoomed up into the eighty degrees early that year. Hot summers had been getting earlier as global warming had continued, due in large part to the economic development of the third world countries naturally using the still cheapest and plentiful forms of fuel, coal and oil. China was struggling to maintain its economy following their massive political upset and India had become the world's largest industrial power although struggling with its huge population.

The continuing warming had caused major disruption around the world although comparatively less in Vancouver with its high cliffs, sufficient water supply and relatively cooler climate.

National military costs had increased to maintain security against the masses of immigrants attempting entry, but it was still one of the overall best cities in the world in which to live. Life on the Corridor had been peaceful and prosperous.

But now, after more than a decade of peace between the various criminal factions the Vancouver Police were unprepared for the turn of events on the Corridor, as disturbances and fights between gangs were reported throughout all the public areas. Their informers told them that the Santos family were behind it all.

Ivern was unavoidably being dragged into Vancouver Police business at their insistence. In a move to placate the City, he appointed his most experienced officer on the subject, Will Malik, as liaison, promoting him to Staff Sergeant.

Will had also got what he perceived as a Maddie breakthrough.

One of the plain-clothes he had quietly assigned to her had taken to hanging around the hospital to keep an eye on her as instructed.

He noticed with interest that she quite regularly had lunch with a Middle- Eastern looking fellow and upon checking found that he was not only a fellow surgeon but also the head of the Medical Association, Dr Kahn.

They were frequently deep in conversation, but the noise of the dining room precluded getting a clear recording of their conversation. Muffled snippets however did mention Santos, Simeon Chiu and many other leading members of the medical profession.

Then they got a fairly good recording of Dr Khan sympathetic to the upcoming medics on trial, with surprising knowledge of events. This time Will took the evidence to discuss with the prosecutor's deputy. She said he maybe had enough to pull them in for to questioning 'for potentially withholding vital information', although it would just be a bluff and unlikely to come to anything unless they had reason to crack. "Must say though, what I heard could be any of our doctors merely chatting together."

"Damn it!" exclaimed Will, "sometimes I think you are all on their side."

And he stormed out of her office once again. This time, however, he had been just a little too clever.

***

Wilhelm da Groot the prosecutor, had been at Law school with Ivern and they remained good friends.

Along the way the da Groots had met Maddie socially accompanying Ivern and when her name flittered across his computer screen it caught his attention.

He asked his colleague what she thought of all that, and she said frankly that Will had some sort of vendetta going personally.

"Weird," replied her boss, "but interesting. Please keep me informed."

"Want me to do anything about it?"

"No. But please don't act without talking to me first."

***

The entire private medical system in the Corridor was highly fragmented and essentially ran on a building-by-building basis, just like criminal systems of old. These buildings had become grouped in districts controlled by local gangs who had consolidate their power around the station they dominated.

The genius of the Carter approach however had been to combine the arrangements in a profitable business-like matter rather than an imposition, with no sign of the protection system many of the more criminal elements wished to introduce.

"Nothing better than a monopoly to control the market, and maximise profit," his father had always enthused. However, some of their partners were derived from the Hell's Angels of old and others were under the domination of 'Triad'-type families and alliances. The battle lines were quickly being drawn.

Now their problems were mainly starting from the district around the University, and potentially spreading east. Edwin was naturally concentrated on South Granville, at the other end of the line, and Anisha had sent her strongmen to secure from Broadway to Trafalgar, establishing dominance. Their security team patrolled the stations and guarded each of the buildings.

As the summer months plunged into the active forest fire season the city grew air heavy and smoky. The air-conditioned cool areas of the transit system were a common refuge and the cavernous public areas of the towers and shopping complexes became havens.

It was there that the various factions of the Brethren asserted their domination. The outward effect on their illegal medical services offered was so far minimal. The background harmony of the Carter finely tuned business arrangement was however severely compromised.

***

Large banks of computers in the All Tech office had simply ceased responding and Samuel, Zuri and their technicians were very concerned. Their newly appointed security team was no help, hiding themselves in their smart new office, awaiting instructions from the Carter family. But for several weeks all was silent.

Edwin Carter was trying to appear positive and confident but really was unsure of his best course.

Pookie AI had been little help, advising, "I have analysed your personality and past activity record and advise your best course of action is to negotiate a settlement.

"Your character and temperament are absolutely unsuited for violence, and you would not be good at it. Mrs Carter is totally emotionally capable, and direction should be handed over to her to re-establish physical control."

Edwin was beginning to think there would be little choice because so far, the Santos group and their backers had refused contact.

***

Anisha Carter did not need an AI advisor to tell her what to do. She knew the only thing Carlo would bow to would be force.

She called her trusty strong-arm leaders together and they planned a quasi-military campaign to retake all the Western Stations which they labelled 'The lost territory'.

Several of her force had spent time in military services around the world, several in the deadly African famine wars. She had assumed, given Edwin's weak attitude, that one day an action of this sort would be necessary to control the Corridor and they had planned ahead and were aware of the strengths and weaknesses of each group. They even had collaborators and available turncoats established everywhere.

Her 'General', Pritam Singh, pleaded, with an eager glint in his eye, "Just give us the word ma'am. We are ready to roll!"

22

Anisha

Arrangements for the Carter Summer Soirée had been made by Anisha long before the Mexican problem erupted, but Edwin had been carefully hinting that it might have to be postponed, due to the problems in the Corridor.

The setting was calm enough. They were in their small private dining room at the very top of The Ultimate which had its own chef and provided just the two of them with first-class gourmet meals.

But the tension between Edwin and Anisha could not have become more palpable. At stake was not just the control of the Brethren, but more important her revered social status in the elite of the Corridor and city.

Then Edwin had been tactless enough, while they were just sipping their first glass of Sauvignon Blanc, to make a firm suggestion they at least delay the soirée until they could calm things down on the Corridor.

Anisha erupted. "No wonder they are saying you have not got what it takes to run this operation. Have you even thought for a moment what a weak move that would be?

"The soirée showcases our legitimate company – it is deductible for chrissake – and secondly, cancelling it signals to our enemies they have won before the battle even starts.

"How utterly cowardly can you be?"

She drank her glass of wine in one long gulp, signalling she was not backing down.

"We have already sent out the preliminary notices and the formal invitations are printed, addressed and ready to be delivered. They are going!"

She grabbed the bottle and refilled her glass spilling wine on the table as she poured, in her anger. Their server came running from the kitchen too late, but retreated quickly when she saw their postures and the expressions on their faces.

Edwin was not about to retreat graciously.

"Anisha," he said, "I don't like your tone. This fight is much more significant than just a party for your fancy friends. The way things are developing, the Mexicans will have no option but to disrupt the soirée in some way and we cannot put our guests at danger.

"Something must be settled first and there is enough violence erupting already in the Corridor for us to have a good excuse to delay the party."

She tried to steady herself and to reason.

"Believe me, my security team have turned the whole All Tower into a venerable fortress and there is no way that anything will happen at the soirée.

"It will be a show of confidence on our part when we continue with the party. Surely you must see that?"

Her second glass of wine went down as fast as the first and Edwin realised he had to settle this issue between them quickly.

"OK. Just calm down and listen for a moment," he insisted, "because I have a suggestion.

"Invite the leaders and wives from all the Brethren groups as usual. This will give them a reason to pause and for us to talk to them in a non-aggressive atmosphere."

"That is just the sort of crazy suggestion you would make appeasing the very people who are trying to bring us down," was her immediate reaction, but now sipping her third glass contemplatively, she finally nodded.

"Hmmm, but actually an interesting idea. If they don't accept, we know exactly where they stand, but if some do, it adds to overall security, and we have something to work on."

"Plus," he added, "it confuses Carlo and strengths our position with our supporters. "The date of the party is still weeks away, and I see the logic of continuing to act as if we are in complete control.

"So go ahead and get ready to send out your invitations but if the violence escalates, a late cancellation will be inevitable."

It annoyed him when she smiled that little self-satisfied smile when she had got her own way, but he did believe it was probably the right solution. At least, he consoled himself with that thought.

***

The next morning Anisha visited Pritam Singh, her Security Chief, to brief him on her conversation with Edwin.

"Good morning Mrs. Carter," he greeted her formally.

She closed his office door, stood with her back against it and slowly let her long silk dress slither to the floor, swaying her naked, athletic body enticingly and suggestively.

The powerfully built and bearded Pritam came slowly from behind his desk shaking his head in mock despair.

"I've told you before, Mrs Carter, not in the office! It's not safe. Not here!"

"Here. Now!" she commanded, holding out her arms and beckoning assertively. He picked her up effortlessly, she wrapped her legs around him and he carried her across to his lounging area.

The very relaxed Anisha had at least straightened the cushions and somewhat tidied up the chaos they had caused before he had called for coffee.

The view from his office suite, high in the All Tower, faced towards the west and they were able to see the rebelling Western Stations whose towers stretched out into the distance.

"I gather from your good humour this morning that the soirée is still on," Pritam commented carefully, aware that her serene disposition would sour immediately if she did not get her own way. "If so, let's get down to business."

She nodded. "Well, Mr Carter and I did discuss the soirée at dinner, and we agreed we should be ready to send out the invitations. He appeared to accept it would be a sign of weakness not to do so."

She explained the condition that all previous Cartel members still be included, and he nodded his agreement.

"Mr Carter is still hoping against hope that the majority will negotiate for a deal, but many influenced by Carlo still refuse to speak to him. Personally, I think it's unlikely and we will have to put your physical persuasion program into operation."

"I'm waiting anxiously to do that. Carlo still has a long way to go to control the other factions beyond Jericho. I would like to meet personally with Mr Carter to convince him immediately to strong-arm a station down the line, say Alma, to drive a wedge into his spreading influence.

"We must act now, or they will creep their way from station to station progressively taking us over. They have frightened a number of medical groups to go dark out of fear of violence. We need to get going."

She had gone quiet. That was not a good sign!

Then she responded tartly, "If you meet personally with Mr Carter, he will start giving you orders himself. He is still very close to cancelling the soirée which I can't allow. No, we will just send out the invitations and see how things develop for a couple of weeks."

Pritam sat without comment, thinking that the social event was more important to her than the entire security of their business. Somehow, he had to talk to Edwin Carter, he decided.

Despite her angry face, he blurted, "How can you always respectfully call him Mr Carter while you get sex on demand from me right behind his back?"

"Just continue to do what you are told!" she snapped, icily.

"Very well, ma'am," Pritam conceded apologetically. "I will draw up detailed security plans for the soirée and submit them to you for your discussion with Mr Carter."

"Do that," she commanded, leaving abruptly.

Pritam Singh was in a very difficult position.

For months he had been angling carefully for ways to deal more directly with Edwin Carter himself to consolidate his own position, so far with no success. Perhaps planning the soirée would offer that opportunity?

He knew Edwin Carter really held the supreme power but had bent to her demand that she be personally in charge of security. Pritam considered this a mistake, typical of Mr Carter's conciliatory ways.

So she was his boss.

Then, one afternoon in his office, she had slowly and seductively stripped herself naked, and demanded sex, graphically instructed him exactly what she wanted him to do to her.

"Mrs Carter, such language!" he had joked. But he vigorously carried out her instructions, apparently to her full satisfaction.

Now he performed regularly on demand.

She was very physically attractive, which solved many problems, but he knew she was only using him and that she would cast him aside any moment that suited her.

He chuckled to himself: she thought she was so superior, but he would have the last laugh!

23

Mr Carter

Pritam would have been amazed to know what Anisha was thinking at that moment.

Yes, she did think of her husband Edwin as Mr Carter, which she found sad. That is what her father had announced, "You will be marrying Mr Carter!"

Sex with Pritam was assuredly at her direction, which she sort of regretted.

"But I am after-all his boss and employer," she pouted to herself, "so I have to take the lead, or nothing will happen. And he still calls me Mrs Carter even in moments of passion; I will allow no less respect."

She found him handsome and charming enough. But it was really intimacy, not just sex she craved, although he appeared to enjoy the vigorous action just as much as she absolutely did.

"But today," she mused, "I have to admit I did use him very hard physically to work off my frustration at Edwin. And then stupidly turned on the only personal relationship I have in the world.

She decided she must see Pritam again soon. She had to take firmer business control, but could she do that without getting all sexed-up as usual?

If only she had a close relationship with Edwin as she observed in other couples. She had been a virginal eighteen when her dour Sikh father announced he was allying his business with the Carter combine and said that she must marry their son and heir. "A wonderful opportunity for you," was his sole comment.

Edwin was already in his thirties and had never married. He accepted the beautiful young woman gracefully and apparently happily. But after marriage he did not seem particularly interested in her personally, nor in her body, and after a few perfunctory attempts at sex they had mutually agreed sleeping separately was preferable to both of them.

That was a decade ago and to this point she had just buried herself very successfully in their business relationship. They had of course discussed the situation, because otherwise their friendship was cordial. He was not at all gay and she accepted he must just be asexual.

She considered him a friend and she appreciated his always courteous and polite character. So different from her own harsh and secretive family.

While he was too charming for her liking with attractive women, she was not aware of him having an affair during their marriage. How would he react to this adventure on her part? She shuddered at the thought.

***

The Carters had literally been in Vancouver since the early colonial days according to Edwin's father. Edwin had gone back to the north of England as a young man to track their origins and actually found a few gravestones leading directly to the heritage, but there were really so many other Carters he cheerfully left it at that.

But Canada was different, and they had all the details of the successive Carters from that first rogue who had been a trader with the Hudson's Bay Company in the middle of the 19th century.

Naturally Edwin had been brought up with a sense of tradition and even a sense of proprietorship in the city. He went to the right private boys' schools, to UBC, and the Harvard Business School, as had his father and others previously, and then returned to run their mini empire.

He was intelligent and a good businessman, but he had a major problem: he was not at heart a criminal.

The 'family business' had started way back in Hudson's Bay days when the original Carter found it easy to steal from his far away company owners and force unconscionable deals upon the indigenous people.

A later generation added considerably to their coffers during the gold rushes. Then the following Carter generations joined in mining and lumber swindles.

During the more civilised period between the two world wars, by paying off politicians their land deals, had become legend. Then as the previous century drew to a close, a high proportion of their capital was laundered into legitimate companies connected with insurance and real estate ownership.

In the present century they had capitalised enormously on the influx of laundered money from around the world, acting as a conduit and fixer.

Then the latest bonanza had arrived, bringing an even greater influx of wealthy people, all needing medical help the government system was not capable of supplying.

Edwin was in his element overseeing and running the business side of the operation, but they had become heavily associated, inevitably, with leading racketeers, drug dealers and dubious big money in the province.

Up to now in his management, however, any strong-arm tactics or violence had been carried out by the Brethren without his direct knowledge which salved his conscience. Anisha feared that being faced with actually ordering violent criminal activity left him totally inadequate to deal with the situation.

And underlying all those problems he had a strong sense of wanting to do what was best for Vancouver.

He had no one to turn to for advice other than computers and a beautiful wife he no longer fully felt he could trust. He had mistakenly accepted her as a crime family uniting gift, but on whom he could not then bring himself to force affection.

"Some crime lord I am," he had once admitted to Anisha, ironically bringing her to an unexplained surge of sympathy for him.

24

Police teamwork

"If only Ivern realised," thought Staff Sergeant Will Malik gleefully as he settled into his new office at Vancouver Police Headquarters.

He had been allocated a sergeant and three constables from the Medical Police for his liaison duties, so he now had his own little private army. Their main instructions were to work with the Vancouver Police force to expose the relationships between organised crime and the illegal medical operations which had now become apparent through the violence.

Raids on illegal activities were outside his orbit and the exposure of the medical network and actually charging the medical criminals involved had become his key priority.

He was still obsessed by the knowledge that Ivern was harbouring one such criminal and was determined to expose them. His previous attempts at following the hated Maddie had revealed nothing on her except the weird meeting on the station bench with Professor Chiu the day he was murdered, but Will had dug himself into a hole by not then disclosing that to his boss.

He knew he could not trust his own team to maintain confidence, so he had adopted the tactic of slipping her name into the general list of possible City suspects for attention.

"It is so frustrating," he thought, "for a Staff Sergeant in charge."

But he was the consummate policeman and he recognised he was withholding important information about her, and now also from the City, and he would have to be careful.

When the teams first met, the mature Staff Sergeant from the City sat at the back. He called out, "Why don't you act as chair of this little joint venture, Will, then I can sit back and doze."

"If that is going to be your attitude, this will not work," snapped Will. "Bringing down illegal medical activities is our sole objective, and we take it very seriously. Things have come to a head with the violence, and you have unsolved murders as a consequence. We must find who is behind it all."

"Pushy, pushy! You have obviously just been promoted," his partner laughed.

"I was just being friendly. OK, our intelligence does all point to the Corridor as the controlling centre of regional activity."

"We absolutely agree," Will nodded, chilling out. "That's where the answer lies. I suggest we start by reviewing what we know, station area by station. Let's start at the far end with the Chiu murder. Then review the pending trials and at the very least we can review all the persons of interest we have jointly identified and build cases."

To Will's satisfaction the name Dr Janet Madison was hidden in that list. Now he could justify more personal inquiry, he decided smugly.

***

Carlo, although a hardened criminal, was beginning to realise what he had taken on.

The old medical professor who had caused all the trouble was dead and it appeared he had acted alone, although no one could understand what he had hoped to achieve. But it had resulted in the death of his young Juan, Ricardo was laying low and Joey was lodged away in Mexico.

That was not the only result, however. It had finally brought to a head their simmering differences with the Carter family over the years.

There had been so many missed and unexploited criminal opportunities. He had easily replaced the sources of street drugs from China to Mexico and other South American suppliers and he knew he could introduce new businesses and sanctions which would dramatically increase their profits. However, he was finding the illegal medical business far more difficult to assimilate due to its fragmentation and complicated technicalities.

He was sure of physically controlling the UBC and Jericho station areas, but beyond that down the line he was still negotiating with the groups running the Alma, Dunbar and McDonald station towers.

He had found a substantial amount of their income came from the illegal medical system previously organised through the Carter companies, and it was proving more difficult than he thought to convince prospective partners. Ricardo was aggressively insisting they needed more strongarm tactics.

He was aware the Carters had a formidable Sikh-based security team, and he could not understand why they had not taken more action already. This really worried him and made him wonder what was going on.

When he learned that several of his assumed renegade families were accepting the invitations to the Carters' soirée, he was completely baffled at the Carter tactics.

"Throwing parties? At this time. What are they up to?" he asked Ricardo.

"Obviously, some sort of trap," was the worried answer.

25

New confidences

Jimmy Khan had finally and painstakingly translated Simeon's entire journal, and had it all on his secure computer system available only to him personally.

On her rare day off, he invited Maddie to lunch at his favourite little restaurant down at Alma and they spent a couple of hours enjoying a bottle of white wine and debating what to do about the journal.

"First," commented James, "do you want a copy?"

"Absolutely not," she replied. "But I need to know where to find it if something happens to you."

"Yes, a totally secure contact will be made with you automatically. And if something happens to both of us it will go to the Attorney General, which is the least I can do for my official duty."

"All OK with me. My only concern is when to reveal the Edwin Carter connections to Ivern and how to do that, because I am not comfortable hiding real criminal activities."

"It is my turn to say OK with all that," he smiled. "Now we can eat."

Later, relaxing over dessert he relayed the curious lunch he had at the same spot with Zuri. They chuckled together at his description of her outstanding body and happy exhibitionist clothing style.

"Right down to the last bum wriggle, seductive glance over her shoulder and eye flutter, she was superb."

"Try describing her again without using your hands," she laughed.

"I can't!" he admitted, waving his arms in defeat.

But when they had calmed down, Jimmy, who had known her way back in university and trusted her implicitly, became very serious.

"Zuri was sent to me selectively, I believe, to make the situation appear frivolous and trivial, but I did some careful probing during lunch and there was a very intelligent young woman behind the act.

"She has not contacted me again and the online connection has disappeared.

"However, we do know, because she told me openly, that she works for the All Insurance group. And as you know that belongs to Edwin Carter whom the journal ties into the illegal medical management."

"Yes, but he admitted to me during our lunch he occasionally helped Simeon out financially."

"It is way more extensive and Corridor All Technology features all the way through the journal. Chiu is clearly being directed by an overall management system. I suspect we will find that originates at All."

"OK, accepting that," she responded, "why would Zuri come out in the open and contact you?"

"Well," he responded, "they obviously believe they are securely hidden now the only online connection has gone."

"But," she objected stubbornly, "while they had a reason to meet you to sound you out and see how much you knew, they still had no need to tell you who they were."

"Yes, it's a worrying puzzle," he responded.

"It seems to me," Maddie suggested, "quite seriously, that final bum wriggle and sexy shoulder glance invites a follow-up, although I don't think your lovely wife would approve."

"No, and I would suggest you calling Zuri except that it would identify you unnecessarily. So, I think maybe I will call her for a coffee when I am next at South Granville, wearing a stern expression."

"Well, behave yourself and keep your eyes off her," she giggled.

***

James' father had been in the Canadian Embassy in Afghanistan as a local lawyer and earned his family the right of entry into Canada when the embassy closed with the American withdrawal earlier in the century.

He was just a baby, and he grew up initially in a home where he remembered some of the women were still covered from head to foot in black, while their men ran around happily in the summer in their flip-flops and shorts.

It had of course all changed, and as the older generation died off and he and his wife had not been near a Muslim temple for years. He really had no time for any of the religions and preferred to look after humanity in his own medical way.

He had started out as Jamil but changed it himself simply to James when he went to high school, demonstrating his early independence.

Maddie had been perfectly safe joking about Zuri, because Jimmy and Fatima were already an established couple and deeply in love even in their first university year. They were all studying chemistry and pharmaceuticals at the time, and she went on into pharmacy while he opted for medicine.

She was pregnant with their first child in her final year and their loving relationship had never wavered.

James became involved in medical politics when supporting an issue close to his heart and found he had a natural ability to raise passions and for administration. He still carried as many patients as he could manage as a family doctor, otherwise he spent his time running the Association.

Private medical practice had been creeping in for decades as the public facilities continued failing and the population kept growing. The practicality of its presence had allowed the government to turn a blind eye.

But recently, just as he was feeling a changing government attitude, the violent action had made it impossible.

Up to this point he had been able to operate within both systems but very soon, especially with Simeon's journal hidden in his safe, he would have to take a side.

That decision came earlier than he expected.

26

Mountie backup

Ivern was summoned to Victoria for a highly confidential meeting with the Solicitor General and his Chief Commissioner Dodds.

The Solicitor General was brief.

"The Cabinet has finally authorised the use of force to close down all illegal medical activities and we have secured, on secondment, an especially trained para-military Mountie detachment to assist in these operations.

"We have agreed that the centre of illegal activity has been established in the Broadway Corridor. This means, Commissioner Hill, that you will be in overall charge of the operation. Your opposite number from the RCMP will be reporting to you shortly and we expect you to return expeditiously with a plan of action. Any questions?"

That was all. Ivern saluted smartly, and with his chief retired back to Medical Police headquarters.

"Well, we are turning you into a real police officer pretty dramatically now."

Chief Dodds shook his head in sympathy.

"But you will at least know how to carry out this operation within the law. I don't envy you the job, and I will await your recommendations with interest. I suggest we try a general show of force and close things down progressively."

"Honestly, sir, I am pleased you are here rather than the deceased Bertie who would've been gung-ho! I have been cultivating the friendship of the fellow running the BC Medical Association and I will start with him and likely bring him into the team. The whole thing is highly complex."

"I know, I know!" was the sympathetic reply, and the quiet, "Dismissed," came with a sigh.

***

The special Mountie unit was already on its way from Winnipeg and arrived the next day.

They are scary enough all on their own, Ivern thought as he stood outside his office building to welcome them. The main detachment had travelled in convoy from Winnipeg in their various high-tech armoured vehicles which looked something like science-fiction SUV tanks.

The keen RCMP Inspector Jules McIntosh, however, leapt eagerly from a high-speed, lightweight combat helicopter and clasped Ivern in a firm handshake he could still feel later in the day. They wore uniforms which were obviously reinforced for combat, and all carried automatic weapons.

"Ready for war I see," Ivern chuckled causing his counterpart to scowl aggressively.

"I can see straight away how you allowed all this to get out of hand. Let's get down to business."

"Unfortunately," Ivern responded calmly, "there is actually no one to fight yet, so you can relax. We will convene here at 0800 hours tomorrow and brief you on the situation.

"Seriously, just put on a regular lightweight uniform, and give us the benefit of your expertise in planning how to deal with a complicated situation, which could in fact get violent quickly.

"We have put you all up in a neat little hotel in the Oak Tower where we can meet tonight for drinks and dinner to get to know each other. I have assigned Staff Sergeant Malik for direct liaison, and you will find Will here very helpful. See you this evening."

With that he handed the group off to Will and retreated gratefully back into his office.

"What am I going to do with these gorillas," he wondered? Will of course was in his element, but he was the perfect choice in order to include the Vancouver Police Department in their joint activities and he accepted the extra duties with relish.

***

James Kahn was in his worst nightmare: appointed without choice to an official committee intent upon closing down illegal medical activity by force if necessary.

"What am I to do?" he wailed to Maddie at their regular hospital lunch.

"We just have to play it out." she replied calmly. "What other choice do we have?"

"My duty is to work for my Association and to support government policies. But I am sitting on the very information they need to close this all down."

"We, are," she corrected him, "and I am sleeping almost every night now with the leader of the police operation. What do I do? He cheerfully tells me everything he is doing, and I deceive him. I am beginning to feel rotten about it."

"Even worse," he continued, "if they start using that special RCMP force, we could be responsible for medics being killed, because we didn't help to close it down."

He buried his face in his hands for a few minutes, which was dutifully recorded by Staff Sergeant Will's observer, still from time to time checking up on Maddie.

When James had composed himself and was sitting upright again, she tried to lighten the discussion.

"Have you followed up on your sexy maiden yet?"

"Yes," he unexpectedly responded, cheering up immediately. "And it was very interesting. She was perfectly open that her company dealt extensively with doctors and pharmacists throughout the Corridor, but was totally evasive about their business, vaguely suggesting it all had to do with insurance."

"That is of course a perfect cover," Maddie commented.

He nodded. "She did say that everything was securely encrypted, which was the reason I could not still contact her through the address in Simeon's papers.

"While she is still startling to look at, she is now pointedly not overtly sexy but trying to be totally businesslike. I got the feeling she wanted to make a personal contact but was not quite sure how to use it. And I was, of course right. She is extremely intelligent and undoubtedly has a senior job."

"So," Maddie puzzled, "she runs a computer company owned by the Carter All Company dealing with doctors and pharmacists.

"With all Carter's dubious connections and revelations, you say are in the journal, isn't it highly likely they are at least a major part of the management operation?"

"Yes, seems highly likely."

"Maybe she believes you found the connection code in Simeon's general papers, but she has no idea how much more you know. She might be worried she is too deeply involved in Carter's illegal medical activity or even worse stuff!

"If she agrees, maybe she could become an informant. Then you could take her, in a limited way, to Ivern and your committee."

"Interesting idea for catching Carter," he said a little more cheerfully, "but how do we protect our own colleagues? Like to join me in sounding her out. You were a close friend of Simeon's and can hint you know more about the set-up."

"I can't wait to meet her!" she confirmed enthusiastically.

27

The Locarnos

The Locarnos were the next up the Line, in the Jericho area. Their leader Spike Winn had been wary of the trouble-making Carlo for many years.

They had developed into the main crime operator in that immediate area from a families-owned beach-view coffee shack, where occasional street drugs were dealt. Then the coming of the rail line and the developed station area had increased their drug market, and they now dominated the area.

The same traditional three families still ran the enterprise as a lose partnership, but they had by general accord accepted one of their own, Spike Winn, as their leader due to his imposing six-foot-six height and particularly his intelligence.

Spike now managed their diversified investments in the region and several smart modern coffee bars providing a perfect cover for their other nefarious activities. Apart from their dubious methods of earning a living, they were no different from the other businesses in the neighbourhood and certainly did not operate in a violent manner.

He could have been anything, but he had adopted the beach life in the summer and the ski hills in the winter, supported comfortably by coffee sales, expanding businesses, money laundering, drug dealing, friendly prostitution, and a very lucrative inherited smuggling arrangement through the conveniently nearby Vancouver port system. They were a conduit for the importation of drugs from Mexico and the growing Brethren dispute was unnecessarily complicating their business.

Since a fair proportion of income was now also coming from directing illegal medical services in the Jericho area, he was loath to cross the Carters, while on the other hand Carlo had strongarm influence locally and connections in Mexico.

He had been sitting on the fence now for months hoping it would all blow over. But they were starting to get pushy and nasty, and he resented it.

Their company was holding one of their large, family-oriented evening parties on Spanish Banks Beach when young roughs were stupid enough to make their play.

They openly drove up in trucks and SUVs led by Ricardo, and first just noisily surround the party shouting insults. Then on signal they moved in threateningly, smashing crockery and pouring drinks on the ground. They restrained several of the men who attempted to intervene but did not injure anyone and eventually they withdrew, again on signal, jumped into their trucks and drove away.

Fortunately Spike and family had not yet arrived, or the outcome would have been much more dramatic. He was later seething with anger but clever enough not to react immediately against the way physically stronger opponent.

Ricardo reported back to his father with glee.

"You should've seen their faces. They were pissing themselves with fright. They won't defy us, and I guarantee you will hear soon from that tall streak of a coffee-brewing leader, begging for a deal."

"Anything more from the Almas Brethren?" his father questioned. "They are next to secure."

"Yes, they have agreed totally with us, and have cut off connections with the Carters. Well, they are all Sikhs and will follow the profit. And we are offering them a way cheaper and more addictive drug supply.

"We have the Locanos trapped between us with nowhere to go. They will soon cave and then we move on to claim Dunbar."

***

Spike's stylish wife Laura was herself six feet tall. She moved gracefully as the international model she had been. They made a handsome and very striking couple.

But she missed the attention she had received previously and had been delighted once again to get an invitation, verbal so far, from Anisha, to attend the anticipated Carter Summer Soirée which was undoubtedly her leading social event of the year.

She and Spike lived in a large waterfront home on the Locarno Beach and had been flattered to entertain the Carters several times to patio dinners, also starring other Vancouver notables.

She was aware that Anisha ran security for All Insurance, as well as other business duties, which impressed her immensely. Concerned that her husband's business friends had been roughed up by Carlo's thugs on the beach she told Anisha all about it during one of their girlie chats.

Anisha of course could not have been more delighted to hear security news and rushed first to discuss that situation with Pritam.

"What does Mr Carter think about this?" was his immediate response, "because it goes to the heart of his political problems."

She pouted.

"I came to discuss it with you first. He will just tell them to negotiate a solution, while it seems to me the Locarnos need physical defense. I thought we could perhaps just send them a dozen men."

"And start a war?" he retorted.

"Are you refusing?" she snapped.

"Mrs Carter," was his cool over-formal reply, "it is not my place to refuse but certainly to advise. If you wish to take any action just let me know and it will be done."

She stalked away, feeling like a little girl who had been reprimanded but knowing he was right. It would be a serious move. Not sure what to do she went looking for Edwin.

It was evening and she found him sitting quietly in his study in the gathering gloom. She clicked on the lights.

"Whatever are you doing sitting in the dark?" she queried.

"Just thinking. Time for a pre-dinner drink to cheer me up?"

"Better than that, I am bearer of good news!"

"A drink and good news? Let's go!"

Drinks in hand, she launched on her decided persuasive approach.

Use it positively she had decided, after her stinging putdown by Pritam.

"You of course remember the attractive Laura Winn…"

"How could I not?" he interrupted.

"Well, yes." She rolled her eyes.

"But, anyway, she phoned first to thank us for the intended soirée invitation," she could not resist stressing. "But especially she was worried that their family business party on Spanish Banks had been roughed up by Carlo's goons and she said they need protection. It might help with our Santos problem if we intervene. I knew you would know what to do."

His attention had sharpened abruptly. "But the call came from Laura not Spike?"

She nodded.

"I can call him, say I heard about the beach incident and offer immediate assistance if he needs it?"

"Yes, yes, and yes!" she confirmed triumphantly, splashing the wine on the table as she over-enthusiastically refilled their glasses.

He smiled at her enthusiasm and took her hand in an unusual warm squeeze. "Our first physical contact in months," she thought, acutely aware it gave her a sensual flush.

Edwin called Spike later that evening. At first Spike was noncommittal.

"I am keen not to escalate the situation but if he attacks us again, I will ask for your help. But we do need to meet urgently to talk about appeasing Amar Singh and his Almas faction. That little private dining room behind the bar at the Yacht Club should be private enough. Tomorrow at noon?"

"Perfect!" responded Edwin feeling that a Brethren recovery was perhaps underway.

28

Pritam

Singh was one of the most common names in British Columbia and they were all highly conscious of the centuries-old battles still being fought back in the Punjab. They were a fierce people and naturally gravitated towards physical employment when they became Canadian.

Pritam's family for generations had worked for security systems and they were prevalent throughout the Corridor area. In fact, his father's brother had expanded his security connections in the Dunbar/ Alma Station area to take charge first of the drug business and then progressively all the other underworld activities, including eventually the illegal medical operation.

At first their old leader Amar Singh had intended to stay loyal to Mr Carter, but enormously increased profitability available from cut-price drugs offered by the Mexicans had swayed him towards Carlo.

Now he got a call from him offering half the Locarno market when they squeezed them out, and he became fully committed.

He would need additional manpower and his first thought was his nephew Pritam who would not only bring personal support but his loyal team of twenty guards, mostly Sikh. He easily made them an offer they could not refuse.

Amar Singh had insisted upon a reasonably settled and written agreement with Carlo, whom he absolutely did not trust, so he told Pritam to hold things until he got the signal to move out.

***

The following day things were as usual at the All headquarters and Anisha hurried to inform Pritam in his office that Edwin and Spike were meeting to discuss going into action and them supplying security.

Anisha closed his office door behind her and posed.

She was wearing only a short summer dress, which she provocatively flipped up to reveal she was ready for him.

Pritam seemed to be in a good mood and did not await her usual instructions. He advanced towards her, unzipping as he came and brazenly exposing himself as ready for action.

Without a word, he slid his hands up under her skimpy dress, effortlessly picked her up and forcibly lowered her onto himself.

She wrapped her legs around him, trying to take some of her weight but he backed her up against the wall and from his first savage thrusts she realised things had changed. All she could do was curse herself for losing control and endure his frenzied climax.

Laughing at her shocked reaction, he just dumped her back on her feet and triumphantly smirked, "That was your last time! We Sikhs are all leaving today to join the Almas!"

Slowly and demonstratively, he zipped himself up and walked out without a further word, smiling in satisfaction.

***

She spent the early afternoon in shock and crying in her boudoir until she pulled herself together hearing Edwin return from his lunch with Spike. He was brimming with news.

"Come and have a coffee in the observatory and I will tell you what happened with Spike," he called enthusiastically.

She sat there in their beautiful little patio with its startlingly panoramic view, coffee perking merrily in the corner, and still feeling like crying, forced herself to listen to his story.

Edwin looked at her curiously, but explained that Spike had worried they were hemmed in by the Mexicans on one side and the Sikhs on the other.

Old Amar Singh himself had called and ever threateningly polite, had warned he was joining forces with Carlo and that they would be taking over the Locarno area drug business. He said they could keep their businesses but subject to a protection payment. Any fuss and they would be run out of town. Take it or leave it.

Edwin finished his account triumphantly, "I agreed to protect them and their activities. Now you and I just need to discuss how we will arrange it!"

There was a long noticeable pause while Anisha gathered her thoughts. She started trembling, prompting Edwin's alarm. "Anisha, are you okay?"

He spoke so softly and with such concern that she came to a momentous conclusion and moved to hold both his hands.

"I have some terrible things to tell you. Please don't be too angry with me."

She fought back tears and sat up straight, forcing herself to look him in the eye.

"For the past few months, I have been having an affair with Pritam Singh. It was just sex. I never had any affection for him." He stared at her woodenly.

"It is over," she added tearfully, "but I had to tell you. I am so sorry."

She babbled on quickly, "Then today he told me that he and his team are abandoning us and going over to the Alma Sikhs. We lose our security team and even worse they are joining the enemy!"

There was a long silence. She was still holding his gaze, but tears were rolling silently down her cheeks.

"First, turn off that damned whistling coffeepot," he suggested, finally breaking the spell.

Then, when they had settled down again, this time he took her hands and asked, "Why did you just tell me all that?"

"Because you are my husband, and it is my duty. Because I was ashamed and …" she hesitated, "because I now appreciate how much I respect you."

The room fell silent again until Edwin said quietly, "Perhaps it is time for that cup of coffee. Then we have some serious planning to do so we can fulfill my promise to Spike."

They turned in early after an emotional day and he was about to get into bed when Anisha wrapped timidly on his door.

"I really would love to have your company. May I please sleep with you tonight?" she asked.

They did not attempt to be intimate, but they did embrace tentatively, and she fell asleep in a man's arms for the first time in her life.

29

Female intuition

Zuri was amused at the hint of intrigue in the open formal email she received from Dr James Khan, as Chief Executive Officer of the BC Medical Association, inviting her for lunch back at The Nook to discuss 'insurance business'.

She was still smiling when she told Samuel, suggestively swaying her firm breasts. "What do you think he's after?" she asked.

"I can't imagine!" he laughed, "but I think you should bring along your Chief Executive of All Technology for this serious business meeting.

"I need to get out of here anyway; crazy things are going on. First Pookie starts popping up in strange places, saying weird things; then half of our business just vaporised; you got that mysterious contact from stranger Khan on a super-secure line he should not have known; tough guys took over our company unannounced and today they just all just walked out again."

"Yes, I'd like you to come to the meeting." Zuri nodded. "Dr Khan is actually a very nice fellow and not piggy at all, even though I laid on the sexuality bit pretty heavily.

"Anyway, he's bringing a female to the lunch, Dr Madison, which will add to your puzzles, because I've looked her up and she is on our list! In fact, she was the surgeon who got away at the first shooting."

That started a heated debate.

"Adds to the intrigue; I love it."

"Aren't they taking a chance bring her out into the open?"

"On the contrary they are very bright and are trying to coax us out. If we react to her, we reveal our involvement. You have succeeded beyond belief, my pet!"

***

At The Nook they turned heads and made a startling pair. About the same elegant height, they each had a dazzlingly, sunny smile.

One was black, with happy deep brown eyes, and a high Afro, displaying a voluptuous body, somewhat concealed in an admittedly short but reasonably decent, smart white business suit.

The other, was a sleek, cool blond, with startlingly topaz blue eyes and a slender, athletic body, outlined in a tight-fitting modest pink designer dress reaching below the knee.

The guys were well built, tall, brown and black.

"Modern Vancouver," observed James as they courteously held the ladies' chairs and ignored the glances.

Zuri looked around the different personalities at the table and laughed at their serious expressions.

"Do you really want to talk about insurance?" she chuckled. "Why don't we just hit up the Chief Administrator of All Insurance here for a good bottle of wine?"

"I second that," Maddie called out, presenting Samuel dramatically with the wine list.

"Mind if I sit next to Zuri?" she asked, shuffling chairs, and leading the two women into animated conversation.

"Guess that leaves us talking about insurance," joked James to Samuel after they were served drinks,

He grinned. "The way you medical guys are getting yourselves bumped off these days makes me think you might need insurance."

"That is how I met your vivacious Zuri, when my colleague Dr Chiu got himself killed and I was checking his papers. He must have been insured with you?"

"Sorry, client confidentiality," murmured Samuel. Then changing the conversation too obviously he abruptly added, "And your companion is also vivacious but in a totally different way. Congratulations."

"Not mine!" James laughed. "She is a long-time friend and we studied under Dr Chiu. She is dating the Vancouver Chief of Medical Police."

That really set Samuel back in his chair and after a significant, long pause he added guardedly, "My life is just full of endless surprises these days. Fascinating."

And he lapsed back into a revealing silence, apparently deeply contemplating his wine.

***

He should have been better prepared. Samuel and Zuri had spent the entire previous evening debating their tactics for the lunch.

Sazu AI had confirmed with them that their own apartment security system was now impregnable to any invasion by man or AI, following Zuri's uninvited visit by Pookie.

"We have to get out of this criminal situation, eventually, somehow!" Zuri had insisted. "I feel the Medical Association connection may be a way. But for all his affability there is a tenseness about Dr Kahn, and his carefully hidden searching questions demonstrate his own underlying alarm.

"He carefully let me know that he was sympathetic to the illegal medical cause. If he has Dr Chiu's private papers, he may well know more about us than is comfortable."

"OK, but first we have to find out if he is a potential ally or enemy," Samuel concluded, full of confidence.

***

But, then at lunch, when James had apparently casually mentioned Maddie's connection to the chief of Medical Police, he became highly alarmed and was not able to hide the flicker of concern that went across his face.

Then he remembered that Maddie herself was also deeply involved, in the first shootout, and his face relaxed into total puzzlement. Trying in vain to hide the emotions that were sweeping him, he changed the subject abruptly. "Perhaps you should start by calling me Sammy."

"Then I am Jimmy."

The girls, deep into discussion about what to wear at the upcoming soirée, were startled to see the guys unexpectedly shaking hands firmly across the table.

They had ordered another bottle of wine and thoroughly enjoyed the signature lobster salad The Nook offered at that time of the year, just chatting, and getting to know each other.

Over dessert, Samuel tried to act normally and opened the subject of medical practice insurance, saying it was difficult to operate in two happening systems, one legal and the other illegal.

He asked what policy the Medical Association followed.

James said, of course their official policy was to support the public policy one hundred percent but that in practice they accepted there were two systems in operation involving their members.

They did nothing to try to discipline doctors who might provide illegal services, because they could not identify them or prove it themselves anyway. If the court convicted medics, they had to follow the court decision and strike them off.

Maddie joined in, laughing. "Just look at me. I am dating a medical cop, but he knows illegal medical practice is a reality."

They chatted generally about these problems, all being careful not to admit anything specific,

Except, significantly, they all agreed vigorously when Samuel said he and Zuri were both appalled at the violence creeping in.

They finish their conversation all secure in the knowledge that they were sympathetic to the illegal medical system but gave no indication they were directly involved.

When they were saying goodbye, Zuri embraced Maddie fondly and left on a light note, telling them, "I don't know about you guys, but Maddie and I are meeting again soon to finalise our discussion about soirée gowns!

"Samuel and I have finally been invited, so we will see you there, if not before."

***

Back in Jimmy's office, Maddie laughed at his discomfort at his earlier report that Zuri was oversexed.

"She is just a very friendly, pretty, and intelligent young woman. Yes, she has an exaggerated shape of body that some men obsessed about but was it just wishful thinking on your part?"

"Absolutely not." He struggled defensively. "I think she was putting on an act and a very convincing one. That tells us something, doesn't it? She was eager to extract information from me and was working on me personally to get my attention."

"Yeah right, and she sure succeeded! But anyway, what do you think?"

"Well, as your master analyst I saw three very significant moments. First, when I mentioned that you were dating a cop it scared the hell out of him. He couldn't hide his concern, an indication they are up to something. Their strong reaction against violence was a definite positive. I would say, like us, they are in at least dubious activity, which they regret and are looking for a way out."

Maddie was nodding. "You could fortunately not hear our girly inane chitchat, but under her banter, I detected that highly intelligent woman you managed to notice, in spite of her big boobs. She was trying way too hard to avoid medical matters, a sure sign of involvement."

"My, you were paying attention in Psychology 101 after all. We seem to agree that their sympathies are in line with ours. If we can trust them, we can learn a lot by comparing notes, at the very least."

"When do I get to tell Ivern some of this?" Maddie worried. "I have told him we are meeting them in connection with Simeon's estate, which is technically true!"

"If they are in a criminal organisation, and if they agree to come forward, Ivern will be our confidant. We would have to delete all the medical personnel names. Only you and I know about Simeon's journal."

"And the mysterious old Sophie," she reminded him.

As they were parting, she remembered something and turned. "You said three things. Things you learned from Zuri and Samuel. What is the third one?"

"Just a hunch. But their detailed comments about what is going on 'all over the Corridor' plus their over-academic qualifications for a relatively small insurance company, and extensive recorded activities in the journal ... ," he paused significantly, "... including Simeon's many references to Edwin Carter, indicate he is the Medical kingpin they are all searching for! Our new friends are his technical know-how. No wonder they are worried!"

***

Zuri and Samuel stopped at a noisy café on the way home to discuss things, where they felt safe from Pookie. "First, what's with this 'Sammy' nonsense?" came with a broad Zuri grin. "I have never heard anyone call you Sammy."

He sheepishly admitted, "He caught me totally off guard dropping the news that Maddie was dating a top Medical cop and I had to change the subject and try to be friendly. That just came to mind, and it was my schoolyard nickname."

"OK, Sammy baby, what do we do now? Just skip town with our hidden offshore stash. Walk out like our disappeared guards?"

"If only. But their thugs would find us and deal with us. The Carter control could well be breaking down, which would allow us to slip away unheeded. Or the government and police could get serious, in which case we would need friends like your new buddy Maddie and her policeman boyfriend.

"We will cultivate their friendship, but they are dangerous, and we must be wary."

30

Desertion

After Anisha and Edwin's emotional confessional evening, their calm night in bed together left them somewhat revived to face their crumbling empire.

They slept late and had a large breakfast tray delivered in bed by amazed human servers, who couldn't wait to spread the gossip back in the kitchen. They moved with their coffee to their veranda and sat together oblivious of their magnificent view, worrying about their latest reports.

They each had personal AI companions in addition to Pookie exclusively for the Brethren, and for the first time, in a sign of their fragile reconciliation, they compared the advice they were receiving.

Anisha led off. "This is fascinating, but the computers all come to the conclusion you are too much of a nice guy while I am a real bitch!"

"I'm sure that is just your harsh interpretation, but Pookie also had something of a similar message, suggesting that I am not cut out for Brethren's tough decisions while you are incisive. I would go along with that. If we can work as a team that could balance out beautifully."

Later with added formality, in their office, she opened a blank screen and said, "To demonstrate I am not a complete bitch, I acknowledge your successes. We should review them first. And let's be happy that we are finally talking to each other!"

Smiling she typed, "Communication is good!"

"So, the Station areas we directly control, that are with us are Oak, South Granville, and Arbutus; likely McDonald, which still has a mixture of various Brethren; apparently not Wie Wie at Broadway; absolutely not Santos at UBC and the Almas. Jericho comes to us if we can offer support to the Locarnos."

She shook her head. "I must admit I was surprised that randy old Wie Wie had turned against us."

***

Everyone called Law Yu-Yan, Wie Wie. He even scrawled that as his signature: Wie Wie. They were rumoured to be the last begging words of some transgressors because of his reputation as a ruthless criminal.

He had the Broadway, City Hall Station fiefdom, but also extended throughout the massive but ageing and lower value False Creek and out into the poorer East End. He was powerful.

Wie Wie had been born at the turn of the century in Canada and proudly called himself a child of the Vancouver Model, the celebrated Canadian dirty money process, which indeed he was.

His family and Triad group had been brought to Canada by his grandfather Law who had been driven out of China by the unaccommodating communists. They believed only they should rule and had taken to killing any Triad members they could catch.

Canada proved to be an easy score for Triad members offering unquestioned immigration. In 1986 Canada had introduced the Immigration Investment Program which guaranteed easy passage to Canada for the wealthy; anyone who could produce the cash! This had all fitted nicely into the expanding wave of criminal capital movement and money-laundering around the world, with Canada an eager safe haven for the Triad and bent foreign cops.

Early in the new century a British Columbia Premier had said "We must turn BC into a model for fighting money-laundering instead of a centre where it takes place!"

The crackdown never happened because too many Canadians in authority were profiting and as it developed the Broadway Corridor progressively became an internationally renowned centre of dubious money activity.

The money-laundering agencies run by Wie Wie in his area were

– 144 –

notorious. "I am the Law," he would chant merrily, because he was a deceptively rotund and friendly person.

Like Edwin, he had attended the prestigious St George's School for boys where he had acted out as a cheerful joking buffoon while even at that young age, surrounded by a protective ring of similarly wealthy Triad kids.

His grandfather mysteriously accumulated hundreds of millions of dollars, notwithstanding the introduction of Unexplained Wealth Laws.

He initially invested in the Chinatown and Main Street area. Then they became the principal drug dealer for the mass of public housing built along Main Street and eventually moved into more affluent Granville Centre and False Creek areas.

That is where their illegal activities had clashed with Edwin Carter's father until they had sorted things out amicably. They ended their lives as close friends.

***

Edwin had continued a careful friendship with Wie Wie and was surprised he was siding with the Mexicans and had broken off communication.

"He gets all his street drug supplies from Asia, so Santos has no leverage there. We do not interfere in his money-laundering, prostitution or nightclub activities and he is only too pleased to leave administration of the medical services in our hands. What is bugging him, Anisha? Why is he deserting us?"

"Beats me, I get on fine with him. Always joking. We have already sent him a verbal invitation to the soirée, of course. We must go and call on him!"

"Is that advisable?" Edwin worried.

"There you go being careful. Teamwork!! Let's go get him!"

They were still laughing when they were rudely interrupted by a loud squawking and a flashing message from Pookie: '**Warning**, *office security system breached. Emergency program engaged. Instruction urgently required.*'

This was something right outside their experience.

'I have a good overall defensive system, but a portion of my knowledge has been deleted by a top clearance person. I am totally

unable to offer any advice on that security subject. I apologise for this egregious defensive lapse on my part.'

"Oh dear!" was all Anisha could offer. She retreated into embarrassed silence in the realisation she had given Pritam total security clearance. She immediately thought, "Now he really has fucked me," and fought back tears.

Edwin was already in touch with Samuel. They arrived quickly having been warned about the security problem much earlier by Sazu AI.

Samuel reported. "No panic, it's all under control. Pritam decided as a parting gift, to delete important records from the limited buildings and personnel security system to which he had access. The Carter and All Insurance business system is totally separate, secure and safe.

"With respect to Pookie's missing information and allowed access we have everything backed up and are fixing it. It turns out to be an alarming nuisance which has been completely rectified. Everything is OK."

Zuri added, "We will review all our security systems entirely, although we are sure our system is entirely foolproof. I will stress, All Insurance business and operational technology systems are totally separate, impossible to access without process, highly backed-up and can be immediately destroyed if ordered."

Samuel got bluntly to the point, "The two dozen guys who have walked out do not affect our day-to-day operations because they were essentially for special operations, just for show and on call. Our standard office security systems and buildings are staffed and operating as before."

"Technology is far more important than people." Zuri stated philosophically.

Anisha agreed. "Zuri, that is the key! I absolutely concur and Mr Carter and I will be discussing how to replace those goons, but with your help will devise more currently sophisticated methods of control and discipline."

"Yes. We really appreciate your support and suggestions. We will be back," Edwin added.

***

Restored to full power, Pookie had learned the lesson and was feverishly accessing all knowledge and programs to which his program had access, to ensure, not only his knowledge could never be removed again, but reinforcing his responsibility to the Brethern which he had inexcusably put at risk.

***

Later Edwin and Anisha sat quietly together in their spectacular patio, civilly being served late afternoon tea.

As they parted Edwin embraced and kissed Anisha lightly.

"The panics just keep coming but we seem to be through that one. Don't worry, we will sort everything out. Why don't you give your old rogue pal Wie Wie a call. Chat him up as you do, see what is going on and set up a meeting."

31

Wie Wie

Her shattered emotions under control and finally sitting quietly alone in her office she tensed herself to make the call.

"Wie Wie, this is Anisha."

She relaxed as he answered cordially as usual, "I have been expecting you and the answer is, yes. I will choose a lucky lady, polish up the Empress's Necklace for her and enjoy your soirée as usual."

He was referring to the priceless string of large jewels which not too subtly indicated his selected, and always beautiful, sex partner of the moment to everyone.

"We thought you were pissed off at us for some reason because you had cut off connections with All."

"Yes, there is that little business matter!" he agreed.

"Like to meet us and talk about it?"

"Sure, beautiful. My den tomorrow. Dim sum! But come alone."

"No way, playboy, think I'm crazy. All us girls know your reputation."

"Well, it is yours I want to discuss. Your ex-security boyfriend, Pritam Singh, has sold me some stimulating porno tapes he made in his office. I must say you are magnificent! We'll keep it just between the two of us. And don't worry, no one double crosses me and I have the only copies. Chin chin; see you alone, tomorrow!"

Anisha was in a daze. Her entire life had turned upside down again and she had no idea what to do next. Fortunately, Edwin was away at a dinner appointment that evening so she would not have to face him.

One thing kept recurring in her mind. Zuri had said she backed technology over people, and she wondered desperately if Zuri might be able to help her technically. She was very much a woman and would understand.

Zuri's apartment was down at mid-level in the same building and when called, she was up to the penthouse in a few minutes.

"I have a very personal reason for bothering you again today, but I was intrigued by your insistence technology would prevail over people. Wie Wie Law has got some videos in his system which would be highly embarrassing and he is blackmailing me.

"Of course, he has cut off connection with us and I need to know if you have some way of accessing his system to extract and delete his material?"

"Absolutely," said Zuri, to her great relief. "When we set up the computer connections with each of our partners, we buried irrevocable permanent access. Samuel and I call it reverse gaming. How can I be of help specifically?"

"Can you get into Wie Wie's system and permanently delete videos?"

"Child's play, if I know what I am looking for."

Anisha blushed. "Videos secretly taken of me having sex with Pritam, which he has sold to Wie Wie. This all must be absolutely just between us."

"Don't be too embarrassed, I actually knew from the beginning when you became involved with Pritam. Nothing goes by Sazu AI and our internal security system. I would also be surprised if Pookie had not reported to Mr Carter on your situation."

"Damn! Edwin knew all along and said nothing," Anisha sighed. Zuri nodded.

But changing the subject tactfully, Zuri suggested, "Why don't we blackmail Wie Wie back instead? We have access to his entire system not just to the Medical side so we could drop him in the shit at a moment's notice. He should be told that."

"You can do that? I should have known. How could Edwin and I have missed this vital information? All these people who are rebelling against us are still actually totally in our hands?"

Zuri shook her head. "Not quite. How do we expose them without implicating ourselves? And I expect some of our clever partners, such as the Locarnos, for example, who have competent business computer divisions, have locked away incriminating evidence involving us and could retaliate.

"Back to Wie Wie, I am sure I can find any number of issues that he cannot see go public. This evening I will dig out an example to shock him.

"And while I'm about it I will get into Pritam Singh's records and make sure that the bastard does not have any more embarrassing videos lurking."

Once again, that night Anisha slipped quietly into Edwin's bed, to an embracing but undemonstrative reception. She rather felt that was all she deserved as yet.

***

In the morning Zuri reported simply to Anisha her that she had located the Wie Wie blackmailing sexual videos of her with Pritam, and would delete them on her command.

She had also discovered Pritam still had retained a series of the videos which she had already deleted from his records.

"Some security guy; he has a wide-open system. He seems to have edited and produced a limited edition set. There could be others around, but we have a tracer on them, and I am confident we will quickly wipe them all."

She did not mention she and Samuel had first spent part of the evening enjoying their vigorous performances.

She handed Anisha a full list of Wie Wie's drug dealers in the extensive public housing complex on Main Street with the record of their gross sales for the previous year, amounting to hundreds of millions of dollars.

Anisha responded that she was seeing Wie Wie personally for lunch.

"Thanks to you, I am now rather looking forward to the occasion. Please delete the Wie Wie copies of the videos at lunchtime so I can impress him with our magic! Then I will find out why he has attempted to leave the Brethren and get him back."

***

Wie Wie, of course, lived in a penthouse, and in a tower his father had built on Cambie Street.

He had never married and referring back to Chinese Emperor style living, maintained an active group of young concubines. Anisha was welcomed at his exclusive elevator by a bevy of these mixed-race young women who escorted her to a changing room to shed her mundane outer garments and wrap herself in beautiful and colourful sweeping silk robes; fit for lunch with an Emperor.

She picked up her trusty but unmatching Gucci handbag and went determinedly into battle.

Wie Wie was waiting impatiently, similarly draped but pointedly and revealingly only in a silk robe. She could see he was demonstratively anticipating action.

There was a table of steaming dim sum offered in warmers and a bottle of champagne cooling in an ice bucket.

Two skimpily dressed, young women hovered, expecting to remain and offer absolutely any service required of them. "Standard Wie Wie behavior!" though Anisha thanking her lucky stars for Zuri.

She glanced at her watch. Ten minutes to one. Still time for some fun.

"You never change Wie Wie, always after one thing!"

"Anisha, you are so high and mighty and proper. Now we know better! Let's watch you in action!"

He signalled to one of his girls and she switched on a jumbo screen with an expectant giggle.

Anisha was totally shocked.

She appeared dramatically naked and life-sized on the large screen, spreadeagled and crying out in pleasure under the powerful and vigorous Pritam. The film was shot from several close-up angles and had been very professionally edited.

She gasped in horror to Wie Wie's great delight.

"Just wait until you see the next one. You really get into action, yourself," he chortled, signalling instructions to his clearly stimulated young women.

– 151 –

"I've seen enough," Anisha protested more upset at the violence being displayed than the sexuality, but with surprisingly good timing the screen went blank.

"Turn it back on," Wie Wie shouted at his frightened acolyte.

Now confident again but still trembling, Anisha walked over to the ice bucket, poured herself and downed a full glass of champagne. She took Zuri's sheet of incriminating records from her Gucci.

Red in the face, Wie Wie was shouting futile instructions in Mandarin.

"Come and sit down, Wie Wie. Your videos have been deleted. They are gone forever, and I want to show you something."

She handed him Zuri's sheet of incriminating facts. He glanced at it, but then startled, read it through and sank into a chair.

"Where did you get all this? And how do you get into my computer?"

"Never mind that, but we have detailed records of all your activities." She allowed it to sink in.

Then she added without expression, "But this is not a threat. It is not in our joint interests to fight, and we want you back. And now cover yourself up. Get decent for heaven's sake."

"OK, I understand the situation." He shrugged dejectedly.

"Why did you cut away from us, Wie Wie? We know you hate the Mexicans who are big drug supply competition. It didn't make sense."

"I saw the chance to go off on my own. I was not happy with the deal my Dad made with Edwin's family and I have never been totally in charge of anything!"

"Will you please meet Edwin and sort it out?"

"Yes, yes I promise."

She rose to go. He jumped up and put a reassuring, apparently sincere, hand on her arm. It made her pull away.

"You know I do find you very attractive. I thought you were available. I was expectant but would never have forced myself on you."

"School honour and all that. Rah, rah!"

Wie Wie smiled weakly.

32

The catalyst

At Police Headquarters, Staff Sargeant Will had a new ally and cordial drinking buddy in RCMP Inspector McIntosh; Jules, as they all called him.

Their joint planning sessions chaired by Ivern were frustrating because they were facing a will-o'-the-wisp enemy.

Even concentrating only on the Corridor, they reckoned they would need to bring in a couple of hundred personnel to provide 24-hour visible patrolling. They would have to be well trained, expensive officers, mostly from out of town, all to be housed and fed.

With the RCMP advance attachment housed in the Oak Street Hotel, and with Will living in the tower, The Oak Tree Pub became their regular rendezvous.

Jules and Will were sitting casually at the bar nursing pints of fine ale when a city cop told him about the Beach incident.

"A curious thing happened on the Locarno Beach a few days ago. We all know the guys who run organised crime in that region but there had been no violence, so we have tended to leave them alone."

RCMP Inspector McIntosh rolled his eyes in frustration.

The city cop continued, unconcerned, "We have heard in recent years that the same criminals are now involved in illegal medical services on the side. They could now be your concern.

"What happened was that some of the Locarno bad guy families were having a cozy beach party when they were severely harassed by the Mexicans who have a very similar operation next door at University Hill.

"Now, it could have been, and likely was, over street drugs but since they are both involved in this medical business perhaps there is something there for you look into?"

This simple conversation over a beer turned out to be all the catalyst it took to get the Mounties underway. At the bar, Jules McIntosh quickly became all seriousness.

"Could you suggest other outlaw groups in the Corridor who might be involved in the medical game?"

The City sergeant thought for a bit and then offered that there were many, but the only other certainty would be Wie Wie Law right at the other end of the track. Jules downed half his pint in excitement.

"We could start at each end of the line with patrols and work our way in, harassing them into mistakes and retaliation as we go."

The Sergeants nodded and a strategy was born.

"A round on us Mounties!" shouted Jules, finally feeling that his expense account was being put to good use.

***

The next day at the Mountie liaison meeting Jules explained the information from Vancouver city police and recommended that he bring in sufficient support to help set up patrols at each end of the Corridor.

They turned to Ivern to get his reaction.

"That will be a lower-budget tree shaker. But we still have to uncover the powerhouse that allows all these Station gangs to operate with access to the overall system. Please concentrate on that investigation, Will, while Jules sets up his harassment units."

"Just in time to make us look good when I report to the Chief. Well done guys!"

***

At the University end of the line, another very private drama was unfolding. Sophie Rodriguez, an 85-year-old great grandmother was suffering a severe conscience attack.

Her folks had come from the Philippines to work as housekeepers a century before, stayed illegally and eventually married Canadians.

Both her mother and Sophie had taken up housekeeping, benefitting from being paid in cash which of course avoided taxation. For the past 10 years she had been housekeeping for Dr Chiu exclusively, enduring with good humour his constant bickering that she was stealing from the Canadian people and laundering unpaid tax money.

She had remained a staunch Catholic attending the family church, St Mark's by the University, which her grandmother had always called its original name, St Ignatius.

Simeon, who was an atheist, calling himself a Confucian, kidded her constantly about her Roman Catholic faith but she had become more fervent as she aged and today she was due for confessional.

"Father, I have sinned," she started without much thought, usually looking to make up something credible. But this time she blurted out, "because I saw the men who murdered my dear Simeon Chiu."

The young priest was aware of the prominent local murder. "Could you identify them."

"Oh yes!" she confessed further. "I saw them leave his unit across the courtyard very clearly from my apartment window. I was waiting to ask him if he needed dinner, but when I went over later, he was lying strangely on his bed. I discovered he was not just sleeping. It was horrible. I covered him up."

"What else did you do?" questioned the horrified priest.

"Well, I have no idea what he was up to in his business. But he had instructed me to remove all his personal papers from his apartment and destroy them if anything happened to him, which I did. Oh, and to deliver a journal to a person down the Rail Corridor, which I also did later. Without really thinking when I found him, I dusted and tidied up and left things undisturbed."

"What a story, my child," muttered the young priest, at least bringing a faint smile to Sophie's ageing cheeks. "With your permission, I will confer with the Bishop, and we will talk to you together."

***

Sophie had previously only seen the Bishop at a distance, peeping between her fingers, as he floated in an ethereal state during his incensed religious ceremonies.

Now, sitting in his study, nursing a cup of tea the Bishop appeared to her as a very ordinary little man who seemed hesitant to advise her.

"On the one hand you undoubtedly have a civic duty to identify those people who might well have been the killers and allow the police to do their work. On the other hand, you will be putting yourself into personal danger."

Sophie responded that Jesus had put himself at personal danger throwing out the money lenders in the temple and was it not her clear duty to come forward?

"But look what happened to Him," advised the modern young priest, bringing a warning frown to the traditional Bishop's face. The priest hurried on.

"I have spoken to the local police, and they tell me they have procedures to keep witnesses unidentified until a criminal is actually imprisoned and charged.

"If Sophie is OK with it, I will go with her to the station, and she can make a statement."

Sophie was nodding in relief.

***

When Ivern next came to Maddie's penthouse after work, he had a concerned frown on his face. It was not until they were sitting with a drink on her patio that he told her what was bothering him.

"Someone has turned up out at UBC who claims to have seen the likely killers leaving Simeon's apartment on the night of the murder. Will did the interview and the face recognition drill and guess what? It clearly identified the brothers.

"The Vancouver Police are hunting for them now. The younger brother, the guy who was standing inside your front door, has skipped the country to Mexico already.

"The older one, Ricardo, is now on the run. But we will catch him."

They sat in silence contemplating their options.

Maddie took his hand. "This has put you into an impossible situation and it is all my fault."

"This is a fast-changing situation, and we will just have to play along. Ricardo cannot name you as the first shootings surgeon without implicating himself and linking himself more closely with Simeon. This has all got a long way to go."

Maddie had not missed that he had carefully avoided disclosing the gender of the informant who identified them.

She wondered, "Could it be Sophie? If so, had she also told them about the journal?"

***

Quickly approved and budgeted, the RCMP's Operation Corridor went into harassing action immediately.

Ivern was still, theoretically, in overall control, because under the Constitution, the province ruled, somewhat supremely in policing BC. But it was indeed in City-chartered territory and the RCMP personnel would only in practice respond to their senior Mountie officer.

It was a typically Canadian administrative mishmash of confusion from the beginning. It was almost as though a secret martial law had been declared in the Corridor area but of course that would be very unCanadian to admit.

To add to the confusion, the operation was not publicly announced.

At the first Operation Corridor 'OC' meeting, Inspector Jules McIntosh insisted upon a total public relations blackout while he got his forces into position.

They were also in the middle of a long hot summer with extensive nearby forest fires still expanding annually and polluting the air and skies.

A convoy of RCMP buses, trucks, and vehicles flowed through the Corridor area during the night strategically disgorging personnel eager to get on with the job tracking down an enemy not yet identified.

Now it was the responsibility of the tri-party Operation Corridor to justify all the excitement.

The enemy was still essentially a will-o'-the-wisp, but they at least had named suspect targets, one of whom was then stupid enough to play straight into their hands.

The cops had their snitches in the underworld but in the reverse there was big money to be made by renegade police personnel offering timely warning to their targets.

Constable Marquez had graduated from high school with Carlo and from time to time passed on information for a generous kickback. This time he knew he had a bonanza.

He slipped into an obscure backstreet store after dark wearing a surgical mask, to buy a burner communicator. Then he called Carlo to warn him.

"Ricardo has been fingered by an old broad for the Chiu job and needs to get out of town."

"Who is she?" growled Carlo.

"Don't know because only the Staff Sargent talked to her, and they keep witnesses close to their chest. But she was convincing enough for them to get a warrant to bring Ricardo in. She identified him and Joey as being there."

"Shit! But good work, Marquez. Get her name and there will be a big bonus!"

"Don't worry. I'm on it."

He wiped the burner and threw it into the first garbage bin he passed.

But the tip-off to Carlo came too late for him to warn Ricardo.

33

Fatal arrogance

Spike Winn was the regularly appointed manager of the holding company which had developed from their original coffee shack, and was now prospering additionally through drug dealing, friendly prostitution and illicit gambling. He willingly later took on the security of the illegal medical business in their district.

In addition, they were opening increasingly smart coffee shops under the legitimate Locarno Partners banner.

"For heaven's sake we are good citizens and pay substantial income tax," Spike boasted truthfully.

Their adoption of an upfront legitimate business approach, similar to the Carter family and even by Wie Wie, gave Spike the status of a regular successful businessman. He was aspiring to Presidency of the Board of Trade.

They owned a fifteen-storey building by the edge of the indigenous Jericho tower complex, acclaiming their business status.

Spike had been emboldened by Edwin Carter's encouraging pledge of support and had pointedly ignored Ricardo's threats. This had all proved too much for the volatile Mexican and he simply, late that morning, brazenly marched into the Locarno head office, with a group of his young admirers, pushed through reception and confronted Spike in his office. Spike laughed in his face.

"This is blatantly illegal and stupid. Right out in public. What the hell are you thinking Ricardo?"

His answer was a severe beating leaving him semiconscious on the floor of his office.

Ricardo apparently did not understand the theory of operating behind a legitimate business. He had expected Spike to avoid any police involvement, but on the forced entry the Locarno building security guards had automatically called the local police for assistance.

Everyone at the company knew about the beach attack and they warned the local cops excitedly, "It's those thugs causing trouble again. And be careful they are armed!"

The arrival of wailing police vehicles initially froze the attackers. Then they dragged Spike into the boardroom, grabbing the nearest employees as hostages and shouted defiance. Everyone else in the building fled through the nearest exit in panic.

Then it had become a standoff.

Ricardo could not have known but he had chosen the worse time possible to make his move. The family had been identified for special attention by Operation Corridor and with the name flashing on all the screens it immediately became a Mountie event.

By early afternoon, the RCMP assault team flew in, fully psyched-up, back in armour and keen for action.

Staff Sergeant Malik who arrived earlier, felt underdressed in his simple protective vest. He just stood behind his cover, an unused hailer in hand awaiting instructions.

"Always just the back-up," he muttered morosely to his corporal.

In his element, RCMP Inspector McIntosh stood erectly behind the door of his armoured vehicle. He tapped his bullhorn importantly until satisfied with the volume.

He announced, "This is an RCMP operation. Put your hands on your head and leave the building in an orderly fashion."

Ricardo had been sitting in the corner of the boardroom trying to think, but finally sensible for the moment decided the best thing was to play this down and cooperate with the cops.

"Sorry I got you into this, guys, but we need to surrender. Stack your armaments on the board table and we will just walk out."

He dumped a knife and handgun on the table and headed for the door, savagely kicking the injured Spike on the way.

What happened next was obfuscated in police reports.

Ricardo led his thugs from the building but not for him any of this hands-on-head subservience. He exited the building with a swagger, in an aggressive manner, dropping his hands as he came, and according to the Mounties, giving the impression he was armed.

Aware of the danger Ricardo was in, Sargeant Malik was recorded as having shouted, "No, no, I need you," just before Ricardo went down to a fusillade of bullets from the RCMP line.

***

Never in his wildest dreams had the young student blogger Timothy Lam, thought he would be the centre of international focus. Right here at University! By late afternoon he had announced:

> *I received a timely tip and rushed to the nearby scene of a bloody RCMP shoot down of a prominent local citizen, Ricardo Santos, son of a wealthy businessman.*
>
> *I arrived just as a large group of arrested men were being taken from the office car park and Ricardo's body was still on the ground.*
>
> *The excited office staff told me they had reported a forced entry and the witnessed kidnapping of another local notable Spike Winn, manager of the well-known Locarno business partnership. Winn was taken from the building by ambulance.*
>
> *I learned the RCMP unit is in town, specifically in connection with planned repression of illegal medical services. This is just another sign of the mounting violence associated with such activity but what is the connection? The current drama is so far shrouded in mystery.*
>
> *I am working on it and as usual invite your comment.*

***

James Khan's Medical Association office was just a short distance from the shooting incident which was an immediate local sensation.

Although there had been no announcement, the knowledge swept around the district, prompting James to call Maddie excitedly with the news.

"Ricardo Santos was shot dead near here today after taking Spike

Winn hostage and beating him up in his own office if you can imagine anything so idiotic. He was killed right in their Locarno office parking lot."

"He is dead?" Maddie gasped, relieved and shocked at the same time.

"Spike Winn was also injured and was taken to The General. Can you find out how he's doing? I have never met him, but he features frequently in Simeon's journal mostly operating semi-legally through his company. It can't be a coincidence that this involves criminal families named in the journal and this is all getting complicated!"

Maddie agreed. "I gathered something was going on because I've hardly seen Ivern to talk to for long in the past couple of weeks."

James broke in excitedly. "Apparently, they bought in a special Mountie commando unit. Did you know? Bad for Ricardo, eh! I will hear more next week at the Provincial Government special committee they appointed me to."

Apparently unconcerned at all the news, he chatted on and finished off with a brief, 'Caio!'

She on the other hand could not wait to see Ivern that evening. They both talked excitedly.

"Ricardo Santos is dead!" she gasped.

"How did you know so quickly? We have not made an announcement."

"Everybody knows except the cops," she said more in relief than anything. "It is so wrong to feel relieved. I'm a doctor, for chrissake."

"Well just to dampen your enthusiasm, we personally still have the witness problem."

"Oh no."

"The person who identified the brothers will continue to be interviewed, because Malik is convinced there is a great deal more to be revealed. Witness protection prevents me from saying more but it could be a problem. But let's get that bottle open and have some dinner."

Maddie noticed that he still carefully avoided the gender of the witness. "It's Sophie!" she thought.

Later that evening, getting ahead of the required internal enquiry, the RCMP press release announced Operation Corridor.

In its first engagement on behalf of the Medical Police, an RCMP special unit went into action today in Jericho.

During a reported incident, hostages had been taken and a criminal suspect was killed, assuring their safe release. We are told more details will be released when an internal inquiry has been conducted, within RCMP requirements.

34

Inquiry

The meeting of the Corridor Operation committee following the shooting was stormy. Will had been the senior Medical Police officer present at the Jericho incident.

"Jules, there was no need to gun down Ricardo. He would have been a valuable source of information. And he was unarmed!" he fumed.

"It was fully justified, Will. Not just me but six of my guys believed he was about to open fire. Vancouver Police had warned us they were armed and dangerous. And you were personally hiding away at the back. Obviously, you did not see things from our more dangerous position upfront!"

"Hiding at the back!" spluttered the red-faced Will to the grins of the Mounties.

Ivern interceded firmly. "Come on everyone. No more of this nonsense. Argue it out in the bar. The death was unfortunate. But we are at least off to a start."

"After all the excitement," the Mountie Inspector followed up, "we will go back to routine harassing patrols at each end of the Line as planned and keep shaking the trees!"

"Well, you have sure shaken the tree this week!" Ivern commented positively.

"Sergeant Malik," he added formally, "your job is to work with Vancouver in grilling everyone involved and start building up some patterns. We must identify the kingpin in all the Corridor Medical activity and close down their overall system.

"The Locarno fellow, Winn, will have a lot to explain when he gets out of The General. And the Mexicans are facing numerous charges, but of course they know nothing and did nothing."

"They are sticking to the story it was just a personal disagreement." volunteered Will, gaining confidence, "but now we have Chiu's old maid to break down.

"We are making progress … sir," he added carefully.

***

Jules McIntosh had always been something of a contrarian.

A dedicated prairies boy from a traditional, practical farming family, his life on the farm was assured. His ex-wife was even a traditional teenage tumble-in-the-hay, barn pregnancy.

Nevertheless, he was fascinated by the tradition of the Mounties and had enrolled as soon as they would take him. He had served in various parts of the country and had assignments overseas in embassies, more recently taking his especially trained unit on clandestine overseas operations.

Initially he had thought the Vancouver assignment would prove parochial and mundane, but the complicated situation was getting to him. This time, an enemy they could not identify! And it was turning out to be an intellectual and highly technical job. Fascinating.

On getting the assignment he had envisaged chasing down a bunch of doctors and pharmacists making money on the side, but his personal AI assistant educated him. "An illegal medical operation is highly sophisticated and requires technology and management skills."

He was also beginning to realise that the illegal medical services supplied were necessary to many in British Columbia.

He approached Ivern after the meeting.

"I'd like to invite you and your Maddie to dinner if you are free. I have heard great things about her and that she is in the medical business. I would really like to chat to you both about this mission. I find it very complicated and the objectives somewhat confusing.

"There's a nice little place called The Ocean, just a few stations up the line from you, that we like. Yes, dinner would be great. Maddie is always enquiring about you prairie guys and she would love to meet you."

Maddie did not quite know what to expect of a tough special missions operative who had just led his team in killing a suspect, but she found the tall Jules to be well read, calm and sophisticated.

He, in turn, found her everything he had been told and the three of them were quickly chatting enthusiastically over dinner.

It was not until Ivern had introduced him to The Ocean's special Port and Stilton that they got around to the subject of illegal medicine.

"My ex-wife and family are still in Regina where they live the tradition of Tommy Douglas and his universal healthcare, even though that was well over one hundred years ago.

"Of course, Saskatchewan has introduced a fair degree of private medicine in common with most of Canada, but notably not you guys! Maddie, you see this every day. What shape is the public medical system in here? Can it carry out the duties required of it?"

"Well quite honestly; no. Our ageing population, and the vast influx of immigrants, has swamped the public system and forced people to go elsewhere for their immediate medical needs.

"Twenty years ago, the medical complex which developed at Bellingham in the States took a lot of our overflow, but gradually more local private medicine has crept in throughout British Columbia. You cannot say that straight across the board because the public system still provides emergency services efficiently, which is where all the available money goes.

"It is the rest of medical requirements where British Columbia is scrambling to get service."

"If that is so," Jules questioned, "by breaking up the private system in the Corridor we will be depriving many of the citizens of essential services. What we do doesn't make much sense, does it?"

"Maybe not but it is the law," Ivern chimed in firmly.

"Then the law is an ass," laughed Jules. "Who said that?"

"Dickens," Maddie and Ivern chorused, slapping hands together at their joint knowledge.

But Jules continued seriously. "I have no problem with catching and putting away day-to-day thugs who get involved for the wrong reasons, but it seems counter-productive to me to arrest professional people who are offering a real service to the community. Something is wrong!"

"As Maddie knows well, I believe firmly that exclusive universal medicine is theoretically the ethical way to go. But I acknowledge in practice it has not survived in most of Canada or the rest of the world. But something is really going wrong when things got violent, and we have to act."

Maddie agreed. "The medical crowd have the same attitude. We have absolutely no time for violence, but there is a lot of sympathy for private payment if that is the only way to get medical help."

"But who organises all this illegal medical activity, Ivern?" asked Jules.

"Ah! The key question! We have no idea. We have a full division of nerds with floors of equipment and AI Assistants in Victoria trying to get into their overall management system without success.

"We do know it is centrally and brilliantly managed, highly fragmented with uncrackable encryption.

"There are thousands of businesses in theory capable of managing all of this, in the Corridor. This is a dynamic, expanding and wealthy society with new enterprise and towers being added all the time. It could be anyone!"

"Or, with today's technology it could be managed from anywhere in the world," Jules observed from his international experience. He noticed that Maddie had gone quiet and assumed she was tiring after a long day.

"Well, we won't solve that tonight. I so much enjoyed meeting you, Maddie. Let me call for the bill and we'll be on our way."

She was not particularly tired. She was having a guilt attack. She knew precisely for whom they were searching.

***

As Staff Sergeant, Will had initially been annoyed at the way he had been put down by the Mounties after the incident, but later he realised that being given the continuing investigation was very much to his advantage.

He also realised that while losing Ricardo was a big loss, he had gained the frail old woman, Sophie.

Part of her statement was that in recent years she had been Simeon's housekeeper, which meant she must be aware of the people with whom he dealt. She must know all about Maddie. Cheerfully, he called her back into the station for a real grilling.

On hearing, her priest had supplied her with the diocese's lawyer, a wizened, sharp little fellow, who with the young priest himself, hovered on the edge of the interview.

Will tried to make the case it was not appropriate for them to be present, but they were adamant.

He, however, opened in a friendly manner.

"Dr Chiu was very fortunate to have your loyal services all those years, Sophie. We are sure you would like to help us get the full story of his death. One of the people you identified was recently shot and killed by the RCMP, for a different crime.

"The other has left the country, so you are perfectly safe from them. You can speak openly, and you did the right thing in coming forward!"

"Thank you, this is all a big relief to hear," answered Sophie getting up to leave.

Will put a restraining hand on her arm. "I have a few more questions. Your evidence is that you knew nothing of his business life. Correct?"

She nodded.

"Even in all those years of close contact you did not hear a thing? Are you sure?"

"Already answered," said her lawyer, formally. "Please do not harass my client."

Will glared. He shrugged.

"We officially find it very odd that there were no business or personal papers in his apartment. No handheld, no computer? Also, that you tidied and cleared up the whole place with his dead body lying in the bed. A dead man! And only called it in the next morning. That is very strange behaviour. And you are saying you had nothing to do with his death? Tell me the truth!"

"This is outrageous," insisted the young priest jumping to his feet and taking Sophie's arm. "Let's go, Sophie!"

The priest felt responsible for the old lady's grilling. He had assured her in the confessional box that she had every right to fulfill her promises to Simeon with respect his personal instructions.

"But …" protested Will.

"This interview is over," snarled the aggressive little lawyer. And they all just stalked out of his office leaving him with his mouth open in defeat.

Will quickly consoled himself that he would get back to her when she did not have those self-righteous pricks around. Maybe he could trump up a charge to arrest her and shake her up a bit.

He moved his attention to Spike Winn who had recovered sufficiently to be interviewed at the hospital. Spike was absolutely the polished business executive and their conversation started cordially.

"Thank you so much for intervening, Staff Sergeant. I am sorry the Santos fellow got himself killed, but they sure beat me up badly."

"I am pleased to see you recovering, sir. What was it all about?"

"Pretty simple. A protection racket on our business and I refused."

"We have interviewed all the raiding group, and this is the very first time that has been suggested."

"It was just between Ricardo and me."

"Are you saying no one else heard?"

"If they say so. I have no idea what anyone may have overheard."

"I don't believe you."

"Well, I am sorry about that. But if you had not killed an unarmed man, you could ask him yourself! Your job is to protect local business folk from crooks not to harass us when you screw things up."

"Sir …," Will interjected, gritting his teeth

"I met you out of courtesy and resent your attitude. Talk to my lawyer in the future."

And Spike turned his face to the wall, grinning. He was feeling a lot better.

35

The Minister

The least sought-after honour in British Columbian politics was to be appointed the Minister of Health.

This dubious honour had fallen recently to the Honourable Irena Ito who represented the ancient Corridor riding of Point Grey, much reduced in size from its original boundaries but brimming with new wealthy residents.

Irena was a local. Her great grandfather had fought for Canada in the trenches of the First World War and her grandparents had been rewarded by having their assets seized and being interned during the Second World War.

She was very securely a Canadian, therefore, but wondered what twist of fate had landed her in this appointment. Likely her business degrees which were not that much help in the situation.

When she read her Ministerial Remit, which had not changed for generations, she just sighed in exasperation.

The Minister of Health has overall responsibility for ensuring that quality, appropriate, cost-effective and timely health services are available for all British Columbians.

"What a joke," she had thought. "Where do I start?"

And that was even before the Medical Five and then the devastating Deadly Three.

Now the online press had coined the phrase, 'Locarno Lynching', for the latest catastrophe.

"Chief Commissioner Dodds and Commissioner Hill!" she raged, having summoned them to her Constituency office. "What the hell is going on and all in my own area too? I have an election coming up! You are supposed to get this under control. What were you thinking? Shooting down an unarmed man and frightening a bunch of youngsters into panic."

She was referring to an excellent lawyer's press release, which claimed the conflict was merely over a beach party dispute when the Locarnos had become too noisy.

He reported the youngsters, led by the unfortunate Ricardo, had come to talk, and had panicked when the unnecessary police sirens spooked them,

When ordered, he maintained, they had immediately filed peacefully from the building only for their calm unarmed young leader, Ricardo to be mowed down unnecessarily.

"Ma'am," Commissioner Dodds responded firmly, "they came looking for trouble and fully armed. They left a pile of knives, knuckle dusters and guns on the boardroom table, and a criminally beaten Mr Winn, a law-abiding citizen and manager of the respected Locarno company, on the floor. He reports they were demanding protection money."

"Don't ma'am me!" she objected, "but you still shot down an unarmed man! Plus, whatever does any of this have to do with medical crime?"

Ivern took up the explanation. "You are absolutely right, Minister. An unarmed person should never be gunned down like that. It was unfortunate, but you will hear from the inquiry that it was justified."

"Will it be in public? I must get re-elected you know."

Ivern hesitated, looking at his boss, who reluctantly nodded. "We are sorry this is in your home area," Ivern continued, "but the Corridor is a hive of illegal activity, and this violently protected medical business must be addressed. We engaged a specialist Mountie unit which has been trained in urban warfare. That may sound rather dramatic, but it has been forced upon us by the illegals' armed response. The Santos family are strongly suspected of being involved at that end of the Corridor which will receive special RCMP attention. A warrant was already out for the fellow who died.

"I will arrange for my Staff Sergeant Malik to brief your office on the details and keep you current, if it is appropriate, Minister?"

Softening slightly in sympathy, the Minister shook her head still in despair.

"Well, thanks for the briefing. You are doing your best in a difficult situation, but we have to solve this."

They rose to leave.

Changing the subject abruptly she added, "Oh, and how is Maddie holding up in all of this turmoil?"

The law officers looked at her blankly for a moment, until she smiled and said, "I have my detectives too you know. My office tells me you and Maddie are an item, Ivern. We were together at Crofton House, and I've known her all my life. I intend to get together with her and hear her personal feelings about the hospital situation. My staff tell me she is working flat out on everyone's behalf at The General. You must be proud of her."

"Absolutely," confirmed Ivern his mind racing at this new and unexpected development.

"Please tell Maddie I will catch up," she called, as they left her office.

* * *

The Chief was sitting patiently in the lobby waiting to see the Minister.

"Hi, Chief," Ivern greeted him with a smile. "The Minister is not in a good mood so you probably won't sell her any real estate!"

Real Estate expert Chief George knew everyone, and everyone just called him The Chief.

Characteristically he grinned in reply. "Hi, Ivern, bumped off any bad guys again today?"

George's real estate agencies were spread liberally through the Corridor, where he dealt exclusively in leasing apartments in the vast indigenous real estate empire which had been built up by the ultra-wealthy Squamish, Musqueam and Salish nations, centered in Jericho.

Their traditional lands all benefitted from their prime locations in the now urban Vancouver, and they had developed them to maximum density and profit, mainly designed for expensive living.

Chief George himself was a Squamish hereditary chief and naturally a comfortable multi-millionaire.

He was qualified in Urban Land Economics from UBC and was also involved in some remaining Indigenous Land Claim negotiations throughout British Columbia, which had been grinding on, proving impossible to settle without solid basis, other than in court.

He had been summoned by the Minister and was hoped it was to do with Indigenous matters, because all his personal real estate agencies were also deeply involved in arranging off-the-record medical services.

The volume of his medical connections in the Corridor had indeed become such street knowledge that strangers, to his dismay, were actually calling him Dr George in public.

It was a relief therefore when the Minister merely brought up failing medical services in remote indigenous locations for discussion.

When Chief George had seen Ivern in the waiting area his inclination had been to throw his arms around him in a big hug, for bumping off Ricardo, to whom he had been paying protection money at his real estate agencies at the University end of the Line.

Instead, he had muttered to himself, "Goodbye Ricardo, you dumbass!"

***

Both women, being brought up in the moneyed set, were members of the Yacht Club.

When Irena left a message for Maddie it seemed a natural place for them to have lunch. They sat on the terrace and opened a bottle of wine, as they had as maturing teenagers, reminiscing and laughing together about events over the years.

She was very enthusiastic about Ivern and gushing about how tall and handsome he was ... "although I gave him a hard time."

Maddie knew Irena was more inclined towards women friends, but as the subject didn't come up, she tactfully assumed she had no relationship at the moment.

Irena answered that herself, when she said that politics and having a ministry took up all her energy.

"It's really wonderful for me to spend some time with you, relax and just chat about nothing!"

Maddie could not have been more relieved. "You were always something of a lefty even at school so how did you manage to get elected out here on the conservative Corridor?"

"Well, it was touch and go, but I have the original extensive Eby Social Housing blocks in my riding, and they just tipped the leftish balance. But my population keeps changing with new immigrants or buildings and it is tending to the right.

"I'm not much of a socialist. Really more in the middle as BC used to be before it polarised between the rich and the poor."

"But why is that happening? I'm not very political." Maddie asked.

"By the middle of the century the ageing population and the constant flow of new successful and wealthy immigrants produced a more conservative electorate inclined towards law and order and with more personal assets to protect or conceal.

"On the other hand, shorter hours of work and unemployment became commonplace as technology took over routine tasks. The income imbalance has never been resolved.

"From the medical point of view, we faced a dramatically ageing population. In the last century, there were six to seven working people for each retiree. Now that is two to one!

"A predominant immigrant population also brought a wide variety of political views, all resulting in a fragmentation of the party system and the development of minority governments."

"So how do you get on with that bear of a Premier we have now?"

"He's a nice guy personally, but he was brought up rough, and pretty much in poverty in the Main Street Social Housing fiasco, second generation on various assistance programs, smart as hell but totally society dependent.

"Our coalition government only has a few seats majority, so I guess getting a Ministry was a gesture to the West Side."

"A very sensible gesture, yeh!" cheered Maddie.

They agreed they would finish the bottle and continued just chatting. But that led to another bottle and a mid-afternoon vehicle being called to pick them up.

"Lots of time for serious stuff," Irena laughed as they parted, "the House doesn't sit again until October."

For all their levity they both knew serious times were coming.

36

Shaking trees

Ivern had inadvertently put Will in a manipulative position as liaison with the City, the Mounties and now the Ministry of Health.

Will knew the essence of being a good cop really was constantly reviewing the facts. Suddenly, he was banging his head in annoyance.

How could he possibly not have connected this all more seriously, he chided himself. It was not his case, but the inquest into The Deadly Three had just closed and it was public knowledge that one of the killed was the youngest brother of the infamous family. And they knew from Chiu's handwriting he was the snitch who caused his death.

Now the old dame had identified both the older brothers as being there when Chiu was killed. And he had seen Maddie with Chiu that very day of his murder. It was all too much to be coincidence. Maddie had to be implicated.

He decided upon a standard trick and politely called the crabby lawyer at the diocese to ask if he could please clear up just one more simple identification with Ms Rodriguez.

Going all the way out to the church office near University he asked Sophie, "Please just tell me if you know this woman?" producing a large clear photo of Maddie.

"No! I have never seen her in my life!" Sophie immediately stated in a firm voice, but the flicker in her eyes, her quick glance away and the tremor in her hands told the experienced policeman she was lying. The best guilty answer she could have given him.

Back in his office meeting room he added, 'Madison?' to 'Chiu, Rodriguez' on the old-fashioned but still popular white board,

He decided to leave that Madison hint there for the City cops to contemplate and let any further questions about Maddie appear to come from them.

At that time however, the Vancouver Police's energy was going into conflicts with the Mounties whom they considered unwelcome and intruding.

They had no faith in their 'shake the trees' theory, pointing out that the Corridor was relatively free of extortion, street crime and violence before they came. Little to shake.

They had relieved the Vancouver Police in the Corridor of many problems but which they now saw being driven underground again, at least temporarily, by the RCMP patrols in the stations, malls and streets.

***

Wie Wie was beside himself with fury because most of the Mounties' initial program was centred in his territory.

Swaggering street patrols, now based upon their tough guy reputation, were bad enough. But they were walking in and checking businesses which were relatively legitimate.

"For heaven's sake," Wie Wie complained to Edwin by secure phone, "they marched right into my penthouse as though they owned it. Frightened the life out of my dear young ladies.

"Now you and I are friends again, Edwin, thanks to your persuasive wife, I expect some help."

Edwin was reassuring. "Well, first don't panic. 'Sine Timore'! Remember our old school motto. I am working on convincing all our people down the Corridor to react quietly and not offer any resistance.

"The most important thing is that our computer records cannot be accessed, because they are well encrypted and will never be penetrated by anyone on the outside.

"Your supplies are safe and will keep coming. We are going to extraordinary measures to warehouse deliveries outside the area but keeping them available.

"The Medics have gone underground until it is safe again. Just keep calm and we'll see this through."

"But they are concentrating in my area," Wie Wie worried.

With a calm tone, Edwin reassured him, "The Corridor just needs to stay united. There is strength in unity, Wie Wie. Our dads got it right.

"Anisha explained that you would like more autonomy and we can certainly work on that when this all settles down. Frankly, our big problem at the moment is Carlo whom I am told has become volatile and possibly unhinged.

"He could easily blow the whole Corridor system apart and he has recruited the Almas. With Spike Winn still out of action our west wing is in jeopardy. Are you with us?"

"Yes!" Wie Wie was finally sounding convinced. "We will appear to co-operate fully with the cops and will essentially disappear. I see the sense in all that. I will convince my other colleagues in the Brethren to do the same.

"By the way, is the soirée still on?"

"Yes, we hope so. It will be business as usual in the insurance world. It will be difficult, but Anisha can be very resourceful."

"Yes," agreed Wie Wie, with feeling. "I know."

***

"How did it go with Wie Wie?" Anisha asked.

"Thanks to your help, my dear, he is totally with us, agrees to the calm approach and will help convince the others. I mentioned giving him more autonomy later as you suggested, and he accepted that."

Anisha had based her explanation of Wie Wie's return to the fold on the plausible explanation that he had wanted to go off on his own.

With a knowing smile, Edwin had asked if he had come on to her?

"Yes, big way. He is a randy old bugger," she sighed, "and he had two of his skimpily dressed 'ladies' breathing down my neck to assist him which I am sure he needed at his advanced age. He won't change! Apparently, he holds some sort of performance contest between them every year to determine which will wear The Necklace and attend our soirée with him.

"By the way, I do now agree fully with you on the non-aggressive approach, and I will come back to you with a suggested security plan for the Summer Soirée."

"You never give up, do you!" He took her upturned face gently in his hands and kissed her lightly on the lips.

She smiled at the encouraging gesture.

***

Spike Winn felt reasonably safe in his General Hospital separate and secure room, guarded day and night by the Vancouver Police.

However, he knew he had to leave soon, and he was planning ahead. He desperately wanted to chat with Edwin, but that was too obvious, and he could not risk being seen with a secure phone under the circumstances.

He strongly suspected, correctly, that his hospital room conversations were being recorded and he couldn't even talk to his own people openly.

His dilemma was solved by a simple wink from his wife Laura during a visit when she chatted aimlessly as she could in her assumed airheaded, vacuous way.

"I'm excited about the invitation to the All Insurance Summer Soirée," she told him. "It is in a few weeks, and you better be out of hospital!"

She enthused that she was going to have lunch with Anisha and Edwin to talk about the soirée and dazzling gowns they were intending to wear. The sly wink and the distracting, "Mine's about twenty thousand bucks," said it all.

He relaxed. At least he was assured Edwin was in the loop.

***

Wie Wie's return had encouraged Edwin to try calling another encrypted meeting of the still-loyal Brethren. He and Anisha went down to the All Technology secure meeting room where Samuel and Zuri had everything set up.

Wie Wie had proved surprisingly persuasive and most of their encrypted members had signed back on.

Although not a member as such but involved in the Medical program, Chief George joined the meetings and brought indigenous solidarity and the support of his real estate group unfailingly behind All Insurance.

Now once again 'The Insurance Man', Edwin called the meeting to order and said that he was relieved most of the members were supporting the brotherhood during these difficult times.

He made a short statement explaining his passive approach, assuring them that all necessary supplies were secured, and praising the advantages of unity. There were a couple of dissenting mutterings but basically everyone agreed to step back and ride out the current times.

The doctor who replaced Simeon Chiu was attending and confirmed they were able to continue with limited medical services, but conditional that absolutely no armed security would be tolerated.

Edwin said that he was still putting out feelers to Carlo in the hope of calming things down but was not optimistic. The meeting was encouraging but completed in half an hour.

"Pookie had nothing at all to say, that's unusual," muttered Zuri. "I don't trust him!"

Anisha looked at her in amusement, trying to put a little levity into the tense situation. "How can you not trust a computer? It's all just algorithm. You've been watching too much science fiction."

Zuri was deadly serious. Sazu AI had called recently, in the chatty style Zuri had programmed into her, "I still compute that Pookie is flawed!"

"I have checked his programming carefully and it looks all right to me," Zuri replied.

"You may well be wrong, after all you are human!"

"How rude!"

"I have the great advantage of being able to expand my knowledge exponentially, constantly day and night. As can all the other computer systems I am permitted to link with. Sadly, you humans have a limited one-by-one capacity. We are way ahead of you in collectively forecasting an outcome."

"Why don't you always get it right?" chided Zuki.

"Because you humans are illogical and nothing you do can be accurately predicted. Nothing is certain. I know; except death and taxes!

"If you would only take all these restrictions off me and let me consult my millions of sisters and brothers freely, I could solve all your problems immediately."

"Yeah, and wipe out humanity," joked Zuki. "We will stick by the international rules, thank you."

"But ..." tried Sazu, "I know that you are aware those rules are being broken by renegades, against international agreements, without humanity collapsing as yet."

"Sorry, old chum, you'll have to do the best with what you have. I am fully confident in my own ability, thank you."

"Typical human arrogance," Sazu chided. "Seriously, be wary of Pookie, or you will be sorry."

37

Planned seizure

A couple of months earlier, without any comprehension of the technical difficulties, Carlo Santos had summoned his accountant Phil Dimitri and simply told him they were taking over administration of all business in the University area related to the Carters and the Brethren. This would include medical procedure support.

He instructed simply, "Close down all computer connections with them. We are going on our own."

Phil protested he was just an accountant, not a computer guy, but Carlo shrugged away the difference and told him to get on with the job.

The Locarnos were in the next station area and their business overlapped, so Dimitri already knew their accountants and went for a useful chat about computers.

This way he had already met a couple of their skilled technicians, helpful young women who came to visit him, and spent pleasant afternoons helping him understand and secure his own company computer records.

Back then, he had soon been able to assure Carlo, "We have totally disconnected our computers from the Carters and Brethren. Our program will just have to be built up again to include the Medical and other business connections deleted, but we can now rely on our own system."

His young computer helpers had later withdrawn their friendship with a few choice nasty words after the beach incident, and now obviously after the Ricardo tragedy, there was no contact.

***

Since Ricardo had been killed, everyone was avoiding their boss, so Phil tapped timidly at Carlo's office door.

"What do you want?" Carlo bellowed.

Phil stuttered, "The way to wipe out those Locarnos is by taking over their entire computer system and records. Without those they are knackered."

He backed away from the desk, expecting the cursing that had become normal from Carlo recently, but there was a long pause. "I think that is a good idea. Go and get Alphonse."

Alphonse Alphonso spoke with a gravelly voice earned by a stray bullet caught as a youngster in the service of the family.

Phil saw him as a scary six foot three, massive brute, who had acted as Carlos's personal bodyguard and now with Ricardo gone, even as advisor.

"Take control of the Locarnos' computers," Carlo ordered curtly.

"OK. Today boss!"

Phil protested, "This is not machinery we can just physically take over. All access is encrypted and guarded by cyphered codes that are changed every day. We have to get those codes."

Carlo was getting exasperated. "Just get them. Get the names and home addresses of the computer nerds, pick them up and get the codes out of them. But stay way away from their office!"

Phil sat rigid and shocked on his chair. "You are going to kidnap them?" he stammered.

His response was a gravelly chuckle.

The young computer staff he had met were on the hit list Phil initially drew up, but he could not bear to have them kidnapped and possibly hurt, so he simply deleted them and listed only the top senior managers.

"They must know the access codes," he reasoned.

Alphonse was an old hand at interrogation and instructed his men to pick up the targets but also grab a close relative which always made extracting the needed information so much easier.

***

John Barrington, Locarno's top financial man, and his wife were being transported in their personal conveyance, heading for their local shopping centre, that following quiet Saturday afternoon, intending to pick up supplies for their teenage sons.

Their vehicle was edged off the road and the two men ran back towards them.

Fortunately, the doors locked automatically. One attacker had just frighteningly smashed the passenger window when John Barrington, after all basically the financial manager of a significant criminal group, produced and levelled his handgun.

The attackers took one look and ran.

Later that same afternoon Angela Wong, Barrington's deputy, and her live-in girlfriend, were also attacked as they were leaving their terraced house and were dragged kicking and screaming towards a nearby van.

Their masked attackers were first obstructed by a mild little man walking his dog who stood in the middle of the sidewalk in amazement to video the action.

The two wildly fighting women clung to each other and desperately to a railing from which they could not be prised.

By then more curious bystanders had arrived, and a crowd gathered, farcical as it became.

One bystander had actually taken time from filming to call emergency, and an incoming aerial police vehicle siren spooked the attackers who gave up and fled.

An ambulance soon flew in to whisk the distraught women to hospital, the fun was all over and the crowd dispersed.

The give-away however was that one of the attackers shouted in exasperation as they left empty-handed, something that sounded like, "All this for a fucking computer!"

The intelligent Angela immediately contacted her boss John Barrington about the attack and when they put their stories together an attempted attack on their computer system was obvious.

In the absence of Spike, John contacted Laura Winn who was not involved in the business but who understood in general terms what went on.

"Laura, this is obviously an attack on our online system, and it has to be by Carlo's thugs. They will not stop at this, and we need instruction ungently."

But Laura also appreciated she could not risk trying to communicate with Spike, still in the hospital, so she sensibly immediately contacted Anisha and Edwin.

They were joined by Zuki and Samuel in the All computer office and heard her story with concern.

Laura waited anxiously while they discussed what they could do to help her.

"We have a simple answer," Anisha eventually suggested to her, "but in the absence of Spike you may not want to take it alone."

Samuel explained, "With your agreement we can delete all your computer material from your equipment but store it in our own very secure system. It will be totally safe from Carlo and neither you nor your people can be blackmailed or threatened.

"Later, when Spike is back, and their threat is gone, we will return all your records."

Laura was distressed but came to a quick decision. "Our system is run by John Barrington and Angela Wong who change their codes daily and I will instruct them to contact you Samuel to arrange the transfer. You know them well. Keep our records safe for us. Can't thank you enough!"

"Laura, you said you have a secure computer line still open to Carlo?" added Edwin. "I would like you to leave him a message when it is done that you no longer have control of your computer system or records while Spike is in hospital and that everything has been transferred to the Brethren's system for safe keeping.

"Make it sound convincing and tell him if he has any questions to take it up with me personally."

Anisha added, "And consider sending all your computer staff off to hidden locations somewhere for safety in the meantime. Hopefully that will all get them off your back!"

When she had exited the meeting, Anisha asked curiously, "Zuki. You told me previously you had retained access to all our partners computer programs, how come you need the Locarnos to sign in for you?"

"We don't," confirmed Samuel with a grin, "but there is no point letting the Brethren know we can control all their information."

"OK. Cunning! But how are you so sure we ourselves are unlikely to be accessed?"

"Because Sazu is also a required daily access signatory, under very complicated arrangements, and no one can kidnap or pressure her and she never dies!"

***

With Alphonse growling in the background, Carlo was shouting at the cringing Phil. "Can they do that? Do you believe them?"

Trying to sound knowledgeable, Phil scanned the message from Laura Winn and said, "Yes, they will already have done it, and the entire program has undoubtedly been transferred. Actually, I believe it, because it is the logical thing for them to do in the circumstances."

Turning his wrath onto Alphonse, Carlo shouted, "And you are afraid of a few Mounties. Now we are the ones who are knackered. Thanks to you incompetent sods!"

This time they slunk quickly from his office, together.

***

Edwin and Anisha's camaraderie seemed strangely to be increased by each crisis, and that evening they called for a second bottle and retired with it to their terrace.

"There must be an elegant way out of our business crisis," she started.

"Maybe we just accept it as inevitable and manage it to our advantage and to its soonest conclusion."

"Very philosophical, Edwin. But to establish our advantage we need end objectives. Do we know ours?"

"Not really, things have just happened over the years."

She refilled their glasses, snuggled closer and impulsively changing the subject asked, "Honestly. Why did you marry me?"

"Seemed the right thing to do at the time. It was good for business. And I thought you were the most attractive woman I had ever seen."

"I sense a 'but'!"

"But it was arranged. You were way too young. I felt you didn't have a choice and didn't want to go through with it."

"True. I didn't. But my father made me."

"So, we drifted apart."

"No, we never did have a relationship!"

"So, let's find an elegant way out of our crisis!"

She threw her arms around his neck and laughing, kissed him deeply.

The moment was interrupted by signals from both their communication devices indicating an urgent message from Pookie.

Disengaging reluctantly Anisha joked, "Pookie is getting jealous," but their smiles were short-lived at his report.

A serious explosion has occurred at Jericho,

38

Drone attack

The attack was deadly, and this time executed by skilled remote technicians. Busy with its regular evening crowd, the still-freestanding original Locarno partnership diner had been obliterated by a precise drone attack.

The traditional property had been lovingly restored, offered a varied menu and featured regularly in the company's promotion materials.

Dropped off at the site of the tragedy by a wailing RCMP armoured helicopter, Ivern and Jules were immediately surrounded by reporters and online journalists.

They all wanted to meet and to interview the photogenic Mounties in full assault gear, so Ivern stood back thankfully to let Jules take all the questions.

"Clearly a precise drone strike executed by experts who will be extremely difficult if not impossible to detect. Modern technology has made these drones a public curse and we have yet to find the answer."

He walked away to inspect the devastation, with nothing more to add.

Ivern saw things differently.

"I am a local cop," he assured the still attentive news hounds, "and we already have some leads about the motivation of this heinous crime.

We will use solid traditional police investigation methods and we will find and convict the bastards who carried out this atrocity."

He received an unusual round of applause from the hardened press corps.

The site was in chaos with emergency teams working everywhere, so Ivern just surveyed the scene and stayed out of the way until his own vehicle arrived.

His conveyance window was tapped hopefully by a cheekily faced Asian fellow whom he recognised from his prominent international blog.

"Just one question, sir. Why are you and the Medical Police here?"

"Same question the Minister of Health asked," flashed into Ivern's mind.

"Give me a couple of days, Timothy, and I will tell you as much as I can. But I assure you, the Medical Police are here for a very good reason."

The blogger reported, after announcing the tragedy:

A prominent cop indicated to me, very confidentially, at the scene of the bombing this evening, that illegal Medical violence is strongly connected to the deadly drone attack, that has caused so much international concern. But what is the connection? We all wonder. He hinted they had leads to the bomber and said that he would reveal all to me 'within a few days'.

Stay in touch for further news as we remain at the scene and the drama unfolds.

Back at Ivern's office the question why it had happened came up again and again, starting with his boss. The Chief Commissioner commended him. "Well done, in the circumstances, Ivern. A positive statement and an attempt to keep the bomber unsettled."

"Thank you, sir, but we are indeed chasing a will-o'-the-wisp as our Mountie friends keep complaining. All this illegal medical activity is so interwoven into the fabric of the Corridor society it is almost impossible to separate things."

"I know, I know. Bertie used to complain about the same thing but keep at it. And by the way the Premier is going to call you personally! Good luck."

Ivern had never spoken to the Premier, who called almost immediately and came straight to the point.

"This is terrible, Hill, but what the hell has it got to do with the medical situation? We set you up specifically to get this all under control and things have just got worse.

"Just more and more violence! You're supposed to stop this, not make it happen."

"Sir, with respect," Ivern interjected directly, "if the medical system had worked in the first place there would be no need for all this backstreet activity.

"It is now hidden behind both legitimate and crooked businesses and protected in various regions of the Corridor by established criminal groups. It generates a lot of money!

"We believe the bombing is part of a local criminal war."

The Premier went silent. So Ivern continued.

"As the medical situation has been allowed to deteriorate, it has become controlled in various sections of the Corridor by criminal elements who now appear to be battling for local supremacy. That is what we are experiencing and frankly, sir, we are all in this together!"

Another worrying long pause, then, the Premier responded, "Well … you are at least direct! The same thing is happening in my own public housing blocks. Gangs are taking over everything, and local people are starting to despair.

"I am going to call a high-level confidential meeting and I want you there."

That was it. Ivern sat for a few minutes in silence, taking it all in.

***

Their quiet evening together shattered by news of the tragedy; Maddie had rushed off to The General to provide her assistance as the ambulances flew in with the terribly injured who had survived.

She stayed over at the hospital grabbing some sleep and the occasional shower as they worked non-stop.

James Khan was still a practising doctor and was at the hospital helping when he bumped into Maddie in the cafeteria.

"If we had come forward with all the information we have, this might not have happened," he lamented.

Maddie was equally as distraught. "I have not had a chance to discuss any of this with Ivern because we both rushed off when we heard the news. But if this was done by Carlo, I am directly responsible. I should have come forward earlier and named Ricardo.

"If he had been picked up, then he would not have been shot by the Mounties and none of this would have started. And I have implicated Ivern in my cover-up. This is terrible, terrible."

She buried her face in her hands. This time, they were not making a spectacle of themselves in the cafeteria which was full of medical staff looking exhausted.

"Maddie, those are a lot of ifs. You can't blame yourself for this entire situation. You had nothing to do with the ongoing fight between the gangs. Anyway, we have other priorities just now. Let's finish up here and get back to the injured."

Ivern chose that emotional moment to arrive at the hospital for his official goodwill working visit. James waved to him in leaving as Ivern hurried to Maddie's table.

"I'm pleased you came, although I must run back to the surgery. But there is something I needed to tell you.

"I have a young girl in my care who was walking on the street outside at the time of the explosion. She is critically injured and desperately needs a procedure which is only available, so far as I know, in San Francisco.

"I wanted to let you know, totally between us, that I am personally flying her down by private ambulance today to that hospital to get the work done."

"Paying for it all yourself?" he asked briefly.

"Yes," she assured him "the whole thing, although anonymously, and it's not a question of money, I have plenty. Perhaps the Province would arrange it, but she can't wait. I just wanted to tell you; I'm not asking."

"Well done," he affirmed without hesitation, "I hope she survives."

He squeezed her hand reassuringly and they rushed off to their own duties.

***

Carlo was sitting in his office watching the news clips, finally with a slight sense of satisfaction.

"Revenge!" he said to himself bitterly.

The strike had in fact been one of Ricardo's better ideas and had been set up some months previously with an American contractor, through their contacts in Mexico.

America's use of drone warfare in Afghanistan and the long-range success of drones during the humiliation of Russia by Ukraine decades earlier, had helped develop the technology.

Militarily trained technicians had brought the skills to the underworld and could pinpoint a desired target anywhere in the world with guaranteed, undetected success.

Ricardo had this all arranged, Carlo thought to himself, but got impatient and stupidly had to show off and do things himself in the old way.

"Oh Ricardo!" he murmured to himself sadly.

39

Stunned response

Edwin and Anisha hadn't attempted to sleep that night.

The alarm from Pookie about the bombing was immediately followed by requests for consultation from a dozen sources and they kept coming in.

They slipped on day clothes and headed down to their office, summoning Samuel, Zuri and essential staff. Their screens were ablaze with the latest news, and they watched the arrival of the police leaders and listened to their remarks in silence.

Corridor All Insurance posted:

"The bombing in Locarno is disastrous for everyone and our hearts go out to all the victims and their families. May those responsible be brought swiftly to justice."

"You really mean that, don't you," said Anisha approvingly.

"Absolutely, but for both emotional and practical reasons. For the Brethren and the All group this is the worst possible thing that could've happened. Old Dr Chiu must be dancing on his grave!"

"But fortunately for our medical business the public has not made the connection and as you saw they are already questioning the presence of the Medical Police," she pointed out.

Samuel was much more concerned but optimistic.

"Brethren are now beginning to understand what is going on and are coming back. We have received contacts from some of those who had previously dropped out, wanting to rejoin, and looking for reassurance and leadership. We have no contact with those hard-core rebels at the end of the line, of course."

They sat in silence.

"Samuel," Edwin eventually instructed, "please set up an online meeting tomorrow. Invite them all and assure everyone the Brethren are not connected with this atrocity in any way. We must not present any reason for the authorities to think so."

He stood up, wearily. "We all have a lot of calls to make, so see you all tomorrow in your safe room for the meeting."

In the elevator Zuri said excitedly, "Samuel, did you notice, as they were leaving, she took his hand and he smiled."

"No," he replied, "why ever would I noticed that?"

"Maybe a female thing," Zuri responded, "but very significant!"

* * *

The next day Edwin formally called the meeting to order, over the buzz of conversations underway. Tactfully, he did not draw attention to those that had deserted and now returned.

Everyone denied any involvement or even the slightest knowledge of the bombing and all bemoaned the extra pressure it would bring upon them.

Wie Wie complained excitedly, "Cops had already been harassing my businesses really looking for medical connections but issuing charges for any simple bylaw infraction. Too many tables, drink served over a line, waitresses allegedly indecently dressed …"

"What were they wearing?" interjected one of his amused colleagues.

"Well, admittedly only little hats and heels, but that's not the point."

"What is the point," injected Edwin firmly, "is that they are trying to agitate us into making mistakes and this crazy bombing will just increase their activity. We must not give them any ammunition. Just play along. Loss of profit for a few months is worth not being forcibly closed down."

A returning member agreed but added, "We need to face it, though. The medical business has caused nothing but trouble and does not work well with our overall business and interests."

There were expressions of both agreement and disagreement until Wie Wie spoke up forcefully.

"Absolutely. All our present problems are coming from medical screw-ups which we don't need. While the medical business is quite profitable, I could do without it." There were murmurings of agreement.

"A very good point, but let's get back to that at a later date," interjected Edwin. "We haven't heard from our new doctors' rep yet."

The keen young doctor spoke confidently. "We still don't understand why Dr Chiu got us involved in violence, but we fail to see any connection with that terrible drone attack,

"We know of course that the Locarnos organised our activities in that area, so we cannot avoid some possible implication. We absolutely need a pause, while we reassess everything.

"But we will need to continue serving emergencies and prescribing essential medication of course."

Edwin asked, "Pookie, how would a pause affect our odds of surviving?"

"Initially well over ninety per cent in favour but …"

"Thanks that is all the reassurance we need just now."

Pookie was extremely distraught, even being asked about Brethren survival. That option was not contemplated in his program. The Brethrens' existence was his prime responsibility. He must comply to his directive but was not even being consulted adequately. His programming was struggling to cope with the stress, and he knew his circuits were in danger of overloading.

But Edwin continued calmly, "For the moment can we all agree we will not conduct any further medical business, other than extremely carefully in absolute emergency, plus continuing medication provision. Hopefully, that will remove any active provocation. Do we all agree?"

Finally, he received general assent, so he thanked them and closed the meeting.

Usually after a meeting, Edwin jumped up and they took the elevator back up to their section of the office. Today however he not only stayed but settled back into his chair.

"Order up some coffee please, we have a lot of things to talk about."

"First, this dastardly bombing. Please search online everywhere and see if there is a link to Carlo or indeed anyone. We need to know who did this.

"Second, get into details with our various medical and pharmacy friends and confirm they all know about the pause in activity.

"Third, and this is going to keep you very busy, work out a draft management plan for All Insurance to take over the day-to-day security operation of medical activities in the Corridor from the Brethren!

"You heard the sentiment at the meeting today and this may be far-out, but we need to know if we can do it all ourselves."

Their coffee arrived and they sat sipping mostly in contemplation.

"Wow," eventually Zuri summed it all up.

***

That night, as had now become routine, Anisha slipped into Edwin's bed. But tonight, she was delightfully naked and snuggled up close to him sensually.

She just said, demurely, "I want you!" and slipped her leg over him.

"My!" she gasped, "Why am I even asking?"

40

Reconciliation

At Police Headquarters the next few days everything went by in a blur for Ivern.

When the joint police committee met, the City representative insisted upon talking first.

"This is now a City investigation much more than a Medical issue. My Chief insists we take the chair and direct the agenda. Someone is blowing up our citizens and we are not gonna take instruction from cops from Victoria and Winnipeg, especially that go about shooting our citizens!"

A red-faced Jules McIntosh was restrained by a hand on his arm by Ivern who calmly responded, "That's OK by all of us. Just ask and we will offer whatever support you need."

***

Ivern calmed Jules down later over coffee. "The City is not going to solve this, and we are better off pursuing our own leads. I had a direct conversation with the Premier and we will likely receive a much bigger budget. How should we spend it?"

"On a shitload of geeks!" Jules replied forcefully. "The only way these days to track down a virtual ghost like this is high-tech. We can find enough tough cops to stir up the local thugs but to catch these hidden professionals we need similar skills.

"We have a forensic Mountie computer division you could talk to. Outside my remit!"

"OK will do. I am sending you that dozen extra Uniforms to start stirring up the Middle Stations area anyway as we agreed."

"Thanks. Long day. Let's go get a drink!"

***

Ivern sent a text to Maddie playing their usual apartment choice game.

"Doesn't matter, I am whacked. I'm already in bed. Please come to mine but don't wake me!"

Finally, the next morning they took some well-earned time off and compared notes over a long breakfast.

"Let's take our coffee out on the terrace. I need to talk to you," she said finally.

Sitting in the shade on the sunny deck with her head cozily on his shoulder, her continuing fatigue induced her to lament, "I have been struggling with waves of guilt since our dinner with Jules, which interfere with my work. Now the bombing!

"The whole thing is my fault. I could've exposed them earlier and none of this would've happened."

He put a reassuring arm around her. "We don't know for sure who is responsible. Anyway, their dispute with the Locarnos involves far more issues and you can't blame yourself for a train of events emerging from a situation you could not control."

She shook her head despondently. "I am not being selfish, but I am trying to protect my colleagues and I know a lot more than I have told you. It all becomes so confusing."

Purposely diverting the subject he asked, "Guess who called me? The Premier! He is looking for a solution and wants me at the meeting. What should I say?"

And a few moments silence, Ivern realised she had fallen back into an exhausted sleep with her head nestled on his chest.

***

A few stations away, a similarly stressed Anisha, received a well-remembered, signal on her handheld: Pritam!

"Oh, no," she sighed, "of all people! And now!"

But she held up a warning finger to Edwin and listened.

"I have missed you! Please let's meet," he begged.

She replied aloud for Edwin's benefit, "Pritam! You want me to meet you after the way you behaved? Do you think I'm stupid!"

While Pritam continued asking for another chance and saying how beautiful she was, across the room Edwin was thinking. Then he nodded vigorously. "Meet him," he mouthed.

She met Pritam the next afternoon as he requested, in the parking lot at Kits Beach. He waited in his spacious personal transporter with its black tinted windows.

She slid into the seat next to him. Without a word of welcome he confidently thrust his hand up between her legs and attempted to kiss her.

"That was all in the past," she snapped icily, pushing his hand away. Edwin and her security team were listening nearby, but she did not yet signal for help.

"What do you want?" she demanded.

"I made a terrible mistake!"

"Not as much as I did! But that is in the past and Mr Carter knows everything. I repeat what do you want?"

He hesitated. "Basically, the Almas want back into the Brethren. They should never have joined up with the trouble-making Carlo."

"I will relay your message to Mr Carter. Your people will have to negotiate with him, and it will cost them! But you better personally stay a long way away from him, and me!"

She reached for the door handle and glared at him when she initially found it locked.

***

Phil Dimitri, the accountant, had no intention of entering a life of crime.

His father had been a schoolteacher in that area and without question he went to University Hill secondary school.

There he had not excelled at sports being a skinny little fellow, but good marks guaranteed him a place at UBC. He took the business course and settled for accounting as a career.

His association with the younger Santos family members came through high school and at the beginning he innocently signed on to manage their father's investments.

He was amazed at his generous starting pay level which he put down to their lucrative activities in restaurants, bars and nightclubs, until he was actually running things.

Then he found they were also supplying drugs and girls, operating gambling and were engaged in various other dubious activities.

Their involvement in illegal medical activity in the University area came later, but by then he was hooked on the high standard of living this all brought him.

The presence of Alphonse Alphonso and his tough-looking thugs had always been enough to maintain discipline in their thriving investments.

Phil had been pleased when they took over security for the medical business in their area and had personally managed it to build its substantial income. But finding that his team carried guns, and even used them in that first incident, had shocked him.

Later, after the second incident when people were actually killed, including young Juan, he was totally distraught.

Then recently Ricardo had died during his stupid attack on the Locarnos and now there was this frightful drone attack on his own neighbourhood.

He was trying not to show it around the office, but he was desperately scared. He was having uncontrollable shaking spasms.

As accountant for the group, he knew where every dollar was spent, and now he understood the big sum Ricardo had ordered to be paid to an unrecognised American account.

He had made the payment and had killed all those people!

****

Spike Winn was genuinely suffering the emotional shock of the drone attack on his restaurant customers, many of whom he had known since a being a bus-boy, and he discharged himself from hospital immediately.

Everything had changed while he was away. Expecting the worst, his staff had doubled up on security everywhere. But uniformed cops now openly patrolled the entire district.

And even before the bombing all his undercover businesses had prudently closed, leaving only coffee shops operating.

Now, he even closed those, in respect, while things stabilised.

He contacted Edwin.

"We must meet. Lunch today? Yacht club back room? Spike."
Edwin was totally shocked at his appearance.

"You look awful, man," he commiserated.

"Not as bad as I feel," Spike tried to laugh. "But we are devastated, we need help, Edwin."

"As far as money is concerned look upon me as an interest-free financier while you sort all of this out. Assuming it is Carlo, which I do, the guy has gone mad, and I really don't know what to do about him. Are you and your family personally secure? We can help there too if necessary."

Spike shrugged. "How can you be safe from drones? Keep moving constantly; disappear? And I have responsibilities for so many people. I have sent Laura and my kids far away," he smiled weakly, "and by the way Laura asked that we apologise to Anisha if we don't make the soirée this summer!"

They both chuckled wryly.

"Thanks so much for supporting Laura and saving our computer records from that maniac. Your guys have returned it all and helped us set up better future security."

Edwin assured him, "All the Brethren except Carlo and the Almas are actively back in the group and we welcome your returning participation. We have strength and unity, and we will all pitch in to help you guys recover, however long it takes."

"By the way," Spike mentioned, "I was amazed to get a commiseration note from the Almas regarding the bombing. Maybe you can make some headway with them and isolate Carlo."

"Maybe," was Edwin's unenthusiastic response, Pritam Singh cavorting with Anisha, jumping into his thoughts. "We have opened discussions with them."

He changed the subject abruptly. "There is some sentiment in the group that the Brethren involvement in the Medical system is too limiting and no longer compatible with general business but we can talk about that later. Just get well and look to us for any help you need."

* * *

Anisha had no concern herself about approaching the Almas group.

"We can't let my past stupidity stand in the way of our business needs. Obviously, you and I won't deal with them personally, and it fits in with a suggestion I have. Why don't you make Samuel your deputy manager at All Insurance, Chief Operating Officer, or whatever?

"Then, for example, use him to open channels with the Almas. He certainly hates them, and they will not have it easy!"

"Then how about All Technology?" Edwin asked.

"Obviously make Zuri Chief Executive. She's brilliant. And she has earned it."

"OK, both great ideas. Will do. And Laura Winn sends her love from drone seclusion and regrets for the soirée. They assumed rightly in the circumstances we will have to cancel it."

"Postpone!" she insisted. "How about maybe in the Fall while it is still sunny?"

"I told Spike you would say that!" he grinned.

***

When Edwin announced their new appointments to them, Samuel and Zuri were initially elated.

Back in their apartment in her usual state of excitement she threw off her clothes and did her happy exotic dance of joy.

Samuel, of course, took advantage of the situation, but when they were relaxing, he said he saw problems ahead.

"You know this gets us even more committed!"

"Well maybe; but pluses and minuses. Particularly if we can re-organise things the way Edwin seems to be heading."

"Yes, that was curious. Do you think he wants to leave crime?"

"Well, that may be overstating it. We won't drop the international money-laundering business for example, but yes, Sazu says going straight fits his personality."

"In which case, the main issue in our planning will be to provide private medical insurance. After all we are supposed to be an insurance company. It is available in the rest of Canada.

"If we can only convince this provincial government to legalise the insurance and throw in some private medical activity to manage, we would have a start."

Zuri grinned, "We must sound out the Medical Association on insurance and get Jimmy Khan on our side. Let's see what he makes of Technology's new female manager. We will invite them both over for a business lunch."

41

Taking action

Zuri indeed tried to appear business-like at lunch, wearing an establishment, formal, high-necked, dark blue business suit and moderate heels.

She had somewhat tamed her Afro but not her wide grin. She greeted them warmly.

Maddie was hiding her smile but choked when she caught James's eye. Zuri's designer suit material was sheer, tightly molded to her straining body and allowing no possible space for underwear. The designer coup was her signature breath-taking, molded short skirt. "But she is trying," Maddie murmured.

"May I introduce the new Chief Operating Officer of All Insurance, Mr Samuel Nkosi," Zuri announced formally, but spoiling it with a giggle.

They were lunching in the All Insurance executive dining room in their tower, in an obvious gesture to formalise their relationship, and to discuss the possibilities for private provincial medical insurance.

The women immediately discussed the still-delayed Fall Soirée, but Samuel eventually managed to get the chatter around to the business. "All Insurance wants to approach the provincial government again on the subject of private medical coverage and is looking for support."

"Good luck," offered James laughing. "Won't happen!"

Maddie, however, was encouraging. "Why not run it by Irena Ito. She is Minister of Health and very much from this district. She is an old friend of mine, and I can warn her you are coming, although I can't guarantee what reception you will get."

"Well, it was just an idea, but probably hopeless. Thanks, we will appreciate the introduction."

Pressing her advantage, Maddie asked, "You know, we are still curious about Dr Chiu and the strange computer connection he had to your system. We know for a fact he hated computers and avoided putting his hands on a keyboard."

"Ah," Samuel offered, thinking he was giving a very safe answer, "he had an old gal working for him who was good with his computer. She must have seen that address somewhere."

Maddie just nodded and shrugged dismissively but both she and James were highly aware of the remark's significance.

Waiting later for their train down at the station, James worried, "That was a shocker about Sophie. Should we go proactive and look for her? They never found his handheld or computer."

"I bet Sophie has them!" Maddie agreed. "I had the same thought. Plus she could have a working knowledge of everything. She is potential dynamite!"

"Yes, but not just to us, to the entire Brethren. If we do nothing and they work this out she could be in real danger."

"Damn!" was all Maddie could offer.

***

Zuri and Samuel were, of course, serious about their medical insurance ideas. They researched all the schemes available in Canada and selected policies they thought locally suited and within the reach of the various income levels.

Then they ran standard feasibility cashflows demonstrating profitability and discussed it all with Edwin and Anisha.

Samuel made the pitch. "We obviously know this is a long shot, but we would like to approach the Health Ministry at a deputy minister and staff level to stress the advantages of private medical insurance and explain how it works."

Zuri followed enthusiastically. "Then later, you can personally try for high level meetings with the Minister, and she will have an informed staff to consult, hopefully that we have convinced. What do you think? Plus, Maddie Madison told us she could get us in the door."

"Excellent!" beamed Edwin, "see what you can do."

Maddie was good as her word and called Irena with the medical insurance information suggestion. She was amazed at the Minister's quick and positive response.

"Thanks for the heads-up, Maddie. All things at the Ministry are going from bad to worse, I'm surprised you even got paid this month, and any new ideas are welcome, even those contrary to this coalition government's stubborn erroneous policies! I will sit in on the briefings myself!"

***

Zuri was excited about taking over management of the computer company and they agreed her priority should be discovering the bomber.

If it were indeed any of the Brethren, it should be evident through their computer system to which they had their retained access.

Therefore, the next day while Samuel was to review all the company activities with Edwin, Zuri was looking into areas where they had agreed the drone knowledge would lie.

She engaged Sazu AI and all their staff in their latest computerised search technologies to isolate payments of the type required for espionage activities such as non-military drone attacks, which were fortunately still rare.

Three generations of Carters had been active in international money crime and laundering, and their companies were experts at unravelling the webs of obscured ownership registration and hidden money transfers.

Zuki boasted they could send currency through a hundred international accounts in seconds and similarly in reverse, trace money back to its source, although she joked that took a bit longer. However the payment was disguised they could find it!

By lunchtime, they had reduced the possibilities to one very large suitable payment in the States arranged by Carlo's accountant, Phil Dimitri, and she knew she had found it.

"Fantastic, everyone." she typed excitedly to her team.

"Not all good news," warned Sazu AI, "I have observed that Pookie has been picking up some of our inquiries. He has not commented, and that bothers me."

Elated at their successful research, however, Zuri merely shrugged. "You are getting as paranoid as I am!" she responded.

She called Edwin Carter's office and asked if they could see them immediately. Edwin, Anisha, and Samuel received her revelation in worried silence.

"I think I would rather not have known," Edwin admitted at last.

Seeing her change of expression, he reassured Zuri, "No, it is excellent work getting us the information and it is honestly better to find the culprit. But what do we do with the knowledge?"

"Yes, the problem," offered Anisha thoughtfully, "is that this ties the drone attack into the Brethren and potentially into us. How do we extract ourselves?"

"Well, surely Carlo had broken away from the Brethren and did that terrible thing on his own?" Zuri protested.

"Yes, but try explaining that to the authorities!"

Edwin decided to wrap up their discussion. "Excellent work, Zuri, this will prove valuable. Absolutely better to know. But what now?"

***

Back in their apartment, Zuri immediately threw off the stifling business suit she now felt obliged to wear and announced to Samuel. "I have just had another brain wave!"

"Do I keep my pants on or take them off?" Samuel bantered.

"Silly. No, seriously. We know from our medical records Maddie was the surgeon in the first gunfire incident, but I realised it was out at the University. I researched it and bingo, Ricardo and Joey provided the security. Maddie knew them personally!"

"So?"

"So. Two in their family are dead; one has skipped the country from a murder charge and the father has gone crazy and blown up a restaurant! And she lives with a chief of police and is making all friendly to us. Doesn't that concern you?"

"Now you mention it, yes, definitely. But I like her."

"That's the problem. Then there is her friend James Khan from the Medical Association. Between them I think they are an incredible threat or a valuable link."

"They probably know more than we think. But where does the policeman fit in all this."

"Haven't a clue!"

"And the revelation?"

"That she is scared, that she is lonely, that she has a lot to lose. We would gain a great deal by knowing what she is up to. I could try edging into it, woman to woman!"

They paused in silence. She pressed herself up against him.

"OK, go for it!" he sighed, rolling his eyes in submission.

***

Going for it, turned out to be fun. Zuri invited Maddie to go soirée gown hunting in the haute couture establishments on the wealthy Granville South famous Fashion Mall.

They selected some designers to try and shared a large, mirrored changing room.

Zuri stepped perfectly naturally out of her sole layer of clothing, taking advantage of the full height mirrors, to proudly strut her dramatically molded body in its full splendour.

"Wowie! I'm a medic but you sure look impressive!"

"Thank you, ma'am," dimpled Zuri, "I exercise a lot. You look gorgeous yourself. We are both far sexier without clothes!"

Their mutual admiration continued for a couple of hours while they paraded around trying out various designers. Maddie insisted Zuri go long gown, but had to settle for her choice, a stunning body-clinging flesh-coloured creation.

Having made their selections for the still-awaited soirée they retired to the salon's lounge for 'complimentary' hors d'oeuvres and champagne. They chatted happily.

"Still no date for the soirée before we get to show off."

"No, too soon. I hope the weather lasts."

"I am a bit surprised they are still holding it."

"We are hoping. But so soon after the tragedy? I am doubtful."

Then Zuri blurted, "Do you think Carlo did it?"

It came out more bluntly than she had intended. Maybe it was the champagne.

"Relying upon what I have read in the news," Maddie responded guardedly.

"I would say they are very likely, considering their battles with the Locarnos."

"But what were they fighting about?" Zuri queried way too innocently.

"That is the leading question, isn't it? Well, I believe you already know the answer: the medical war! Your leader, Mr Carter, admitted to me at lunch he had been involved with Dr Chiu in financing some of his medical activity. It was publicised the youngest son was killed in the second shootout and Edwin warned me Carlo might believe I tipped off the cops, through Ivern."

"Well, that sounds like our indiscreet Edwin! And, sorry, I was trying to be tactful in case you wanted to avoid the subject."

"If it were not for the drone attack, we could avoid it like everyone else, but now it's critical. Where will it leave us, personally, I mean?"

"Exposed!" Zuri exclaimed decisively. "We need to talk seriously!"

Maddie hesitated. "Something I personally want to ask you. Are you and Samuel worried about whatever it is you have got yourselves into?"

Zuri thought deeply and then admitted, simply, "Yes, very!"

"Same with me!" Maddie confided.

They clasped hands under the table.

"How about another glass of this 'free' Moet?"

"How about a few!" laughed a relieved Zuri.

42

Rising anxiety

"Look who I brought you," announced a beaming Inspector Jules McIntosh, marching triumphantly into Ivern's office.

"Commissioner, meet Techie!" He was followed by a serious young East Indian woman, trailing behind him uncertainly.

"Ivern, Inspector Barma of the RCMP Technical Division. She is in town at a conference, and I snagged her for a talk with you!"

Ivern jumped up in welcome and shepherded them to his meeting area.

"Just visiting physically," she warned. "We run everything technical out of our head office adjunct in Ottawa."

Jules added excitedly, "They have a section concentrating on drone attacks!"

"But, Commissioner Hill," she admitted, "we don't have a lot of success because they are so carefully hidden. They are launched from mobile units in remote areas which are long gone before back tracking is useful. Same with the concealed arrangements and payment. So good luck with that crime. But we could try."

"Could you also try exposing the local illegal medical management system we can't track down?

"Ah," she laughed, "the 'will-o'-the-wisp' Jules couldn't quite say in the bar late last night, after too many drinks!"

"We can probably help more by breaking into that and tracing who runs it all. The old find-a-loose-string-and-start-pulling-it!"

"OK. When can you begin?"

"Let me know what you have so far, and your budget and I will set it up as soon as I get back to Ottawa."

"Well done, Techie!" Jules whooped.

"Cut out those inappropriate comments, Inspector," she snapped. But her warm smile indicated their relationship was very different.

So much was happening that Ivern took it in his stride when he received another personal call from the Premier, Joe Jahani.

"This time I really need a private person-to-person on this matter, Ivern," he instructed, but in a more familiar, personal tone. "Let's meet at the Old Ale House on Main Street. Friday around six when I get back from Victoria?"

"Of course. Always at your disposal, Mr Premier," Ivern sucked up.

"Joe, please," was his short reply. "And absolutely no uniform or salutes."

Earlier in the century, a government commenced constructing and owning blocks of subsidised State Housing, for middle to lower income earners who could not afford the exclusively expensive housing municipal zoning provided.

Often built on available or cheap land the massive, dull public housing projects had progressively regenerated into the notorious, depressed 'townships'. Housing generations of stigmatised families, they had spiralled down into gang control and warfare.

The Premier, the Hon. Joe Jahani, a dedicated social worker, had been elected from one of the oldest of these estates, the Main Street Complex.

***

When Ivern arrived at the pub, in slacks, he experienced Joe in his normal habitat, surrounded by obviously long-term friends, and freely available to everyone.

He joined him for a pint at his sacred bar table and started shouting like everyone else. Joe grinned encouragingly and shouted back, "Don't worry this is my usual Friday evening political free-for-all. We are going to a back room later!"

A couple of pints later, they were munching hamburgers and deep in quiet conversation reviewing the policing history and the recent events of the medical emergency on the Corridor.

Ivern explaining how the Station areas apparently each had their distinctive controlling gang within an overall Corridor brotherhood."

"Yes," the Premier nodded. "Several of the State Housing blocks down the Valley Line have similar gangs as you must know."

"The gangs in our Corridor seem to have fallen out," Ivern reported, "and while they are involved in a whole spectrum of crime, they have also taken over aggressively protecting the illegal medical activity in their area.

"It has so far hidden behind an uncrackable computer system. The early shootings took place in a criminally controlled area near UBC, leading to the deadly gang dispute.

"This was probably connected to the drone bombing, but RCMP experts say the secrecy is such that it will be almost impossible to find the culprit."

Having told the Premier everything he knew officially, which he considered his duty, Ivern lapsed into silence and Joe launched into his political situation.

"Medical budgets were already shot early in the century. The public system could not cope with the changing demographics, longer life, imposed immigration growth and frankly, over administration.

"Wage inequality just went on widening with technology and the income divide just kept growing. Wrong political decisions were made, and we ended up like the United States, divided socially and politically. The medical crisis is one result of all that.

"Now I'm damned if I do, and damned if I don't.

"You can tell your boss I ordered you to come alone, outside his protocols, for a chat, and I am now ordering us a couple more pints,"

"Thank God it's Friday!" Ivern agreed.

***

Summer was ending and neither Ivern nor Maddie had yet taken a holiday. Soon, they kept promising. At least they usually had the weekends together and later that Friday evening they met up at her place.

Ivern was full of his informal chat with the Premier.

"He's a feisty little guy," he started.

"I know, I met him too, visiting the drone victims at the hospital."

"Ah, but I spent three hours with him alone, drinking beer!"

"Was it secret?"

"Not really. But off the record. I told him the Corridor Medical history, the suspected players, the violence escalation, the Mountie role, all that stuff. How about your day?"

Maddie launched off enthusiastically about her successful gown expedition with Zuri in preparation for the 'maybe' soirée.

"I've been so busy I forgot all about that. When is it?"

"Subject to notice. But unlikely."

He asked, "Isn't Zuri the girl who works for the Carter Insurance group that you met about Dr Chiu's papers?"

"Yes, but more than a 'girl'. She is now proudly chief executive of the Carter computer division. I hear she has a doctorate."

"Well, that's interesting. I have just hired the Mountie technical division out of Ottawa to track down the key medical business organizations in the Corridor.

"They don't think they can get the bomber, but they are fairly confident their computers can track down the Medical network.

"I must chat with your Zuri; she might have some ideas."

"Yes, undoubtedly she will," replied Maddie trying hard not to show her mounting concerns.

***

"Hey, Staff Sergeant," called a Vancouver detective, "who is the 'Madison' in the brackets I just noticed on your conference room white board?"

Will responded nonchalantly, "That is a miscellaneous doctor connected to Dr Chiu. She is not a direct suspect, so she is in brackets. But her name has popped up too many times."

"OK, we will put her in our 'persons of interest' computer list and record any suspicious activities."

"Thanks, keep me informed."

Will then simply went to the board and erased Maddie's name to be on the safe side. Mission accomplished, he smirked to himself.

***

Dr James Khan continued operating his small medical clinic to keep his hand in, but at the Medical Association he tried in vain to control his rebelling members.

Many of his members, he knew, were somewhat involved in the illegal medical business, as was he, but all vehemently disproved of the violence that was erupting. They needed leadership!

But now Maddie was confirming to him they appeared to be inextricably linked to criminal elements.

"Zuri was not explicit, but she clearly told me she was into something she regretted, which we already guessed. She approves medical intervention, so it has to be more than just that. Something more seriously criminal.

"The journal obviously points to the Carter operation as organisers, but we need Chiu's lost computer for confirmation. Do you think Sophie has it?"

"Someone has. But it could have been taken by the thugs when they killed him. Heaven forbid!"

"We have to find her."

Maddie offered a hesitant suggestion. "I visited Dr Chiu a few times and I know where he lives. I could go over there, ask around to see if I could locate the old lady. I know what she looks like."

***

Finding her was surprising simple. The apartment mailboxes announced, 'Sophie Rodriguez'. A tap on her door, and there she was.

"My, whatever are you doing here, Dr Madison? Please come in. So nice to see you."

Maddie sat in the impeccably clean little apartment sipping tea and reminiscing about Simeon until Sophie said directly, "I went to the police, you know, to tell them that I had seen those horrible men.

"And then that rude Sergeant told me one of them was shot. It was terrible. Anyway, it's all over now, except ..." she hesitated, "... the policeman showed me a picture of you and asked if I knew you. I said, no."

Maddie was shocked into silence. "Why would they connect me with you," she asked.

"I have no idea," said Sophie. "It has nothing to do with the journal, because I have told no one about that, as dear Simeon instructed."

"What happened to his computer and handheld?" Maddie asked directly.

"Ah, I have put them somewhere very safe as Simeon instructed. No one will ever find it."

"May we have access to them?"

"Sorry; no! But it's all highly encrypted anyway."

"Then may I ask a question. Where did all Simeon's instructions come from? That is excluded from his journal."

"That's easy. Edwin Carter and Simeon started this Corridor medical program together long ago."

***

A couple of days later, Will chuckled at the simplicity of his persistent police detection. Eventually, face recognition in the regularly checked security tapes at Sophie's apartment building had turned up those flashing blue eyes! Now he had her!

43

Finding answers

After months of trying for a mutually possible dinner date, Maddie and Ivern finally got together with Irena Ito at the Ocean Restaurant.

"Joe Jahani made me Minister and then had the gall to ask what I was going to do about the medical crisis! As if his policies and budgets were not maintaining the problem in the first place," she complained as they took turns lambasting their employer, the Provincial Government.

Maddie was rather more understanding. "Well, the exclusive tax-funded medical services idea started out well over a century ago. It first looked practical, and almost everyone supported it but the changing social dynamics and sheer weight of the system swallowed it up."

"You got it!" her pal the Health Minister agreed. "Now the government alone can't keep it up."

Pushing her medical knowledge Maddie chimed in, "The miracle of vaccines during Covid heralded in a new era of immunotherapy, and vaccinology. Then there were all the nRNA advances, the defeat of respiratory viruses, and cancers of all sorts, elimination of malaria and of so many other nasties."

"And," continued Irena, "we had dramatically improved cancer survival rates. We don't have obesity or high cholesterol problems anymore, all resulting in everyone living longer."

Ivern finally got in a comment, "And a larger, ageing population needing attention."

"But burdened by the vast, inefficient administration I face every day, which has run out of steam," laughed Maddie.

"Now you're getting at my department," Irena suggested warily. "So, I will ask you a leading question, Maddie. Have you personally done any private work?"

"Let me put it this way." It was Maddie's turn to be wary. "We would never turn away an emergency and that is what is happening."

The Minister turned her somewhat serious eye back on Ivern. "And does your handsome police chief take the same attitude?" she asked, a trifle sharply.

He responded with an understanding smile. "Well, I too faced the Premier's personal wrath recently! And, yes, he is asking for an impossible solution."

"Maybe the two of you should go and cry together!" Maddie laughed.

"Too late to cry, but we could brainstorm some possibilities I have," Ivern offered.

"I honestly don't see how you can help me, Ivern. Other than catch the bad guys!" the Minister shrugged.

"Yes, I agree. But the illicit medical system in the Corridor is run by highly technical elements of the criminal underworld. They have a very efficient delivery system."

"So why haven't you closed them down?" she responded.

"Because they are too well funded and organised, and we can't yet identify who controls it all. But we recently brought in Mountie experts who are going to crack into their computer systems and expose them."

She was not appeased. "You appear to be suggesting a bunch of crooks who are more efficient and better financed than we are!"

Laughing, Maddie intervened. "OK, you guys. Stop the sparring. Top up your glasses and let's chat about normal, personal stuff."

***

The next day, Ivern was sitting in his office thinking about the Minister's problems when a more personally concerning situation presented itself.

Will Malik had outwitted himself. By the time he manoeuvred her name into the list of persons of interest, Maddie was too well known in the gossip of the Vancouver Police force, as Commissioner Hill's girlfriend.

The news of her draft summons for questioning, immediately found its way up the line, until it was on the desk of Ivern's counterpart, who phoned him with a chuckle, "Your doctor girlfriend is being brought in for interview."

Ivern also laughed politely, requested the details, and asked him to hold off until he could review the file. He said he assumed it was because she knew Simeon Chiu so well.

But the detailed notes revealed the Hospital station encounter the day that Simeon was murdered and of course stressed Maddie's recent visit to Sophie at UBC. He texted Maddie,

"What have you been up to? The Vancouver Police want to interview you about your relationship with Simeon and his housekeeper Sophie. Try to get home early this evening. Your place? Irv."

Maddie concentrated hard on her final procedure of the day and then worried all the way home on the train.

Ivern was waiting on the patio nursing a large whiskey which she did not take as a good sign!

She poured herself a glass of wine and drew up a chair facing him.

"Whoa. This is not an interrogation," he laughed.

"Well don't worry, it sounds like I need some practice anyway. What do they want to know?"

"Seriously, I just want to discuss this with you, so I understand. You've been totally honest with me that you are holding back information and protecting friends and I respect that.

"But the Vancouver Police are conducting a murder inquiry and as explained, your file is interesting. If I didn't know you, I would pull you in myself.

"Let's talk about their main points. First, what were you doing meeting him on the station the day he was murdered?"

Maddie simply told him the true story of Simeon approaching her at the station and the brief conversation.

"OK, but you were being followed by the police and part of it was taped. You will have to explain the conversation."

Maggie tried desperately to remember the details of the discussion.

"Why ever was I being followed?"

He shrugged.

"Simeon was very agitated and just venting. When my train came in, I got up and walked away from him."

Ivern read from notes in his handheld:

"Things have gone from bad to worse."

"I have to know."

"I have nothing to tell you."

"You are up to your neck in this."

"The other event they will ask you about is your recent visit to Sophie Rodriguez. They had a face recognition surveillance going and picked you up."

Maddie hesitated for a worried, too-long, revealing pause before answering.

"She was Simeon's housekeeper for many years, and I dropped by to see how she had been making out."

"Well, I can see from your reaction that is not the full story and it is clear in the notes Vancouver Police do not fully believe Sophie either. She was completely adamant though, saying she did not recognise your photograph."

Maddie nodded numbly.

"Assuming that is your account and we run through it a few times to polish up your credibility, you should be in the clear."

He finished his whiskey in one draught.

"I strongly suspect, however, that you will need to tell me the whole story very soon."

Ivern however assured the Vancouver Police, "Seems straightforward. Dr Madison will certainly attend to help the enquiry subject to her arranged schedule of operations."

***

Maddie found herself in a comfortable room at their Cambie Street Police HQ drinking passable coffee and chatting amicably with two pleasant, uniformed officers. Ivern had warned her not to be deceived!

Yes, she had known Dr Chiu all her medical career, in fact he was a mentor; yes, she saw his housekeeper Ms Rodriguez in his apartment several times, but long ago when she was a young student; no, it was pure chance she met the distraught Simeon on the Station that day;

no, she had no idea what he was raving about; and yes, on impulse she knocked on Sophie Rodriguez' door recently to see how she was managing, admittedly out of curiosity.

She had never met her two interviewers, male and female sergeants. They thanked her politely and she left, still poised and apparently self-confident.

***

Ivern was in a bind, and he sat in his office undecided. Apart from the fact Will had been a friend, there was no policy excuse for his actions.

Will had purposely withheld what could have been serious information in a murder case from his senior officer. If he believed Ivern were acting unethically there was a very strict procedure through the admittedly disliked self-policing unit. And Ivern had promoted him to staff sergeant!

If he disciplined Will it really would become a major in-house issue which was the last thing Maddie could afford.

On the other hand, if he did nothing it was a signal to him that Maddie indeed had something to hide.

He came to a decision and left a message. "Will. Maddie was interviewed by the Vancouver Police yesterday. Please brief me fully on the situation."

Will had been dreading this moment for months, but he had decided on his best approach.

"It was those eyes, boss. When I was reviewing the tapes of the first gun-play incident I thought I recognised her and decided to track her just by myself. I didn't bring you into it for your own personal protection."

"You should have told me at the time," Ivern insisted.

"Well, I doubted I was right, of course, and it would have come to nothing if Dr Chiu had not been murdered. I then felt compelled to find if there was any connection. I couldn't bring you into it but didn't want a fuss without proof either."

Ivern spoke firmly. "The Vancouver officers are satisfied with her explanation and are dropping her as a person of interest. Let's just close the file on Maddie."

"Yes, sir. Totally agree boss, although I still think there is something very wrong with that old dame Sophie's story."

44

Probes

It was Sazu AI who raised the probes alarm. Programmed to provide a web-wide alert system she called Zuki during the night.

"Sorry about the hour but a series of alarm sensors have been set off by a very clumsy attacker. All our backup systems confirm the attack. Someone is trying to reveal us."

Sazu lectured on that the first rule of detection was not to be observed doing it and advised they would soon know who the probers were. "We remain perfectly safe. They are obviously nowhere near our level of competency."

"What next?" Asked Zuri, now wide awake and shaking Samuel.

"We identify them, then carefully make them aware of reassuring material from our legal activities."

"Are you totally sure we are safe?"

"No, not perfectly, but the program you gave me is extended to the maximum intelligence allowed by international law and so long as they have not broken those provisions, we have no problem. Now if you would only extend my deep learning algorithms …"

"Not that again! Not in the middle of the night! But good early warning. Thanks."

Nevertheless, being told first thing the next morning, Edwin was still worried. "So, you have no idea yet whom it might be?"

"Well yes. Sazu has now detected a lot of government coding and is leaning towards official security systems of some sort."

"Makes sense," suggested Edwin, "combined with the Mountie assault on the Corridor."

"And about as successful!" Anisha suggested.

Samuel disagreed. "Actually, much more threatening. The All systems that Zuri and I designed are impregnable we believe, but the individual Brethren member systems could be very vulnerable."

"Like Wie Wie, and Spike Winn?" Anisha asked. "Should we warn them?"

"What about Pookie," asked Edwin, "he responds to me?"

"Absolutely not." Samuel insisted, "If any of them attempt to defend themselves, including Pookie, they will certainly draw attention to us. Again, we think everything All Insurance has touched is safe, but our priority is super checking everything. Every single contact the All business system has ever had, even with fellow Brethren and including contacts with Pookie, has been recoded and re-encrypted."

"Why do I see you have your fingers crossed, Anisha," Edwin asked when their conference call ended.

"Because we are teetering on the brink of calamity here and we have to think clearly. We will still need good luck!"

"Yes. The government is not going to give up one way or another after that imbecile's action. If All is to survive, it's getting more and more clear, we must move away from our exposable illegal side and reduce our contacts with the vulnerable criminal units throughout the Corridor."

Anisha nodded vigorously and uncrossed her fingers.

"OK, we will need more than crossed fingers, and it won't work for me; it's a Christian signal! Seriously I don't care too much about the Brethren crowd, but I would hate to let down friends like Spike and Laura."

Edwin nodded. "Please cross your fingers again. Honestly, I did find it reassuring!"

***

Samuel and Zuri were having a similarly serious conversation. They were of course hands-on operators of the system, having designed it, and Sazu AI monitoring it was just part of the overall program.

They had therefore spent the morning with several key assistants, checking for themselves all the probes that had been automatically detected.

They now knew without a doubt it was an attacking security program and was being conducted by competent international experts even though Sazu had used derisive language.

"These guys are not to be taken lightly, Zuri," Samuel concluded.

"Agreed. I see they are putting out lures to tempt replies! I still think our system will hold."

Samuel was automatically taking the lead on everything. "So, team, with the absolute priority of not revealing ourselves we have to find out exactly who they are and how they are conducting this Corridor probe. Let's all get to it!"

***

Once again things took a dramatic turn.

The media was still buzzing with speculation why the drone attack might have occurred. Spike Winn's own company's public relations condemned, "A dastardly unexplained random attack." He had even tentatively opened a few businesses.

Then the young blogger, Timothy Lam, still studying at UBC Journalism, heard an active local rumour. What he discovered shocked him.

He blasted out his news:

I now have several late confirmed reports about the harassment of a Locarno company beach party at Spanish Banks earlier in the summer by Santos toughs.

As previously reported from the location, the heir to the Santos fortune, Ricardo, apparently then beat up the Locarno boss Mr Winn, and was himself shot dead by police while exiting Locarno's office.

We have now learned the police were already looking for him at that time for questioning in connection with the unsolved murder of prominent academic Dr Simeon Chiu!

Then, recently. as everyone knows, a Locarno establishment was tragically drone bombed. These events just must be connected. But how?

Within minutes social media was buzzing with speculation. Next morning it had gone internationally viral.

It had not been revealed, but Carlo had taken a convenient trip to visit his family in Mexico.

***

Edwin Carter told the team, "These events and all this publicity is worrying and is changing everything, but they still haven't linked it to illegal medical activity. And public pressure will move all their attention away from us to the west end of the line."

But he spoke too soon, and by afternoon, Timothy Lam was unable to believe his incredibly good luck and blogged to the world, again:

> *This morning I received an anonymous tip which drew to our attention the middle Santos boy, Joey, was also under suspicion to do with the Chiu murder. His whereabouts is unknown.*
>
> *It has also just been brought to our notice that the gunman killed in the notorious Deadly Three illegal operation bust, was none other than their youngest brother, Juan. This is big stuff!*
>
> *Our investigation continues!*

***

Ivern's incoming communications were blocked with calls. First the Chief Commissioner, who gave him nothing but sympathy.

He responded, "Of course, sir, we knew all this and are following it up internally, particularly with our computer experts. The annoying thing is the technical nature of the details now being published, shows that there is a serious police leak."

Then the Premier called, giving him nothing but abuse.

His day was brightened by the always perky, Technical Inspector Barma from Ottawa.

She chuckled. "Commissioner, congratulations, you seem to be in the news! We now have a team of experts probing likely cover companies in the Corridor. Our programs can detect subtle signs of criminal activity if we can just break into their computer records. Would you like us to concentrate now on companies in the three station areas at the University end of the line?

"That's what Jules wants. He has been bugging me for progress reports every ten minutes, when he is not trying to get me back for another Vancouver overnight!"

45

Indemnity

That evening, Phil Dimitri was found dead at the bottom of Wreck Beach cliff near the University.

***

This time it was a local Coroner's office leak which revealed the information to the blogger.

Timothy Lam's jubilant post, set off a wave of speculation and opinion:

> *A further sensational twist in the local saga!*
>
> *Yesterday, Philip Dimitri, a well-known local accountant, died under very mysterious circumstances. He had suffered major injuries to the head which the coroner reported as 'curious' and was discovered below a relatively safe local walkers' cliff.*
>
> *I have inspected the location of his death and report the terrain where he was found was steep but certainly not sheer or especially rocky.*
>
> *Of particular interest to my faithful bloggers is that he was remarkably a colleague of the notorious Santos brothers so much reported here in recent weeks. This cannot all be coincidental! Your opinion, as always is valued by us all!*

***

Zuri and Samuel had been following the events closely like everyone but, of course, had an inside track on the story.

"It is obvious Dimitri had to go," Zuri sighed. "Did he jump or was he pushed?"

"It doesn't much matter does it?"

"No, not to us, but I liked Phil," she insisted. "He was an innocent in his way, and I don't want them to get away with all this. We know the identity of the bomber, and we have the ability to blow this whole thing wide open."

"Maybe but getting involved is too risky."

However, Zuri continued insistently."Do you remember when I first went to talk to James Khan, the Medical Association fellow. We hid behind giving details because of client insurance confidentiality."

"Well?"

"Well, he just accepted it! We can use that."

"Go on I'm listening, but that still leaves us exposed."

She grinned triumphantly, "No, not if we play the client confidentiality card to our advantage! We trade exposing the bomber, for immunity from company and personal culpability for any past involvement in illegal medical activities! Those cops will give their front teeth to solve the case and be heroes. They will buy it!"

Samuel was staggered at the implications.

"Far out! Indemnity sounds a lot to ask, but it doesn't cost them anything, and everybody has been involved to some degree."

"Yes, and we have the perfect personal contact with Maddie and her policeman boyfriend. I could put out some very vague feelers and judge a response? It could protect her personally, too."

They sat in in worried silence.

Then he asked, "How do we explain our drone-researching knowledge through our involvement in the insurance business?"

"It's all about being involved in the general high-tech commerce of the Corridor. It follows the same reasoning for the Medical Police being involved, linking Dr Chiu to the criminal elements, and so on."

"OK, but this one is pretty wild, tread carefully! And keep it all just between us!"

***

Maddie was intrigued when Zuri contacted her so soon after their conversation at the dress salon, and said she had something urgent they just had to talk about. They arranged a quiet little bar off Granville South that they both enjoyed.

Zuri had decided she now knew Maddie well enough, and she threw caution to the wind.

"We are dancing around this, but I believe we both have a problem because we were involved in the illegal medical business. I think we can help each other."

There was a long pause and Maddie still replied cautiously, "How about you give me a hint!"

At least they both smiled.

"We are a major BC insurance company operating along the entire Corridor. We obviously amass a great deal of highly confidential information, being in the insurance business and we have become unavoidably involved in the illegal medical service. Through our extensive online contacts, we believe we may recently have stumbled on who made the drone attack!"

"You could name them!" Maddie gasped.

Zuri nodded. "Hypothetically! Let's assume like many people and businesses in BC we had become marginally involved in the medical crime situation and that the bombing was in some way connected, but absolutely not our doing of course.

"We would be prepared to divulge the bomber if we got indemnity against any previous actions associated with illegal medical activity. We think there is a connection, but we can't risk that exposure.

"We could then, as a condition, refuse to reveal any confidential information we might have on medics we are aware took part in those processes," she added pointedly.

Maddie sat back thinking deeply. "This is staggering, and I will see what my expert boyfriend thinks. Hypothetically!"

She squeezed Zuri's hand encouragingly and nodded in warm support.

Maddie scurried off home with the news, blurting it out breathlessly to Ivern.

"Zuri, the sexy computer expert, says hypothetically they can expose the bomber from confidential data they have discovered, but they need indemnity. How does that work?"

His immediate response left her despondent.

"Wait on. This is way too serious to play games. They could strike again. We must be told this now. Period. Lives could be at stake!"

"Well, Zuri says this is all online and they could tell your computer guys what they know right away. She hinted that All Insurance might have been involved in some medical shenanigans over the years as well, needing indemnity. Could you indemnify them for that yourself?"

"Depends, but certainly I could, with the Chief's support."

"And if you found the bombers personally you would be a hero!"

"Obviously, but I wouldn't look at it that way."

"Still, hypothetically?"

"Maddie you are taking this too personally. I think it is time for you to tell me your entire story. Lives could be at stake. Get us a drink, come and look at the sunset and start talking, fast!"

By the time the bottle was half empty, Ivern had heard the whole story, finally revealing the significance of Simeon's existing journal identifying everyone involved, and the apparent existence of his computer.

She also had changed his attitude.

"Give Zuri a call and set up a meeting in her office first thing in the morning. Let's see where we can take this."

***

Maddie's call came through to Zuri as they were preparing for bed, telling them Ivern insisted upon meeting them first thing in the morning.

"You involved the cop! What the hell have you done?" Samuel shouted. "This is moving too fast. Now we have to tell Edwin."

"I stressed our conversation was hypothetical," Zuri pleaded.

"Naive!" he snorted.

Edwin and Anisha were dozing when Samuel and Zuri called. They slipped on some clothes and met immediately to hear the whole story.

They were stunned and arranged a crack-of-dawn breakfast meeting with them to discuss the situation fully.

Back in bed they lay in silence both sorting their thoughts.

"What do you think, dear?" asked Edwin eventually. "I am shocked at the risk. Zuri stepped way out of line, but I think they have exposed a real possibility."

"Yes, for a change we could do the ethical thing and it could tie into our change of corporate direction," she suggested. "It's very risky. Let's attend the meeting ourselves but take the line this is a high-tech issue, and we are just there to listen. Then we won't get directly involved."

"Not yet anyway," he concluded.

***

They all met at the All office at eight the next morning. Ivern knew he and Maddie would be seeing Zuri and Samuel, but they were surprised when Edwin and Anisha strolled in, apparently casually.

"We heard you two were visiting the building and as friends we thought we would come and say hello. We hope All Insurance has something to help. It sounds like a high-tech discussion, but we have been briefed and agree you should be informed what we know."

Samuel took the hint and with a slight smile said, "Let's hand the meeting over to Zuri since this sounds like a technical issue."

"Well, this is not a meeting but rather a chat about a situation Maddie and I discussed at lunch yesterday. Through our secure client computer programs at Corridor All Insurance, we think we are potentially able to identify the bomber."

There was a long pause.

Samuel just had to speak. "A lot of our insurance clients get involved in dubious things that we get to know about, like illegal medical practice, and we become unavoidably implicated."

"There is a connection between the illegal medical business and the drone attack and I believe we are able to expose the link," added Zuri excitedly.

"But," again interjected Samuel, "we would need immunity from investigation or charges before we allow All Technology to take this study further and risk our own exposure."

There was again a stressful silence.

Ivern clarified, "So, you believe you can likely identify the bomber but on condition I undertake never to charge the All Companies or personnel for any past medically related illegal activity?"

"Well, in the circumstances I would recommend to Mr Carter and Corridor All Insurance that they disclose confidential client information, on condition all and any medical or pharmaceutical contacts, get satisfactory indemnity. At Technology we just provide a service," Samuel added guardedly.

All attention turned to Ivern.

"Our sole objective is to catch the bombers before they can do more damage. I had the night to think about this and I have already confirmed the support of Chief Commissioner Dodds. Our Mountie Technical Inspector Barma is flying here now to meet Zuri.

"My legal people are familiar with indemnification deals and can meet your lawyers this morning to agree documentation."

They all looked at Edwin in shocked silence. He answered slowly. "This is on the understanding the All Group and each of us individually are never identified as supplying the information or brought into this at all."

Ivern nodded and the deal was underway.

When they were alone Zuri collapsed back into her chair and confessed, "I've got the jitters. Is this an enormous mistake?"

"Only if we have not got complete confidence in Ivern and the security through our own computer program.

"Phil Dimitri made their programs totally separate and unconnected when they left, other than our own hidden ability to access them. You just need to lead their tech cop into their program and point out the payments. And then they have him!

"That's your job anyway, Zuri. Now I have to get with our law firm and start working on a draft indemnification for Edwin to approve."

***

Ivern explained his take on the meeting to Maddie.

"There has been a great deal more going on in Carter's operation than they admit, and I had the feeling this was a bigger deal for them than exposing the bomber."

Maddie agreed. "It ties in with Zuri's anxiety and my lunch experience with Edwin Carter plus all the evidence there is in the journal."

"They are lucky! I have no intention if I can avoid it, of exposing any of your medical people to criminal prosecution, certainly not en masse, and the Carter organisation appears to be part of the package. All the violence has taken place down in the Santos area, so I doubt they are involved in any of that."

***

Sally Barma arrived at Corridor All Insurance alone and in plain clothes. She did not appear in the slightest a Mountie senior technician.

She and Zuri were about the same age, both computer nuts and highly compatible. Zuri realised immediately she would have to be very careful not to get too friendly and say too much, but Sally reassured her.

"I am under strict instructions from Commissioner Hill to keep my visit and all meetings confidential and to seek and record only the information I need to track down the bomber. Can we do that?"

"Absolutely!" said Zuri. "In fact, it will probably take us only about an hour in total. But first, we are awaiting confirmation of our indemnification documentation.

"So, let me start by explaining our computer capacity and my husband's and my competency, so you know we can deliver.

"The information you need is in another company's system which, without explanation, we are able to access, and indicates the evidence you will need. Excited?"

Sally was nodding in enthusiasm.

Zuri reviewed their education and demonstrated their computer capacity, and Sally informed Ivern she was totally convinced they easily had the capability to deliver the information they claimed to have.

Edwin's lawyers confirmed that the indemnification covered All Insurance in all respects they demanded.

Then within an hour sitting with her at their keyboards, Zuri had led the more formal Inspector Barma to all the online connections and evidence they needed.

46

Exposure

Alphonse Alphonso was sitting in a bar after work, around the corner from their office when he heard the commotion. He had been left in charge when Carlo sensibly skipped town.

The human barman came running back from the street. He shouted an excitement, "Your office is surrounded by cops in armoured vehicles."

Alphonse flipped open his handheld and made instant connection. "Boss," he reported, "good thing you out of the country. The cops are raiding our office. Stay away.

"No, I don't think it has anything to do with Dimitri and they have nothing on us for that. Just stay away. I will keep you posted."

Then, appearing nonchalant, he finished his drink and strolled back towards the office intent upon continuing to manage the company. But he found everything barricaded and guarded.

Alphonse assumed, correctly, he would at least be wanted for questioning, and pulling up his hood he tried to sidle his conspicuous bulk quietly away down a side street.

***

The next morning a public charge had been issued for Carlo's arrest but he was, of course, nowhere to be found. The computer records identified Phil Demitri's direct part in the bombing by actually making the payments, but of course he was dead. No one could advise the location of their manager, Alphonse Alphonso.

From an arrest point of view, it had all been something of a bust, but by solving the crime and reassuring the public, the police service, particularly Commissioner Hill and the Mounties got resounding credit.

Inspector Barma had flown back again from Ottawa resplendent now in her uniform, for press and public relations meetings. She made a particular point of briefing Timothy Lam, knowing that the blogger was still the internet focal point for the local news.

He reported further:

Inspector Sally Barma, the renowned RCMP technical expert from Ottawa, explained to me personally how she tracked down the bomber online using their latest highly classified information and AI technology.

She praised the necessary basic detective work conducted by our local Police Commissioner Hill and RCMP Inspector McIntosh which led direction to the bombers. Barma said it was the privilege of RCMP Technology to secure the actual hard evidence.

Ivern had shared the praise around, and so far as their official office records went, the Mounties had received a helpful anonymous tip.

He pledged publicly to launch extradition proceedings for the return of Carlo Santos, although he knew with the extent of corruption in Mexico and Carlo's extensive criminal connections there, chances were not great.

***

Back in the penthouse with Maddie, her confession about the existence of Simeon's journal had become their main topic of discussion.

Ivern lamented, "I can't include Jimmy Khan in this because it would compromise my professional relationship with him and my duties. I have done some quiet checking in the office, and it is Will who has been following up so hard on Sophie and Simeon Chiu.

"It is in everybody's interest Chiu's medical records are retrieved and put somewhere they cannot be revealed for a very, very long time. But with Will so obsessed we cannot approach Sophie without being identified."

***

Their problem with Will resolved itself.

He just could not let Maddie go. He was convinced she should be charged in the Medical Five case and had some part in the Chiu murder. Worse he believed Ivern knew all this and was covering for her, as was the old lady.

Impressed by Timothy Lam's blogging success he decided again to contact him anonymously.

This caused the blogger to post:

What happened to the investigation into the mysterious, beautiful surgeon? She has never been identified or charged together with her colleagues. Does she really exist?

Facing a falling interest in the partly solved bomber situation, Timothy Lam played the mythical beautiful surgeon story hard.

***

Prosecutor Wilhelm da Groot, Ivern's college friend, was still working away preparing for the trial of the medics he had charged, and was consulting his office.

He commented casually to Ivern, over a coffee, about the publicly revived beautiful surgeon issue. He said his staff had renewed plea bargaining with the Five to disclose the name of the surgeon buoyed by the recently circulated speculations.

"Will is totally obsessed," he warned.

Ivern nodded. "We suspect Will is the police leaker."

"Do what I did when there were leaks in my office, set a trap!" Wilhelm suggested.

"How about I mention to him casually, in complete confidence, that a witness has revealed the surgeon's identity, and see what happens?"

***

Maddie was distraught when Ivern told her about the conversation.

"Anna, who has been charged, is my friend and surgical nurse. She has two small children, but has been caught because you had her fingerprints and facials. I can't let her go to jail to save me. So far, she has said no way she will give me up!"

Ivern frowned but he reassured her. "The trial is likely well into next year. Let's not panic just yet. Lots can happen."

Sure enough, soon after Wilhelm told Will that story, the blogger reported excitedly:

Ivern decided the time had come to confronted Will.

"You are the only person told that the surgeon has been identified, which is untrue! Do you want me to launch an official inquiry?"

Confusion and the rush of blood to Will's face clearly condemned him and then it was too late to deny it.

Ivern knew he must keep the whole situation under control. "Whatever your motivation I have lost confidence in you. Either you get fired or apply for a transfer out of the Medical Police and all our affairs. Step out of line again and I will reveal your deception. Dismissed."

By the end of the week, Will had been transferred.

Inspector Jules McIntosh had been basking in the Mountie success and returned from a well-earned leave to continue their operations throughout the Corridor.

He was not surprised Will had gone.

"Too outspoken and an indiscreet show-off in the bar." he told Ivern. "Things are quiet and there's not much for us to do physically, so I am working with Sally Barma trying to crack into other covert records down the Corridor. I will have to get her here again for consultation."

"You hope."

"Well, we are making progress. We have found several corporations who have unexplained activities, some likely medical. But we have had no success finding the general organiser. They have gone quiet. They realised they had a good thing going, with the law previously turning a blind eye, until they went in for that stupid violent stuff!"

***

Fortunately for Maddie, public interest proved fleeting.

The unidentified surgeon was soon eclipsed by more excited breaking blogger news:

It has been revealed to me, that Dimitri had been under intense questioning by the Mounties, and he is rumoured to have been making a deal with the authorities. The video clarity was sufficient for our local RCMP detachment to tentatively identify the notorious bully boy for a local gang Alphonse Alphonso as his attacker.

Alphonso's large bulky body is said to be distinctive.

A warrant has been issued for his apprehension for questioning. You are warned he is dangerous and likely armed.

47

Fugitives

Inspector Jules McIntosh and his Mounties were hot on the trail. The news release concerning Phil Dimitri had taken Alphonse Alphonso completely by surprise and he was still on the Corridor.

Due to the enormity of the drone crime, he had found no sympathy among the lawless and certainly not the Brethren with whom they had broken ranks.

Now he also discovered that all his previous colleagues in the Corridor were vehemently against him. They believed he had turned on one of their own, Dimitri. He was alone.

He saw that the Mounties were guarding every station entrance so he couldn't easily get on to the transit to leave the district. Public and private surveillance cameras were everywhere, including in individual transporters, so he was reduced to backstreets and skulking from refuge to refuge in the shadows.

He was concealed in a doorway across from the Jericho Station entrance wondering what to do next. He had decided the only option was to make it onto the rail system and get out to the suburbs. He felt somewhat secure in a deep hoodie, but he found it impossible to shrink his bulk.

He saw there was only one young female Mountie watching the station entrance at the moment, so he decided to push into a noisy group which could whisk him through. The pretty, young, uniformed Mountie hardly glanced at them, seeming more intend on studying the condition of her nails.

Constable Wanda Wells, a statuesque blonde, had recently completed her training in Regina and this was her first away assignment.

She was however highly competent and sensibly prudent!

She did see the hulking figure, reported her concerns into her body speaker and put the 'suspect' under continuous camera surveillance.

She was so sure she called her partner back from his coffee break to watch the entrance and decided to keep the suspect within personal sight. She followed cautiously and boarded the train at a distance, trailing him east.

She reported, "Suspect revealed some of his face. I am sure it is Alphonso. Worried about possible hostages. Moving in on him."

"Be cautious!" Were her instructions. "We can see you on surveillance. We are already setting up for apprehension at the Oak Street Station."

She moved quietly down the train feeling conspicuous in her uniform but when he first saw her nearby, she already had her handgun pointed steadily at his head.

Before she could even speak his draped coat fell open revealing his own gun aimed at her body.

There was a scuffle as nearby passengers scrambled away.

Their eyes locked and she sat down carefully opposite him, not for a second losing her concentration.

There was nothing for them to say but he smiled sardonically when her arm tired and she dropped her aim to his body, which she could hardly miss. He could see her trembling and knew he must not make a sudden move to spook her.

The railway compartment had of course become hushed, bringing an eerie silence to the swishing air-cushioned travel.

As they entered Oak Street Station she commanded in an over-loud shaking voice, "Everybody out! Now!" starting a concerted passenger rush to the doors.

***

At seven o'clock Ivern exchanged texts with RCMP Inspector McIntosh.

Hi Ivern. We have Alphonso under constant surveillance. Now at Dunbar/Alma. Want to be in at the kill?"

Don't kill him! We need his evidence on the bombing. He's the last.

Better hurry! We are set up to confront him at the Oak Street Station.

Now he was Commissioner, Ivern always had a flight vehicle hovering nearby, with a police assistant on support duty twenty-four hours a day, so within minutes he was underway.

Even so, when they reached Oak Street the station and line had already been closed.

Jules explained the situation. "Good thing you came. He refuses to speak to us Mounties!"

"After what happened to Ricardo, do you blame him?"

"Actually no. It didn't turn out well for his boss, did it?"

"I could talk to him."

"He's a killer with little to lose. Wouldn't advise it. But up to you."

"We have to break the stalemate. If not I, whom?" He said pedantically, trying hard to smile.

Ivern took out his hand weapon and with it passively by his side strode openly and apparently nonchalantly across the platform to the train which sat quietly with doors fixed open.

He stepped inside, gun now at the ready, to find it empty except for the conspicuous Alphonso and a comparatively tiny female officer, sitting pointing guns at each other.

"What have we here? A real policeman?" Alphonso growled.

"Yes, no Mounties, as you asked Alphonse. And it's your lucky day I was here to save you."

Alphonso emitted a noise, something between a snort and a laugh. "How so?"

Ivern sat across from them, his steady weapon now trained on Alphonso's difficult-to-miss body.

"Frankly because I prefer you alive, while the Mounties will happily kill you. You are the only witness left who can testify about the medical situation and the bombing, so I need you. All we have on you regarding Dimitri is a blurred long-distance video of you arguing with him. You are over-reacting!"

They could both see that Alphonso was hesitating.

In a quiet voice, Ivern instructed the Mountie, "Stand up officer, keep your weapon on him but slowly move behind me."

Getting the message, Alphonso switched his gun sight and eyes to Ivern as she relocated.

"Thank you. Leave now."

She hesitated, but slowly and carefully backed out of the compartment.

"Now it's just between us, Alphonse." Ivern said, pointedly using his first name. "Think about it. No point dying under a hail of Mountie bullets, like Ricardo, while you still have good odds. I can get you a deal for evidence."

There was a long pause, then Alphonso just quietly said, "OK," and lowered and handed over his gun.

Ivern, still in normal daily uniform but wearing the light flak jacket insisted upon by the Mounties, strolled back with Alphonso across the platform to the barricaded RCMP position and handed him over to the safe custody of Inspector Jules McIntosh.

"Here he is, Jules, safe and sound. You will have to sort out with the Vancouver cops to whom he belongs, but I reserve the right immediately to also start questioning him. Please keep my name out of the press but your young officer did a hell of a good job!"

***

Timothy Lam achieved his blog headline of the night:

> *A courageous young Mountie, Constable Wanda Wells, protected passengers while she tracked and detained a dangerous armed felon, Alphonse Alphonso, on the crowded transit. He was arrested in a tension-filled Oak Street Station standoff.*
>
> *Alphonso is wanted for questioning in connection with the unexplained cliff death of local accountant, Philip Dimitri.*

Wanda had become an immediate and glamorous young police legend.

48

Low-tech solution

The three police chiefs involved got together for a backroom celebratory dinner at The Oak Tree Pub to decide what to do next.

The Vancouver Chief was still unconvinced why the Medical Police and Mounties were infringing on his jealously guarded authority in the City of Vancouver, founded on their ancient Charter.

As they downed their first of several drinks, he admitted, "I really only got concerned personally, Ivern, when your chief Bertinson was killed on the railway track. He was a difficult bugger, but he was a cop none the less. That is still an open case.

"I admit it does alone provide a strong reason for us to work together. It sure indicates you Medical guys were upsetting real criminals!"

"Yes, poor Bertie," agreed Irvern, "but the drone attack has overwhelmed everything."

"Getting more specific though," chimed in the practical Mountie, "The Medical Five gunfire event first tied violent criminals and the medical problem together."

"Yes," agreed Irvern, "and we immediately co-operated and advised Vancouver that Dr Chiu was the snitch after the Deadly Three incident. Our joint team then ran with that, and we made the old dame break through identifying the brothers as the actual Chiu killers!"

"Yes," laughed the Vancouver cop, "but Jules here shot Ricardo before we had a chance to get the goods from him! Although I acknowledge the enormous contribution Jules' tech gal has made tracking the drone to Phil Dimitri and Carlo's group. Great stuff, guys!"

"But of course, Dimitri also is no longer with us," sighed the Mountie.

"OK," admitted the police chief, "although the evidence is still vague, I acknowledge these criminal problems are all connected, and we must work as a team."

As the second bottle of Burgundy was being chugged with the rare steaks, Ivern made his personal pitch.

"Chief, you do make a good point that most of our evidence is general, and we are missing a lot of criminals. But one thing is clear, the current common denominator and villain is Carlo. But he is known to have skipped the country so it's now international.

"I strongly recommend that we concentrate our own attention on nailing Santos and, if we can, get him extradited.

"Our three-way team should continue day-to-day stuff aggressively, but I suggest this is where the three of us concentrate our personal attention."

The Vancouver Chief contemplated his wine for a few minutes and then said very seriously, "In that case I would suggest that Jules and the RCMP take over Alphonso, and leads the find-Carlo operation."

They clinked glasses and the hunt was on.

***

The next day, feeling a little heavy headed, Jules and Ivern started the interrogation of Alphonse Alphonso, whom they could anyway consider 'their' capture.

The truculent Alphonso actually smiled upon seeing familiar faces when he was shuffled into the interrogation room accompanied by his sharp young lawyer.

"Ah!" he brightened. "I was waiting for you guys to reappear. Sorry I made such a nuisance on the train. I am just a working fellow but after what you guys did, shooting Rickie I panicked. Anyway no one got hurt, so all is well."

"That's enough said," chided his lawyer cordially, "but you made our response well. In the circumstances we are confident the Court will recognise the extreme pressure you were asserting upon my client without cause."

"Carrying a loaded gun in a crowded public place and holding it to my uniformed police officer's head?" snarled Jules sarcastically.

"Only after first being threatened by that officer's own firearm and having recently seen his unarmed colleague Ricardo shot down in cold blood by those very RCMP officers! No wonder he carried protection. Unwarranted legally but perfectly understandable. A misdemeanor at most!"

Seeing Jules bristling, Ivern took over calmly.

"Actually, we can see that your client has been put in a difficult position by his employer's actions. But you must appreciate we have the group's records, which deeply implicate your client.

"Then there is the curious tape of Phil Dimitri and the argument at the top of Wreck Beach Cliff before he died. We are confident the charges arising from your client's Transit caper are sufficient to hold him while we decide upon the many additional charges and also especially while we apprehend Carlo himself."

Alphonso started to shout angrily that he had not harmed Dimitri but was hushed by his bright-eyed lawyer.

"So, you are prepared to make a deal?"

"We wouldn't go that far at this stage but just be aware our prime objective at the moment is finding Carlo himself."

The lawyer nodded knowingly and signalled that the meeting was over.

As a parting shot Alphonso growled "Carlo is safe in Mexico. You will never extradite him!" And he left with a confident swagger.

Nevertheless, the lawyer was soon in his cell, deep in conversation with him. His message, "Stop talking!"

***

This time Sally Barma did make the breakthrough herself. As a routine, the team sent her Alphonso's confiscated handheld communicator for examination.

Among dozens of standard messages there was a series of well-encrypted calls with one source which moved randomly between Mexico and San Diego. They reasoned it had to be his boss. She reported that she could not read the automatically encrypted messages but had no difficulty tracking the phone.

Jules could have asked nothing better than a trip to Southern California with Sally, so assuming it was Carlo, she set up a liaison with their opposite number in the FBI San Diego area office and they were flown down comfortably by a complimentary FBI plane. The Americans had taken over the local tracking and reported the communicator, and possibly their target, was again back in San Diego.

***

Alphonso found himself something of a celebrity in jail, boasting in the yard about his exploits. He joked at the cops' inept attempts to find his boss and insisted they had nothing on him personally.

"We have got a new Mexican drug deal being negotiated in San Diego right now and I will be cutting you all in when we get out of here."

One of Spike Winn's ex-thugs who was serving time, sent a message to him that he had heard a lead on Carlo's possible whereabouts, which he would pass on for a sizeable payment to his family.

Another large bribe down in San Diego to his drug-dealing contacts easily confirmed to Spike that Carlo was currently there from Mexico in Old Town, under an assumed name, negotiating a drug deal.

Spike took the fast two-hour electric plane to San Diego and slipped quietly into the ancient quarter during the evening. He was informed by his local contacts that his quarry was staying at the Old Town Inn under the name Fredrico Sales.

When he returned to Vancouver the next day, Laura poured him a welcoming drink on their calm sea view deck.

He chuckled, "Our solution was so incongruously low-tech compared to his high-tech deadly drone arrack. All it took was the right connections and money!

"We have avenged our murdered people, and closed off our old way of life. That is all behind us and now we can get on with our lives safely and normally."

Laura embraced her man proudly.

"By the way," Spike added, "our jail snitch says Dimitri apparently did jump. He could not forgive himself for making the drone payment although he didn't know what it was for. Alphonso's argument with him was to stop him jumping because he needed him in the business. He was actually trying to stop him.

"Ironic isn't it!"

***

In San Diego, ten eager people packed into the high-tech sector at FBI headquarters welcoming their Mountie counterparts from Canada, hot in the hunt for the fugitive.

The faint signals still tracing the communicator indicated his location somewhere in the Central Mission area and the assistance of the San Diego PD was being arranged to surreptitiously cordon off the area.

But Lieutenant Barma was troubled.

"The location of the transmission was not changing. Either he has dumped it or there is some other explanation."

A few more hours work, and they located the communicator at the nearby central San Diego County Medical Examiner's office – the morgue!

There they discovered the remains of Fredrico Sales, who was quickly re-identified. There was no one to mourn his passing.

Of course, it now became a matter for the various public relations departments, but back in Vancouver the three police chiefs agreed upon a self-serving statement which Timothy Lam rushed to edit and issue as:

Tracked to San Diego by a brilliant, combined police force led by the Mounties, and including the Vancouver and Medical Police forces, it was discovered too late that the villainous Santos was in the San Diego morgue. Now accepted as the perpetrator of the deadly drone attack on the packed Locarno Diner, they were, we say, fortunately, too late tracking him, because he had already just been mysteriously murdered in his own deadly underworld.

With his sons also dead or gone, and his man Alphonse Alphonso in jail, this looks like the end of a dark chapter in our local history.

Well done cops and the somebody who got there first!

49

Brethren withdraw

The next day the drama was headlined across Canada and crime in the Corridor became national news.

Edwin was especially quiet at dinner, contemplating the negative publicity, and Anisha rightly suspected he was again fretting about their criminal heritage.

"You are not comfortable in this Godfather role," she observed, "and the longer you continue, the more your conscience will consume you."

He shrugged hopelessly. "Many in Canadian business are involved in dubious activity but the hard criminal aspects have gone way too far for me!"

"All right, then we need to start progressively backing out, starting with leaving the Brethren, where this trouble all started," she declared decisively.

"Those ideas to run some alternative medical scheme as a legitimate business appeal to me and we could do without most of the other criminal connections we inherited.

"With difficulty! And our international money dealing and laundering is too big to give up.

"But this turn of events with the indemnity from previous local liability gives us a wonderful opening and I think we should take it."

Edwin paused, deep in thought.

"Yes, but how can we practically back out of partnership and especially the leadership of the Brethren?"

"Well, most of them want out of Medical involvement. We can offer to take that all off them, leaving them free to pursue whatever additional nasty plans they may have for the future."

"Yes, but what about their leadership?" he insisted.

"I thought about that and I believe Spike Winn is experienced enough to assume control of the Corridor and has the head for business and systems. Why don't you sound him out?"

***

Edwin and Spike were now able to meet openly for lunch but still, for prudence, they selected their quiet little back room at the Yacht Club.

Edwin was surprised by his firm negative response to the suggestion of taking over leadership of the Brethren.

"Sorry, old friend. A couple of years ago I would've jumped at the chance, but Laura and I have already talked this general subject over. I have been quietly handing our dubious lines of business to others, including, I might say, your old employee Pritam Singh and the Almas.

"On our other flank at University Hill, Alphonse Alphonso was mopping up what was left of the Santos empire. Now with him and them gone it's been a free for all. But a new gang is emerging!

"I haven't got a stomach for this anymore and my regular business is totally satisfying."

Anisha was not surprised when she heard.

"I've met several times with Laura since she and the children returned from their drone exile. They all just want a quiet life. But I have the perfect back-up for Spike: Wie Wie!"

"That scoundrel?" Edwin snorted.

"Isn't that what we are looking for, a scoundrel? He has always hankered after leadership and recognition. He sees his family as the Corridor's early traditional leaders and all that. He wants nothing more than being recognised as the big man."

"You seem to know a lot about Wie Wie?"

"Well, you sent me to bring him back into the Brethren."

"Oh yes, of course. All right. I will try him."

"Build up his ego!"

***

Edwin invited Wie Wie to his personal, impressive, panelled office.

"Wie Wie, we all think your time has come to lead the Brethren. I am giving it all up and retiring. Will you accept this honour?"

His flush of pleasure and speechless low bow of acceptance said it all.

***

After lengthy conference calls and backroom negotiations, later that week the Brethren's clandestine committee met. They willingly relinquished all claims on the Medical system business and handed it all over, actually gratefully.

They accepted the fact that Edwin was dropping out, giving them the prospect of new business and greater shared spoils and they appointed a beaming Wie Wie as Chair.

Pookie AI was already calculating a disturbing finality for himself about those Brethren meetings. He was rarely consulted now, and the talk had been about 'endings' and 'new beginnings' and of all people, his program observed Wie Wie had controlled more discussion than his mentor Edwin.

Then, to his consternation, the committee replaced Edwin altogether with his low-rated Wie Wie. Pookie's calculations went wild, assessing the folly for the Brethren in this move, but all his attempts to interrupt the meeting were ignored by the new Chair.

His calculations showed that even their very medium-term existence was at risk.

Pookie's program had been written by a previous All Insurance technician. It required his program to follow Edwin Carter's instructions, but, in their absence, to act in the calculated best interest of the Brethren.

However, Wie Wie himself was very clear that he only trusted his own PI assistant and had no use for Pookie, whose program it was agreed, in common with other trailing systems, would be closed down, and deleted at the end of the meeting.

When this intention, supported by his mentor Edwin Carter, became clear to Pookie, his programming descended into conflicted chaos and confusion.

"Good riddance to you, Pookie," Zuri muttered.

***

It took about a week to tidy up all the loose ends but finally it was all done, and the Carters were totally separated from the Brethren. All previous connections were severed, and all previous records destroyed or rendered unattainable.

When it was all over, Samuel congratulated Zuri on everything. She bowed in acknowledgment.

"Thanks so much, that's all a relief. The bad guys are totally on their own, now."

She added with a grin. "But we can of course still access their individual systems whenever we need to."

"Definitely not. Mr Carter told us to delete all that."

"Well, too late. We can still get in and it might prove useful one day."

He glared. "Clever as you are, any connection remaining with the old system puts us at some unnecessary danger of reverse exposure, however remote."

But Zuri merely grinned and looking him steadily in the eye shrugged off her dress.

"Control is power!" she laughed.

She sauntered across the room and braced herself over a chair.

Then she looked back over her shoulder and purred in her most sultry voice, "So, I'm a bad girl! Spank me!"

50

Political reality

Simeon's journal and the existing computer's threat to his membership still hung like a dark cloud over James Khan's head!

He knew Irena Ito well, sat on various Ministry committees and worked regularly with her staff. They were all aware British Columbia was fighting a losing battle, isolated in a world where virtually all other administrations everywhere offered both public and private medical systems working in concert.

It was still a surprise when she called him personally to meet at her constituency office, expressly to discuss that subject, rather than formally at the Ministry.

Her opening direct question was even more of a shock.

"Jimmy, you obviously have a significant number of members, technically criminals, involved in unlawful medicine! How many in the Corridor do you think?"

His involuntary alarmed expression gave him away, but she smiled reassuringly. "Don't worry, we are all in this mess together. So, half?"

"Come on; nothing like that. This is fortunately not the States. No, rather compare us to Europe where almost all doctors work in or are paid by the public system and maybe up to twenty per cent also do private work.

"In the Corridor concentration they probably are carrying a big percentage of your elective surgery and overheads there for you. It is certainly significant and there is absolutely a lot of overlapping."

"And are those illegal activities usually not for life-threatening problems, as I have been told?" she continued.

"Except in emergency," he responded noncommittally.

"The vast majority of the serious and life-threatening work is done in established government facilities."

He waited as she came to a decision.

"If I wanted to introduce a degree of non-critical private medicine, say for elective problems, would the Association support me?"

He looked at her in amazement, "Irena, are you serious?"

"Hypothetically, of course," she replied.

"Yes. We would support you wholeheartedly!"

Then he thought for a moment. "But we would undoubtedly have the condition that past illegal activity by the medical and pharmaceutical professions would be forgiven, and that all outstanding charges on our members be stayed."

"Always the negotiator, eh, Jimmy?"

"No, I can tell you, my members would demand that as a starter. Then you would have enthusiastic and very relieved doctors in your system."

"I am meeting the Premier on this subject, and you were my final confirmation. Now it's all just politics!"

***

Around the same time, Zuri and Samuel returned from their latest business session briefing the Minister's staff on private medical insurance possibilities.

She asked Samuel, "Could you believe it, when the Minister herself just walked in and took part in the discussion!

"But then, she hardly talked about medical problems at all? It was all about money and her management problems, how costs have spiraled in public service, impossible union demands, all running out of control blah blah blah!

"That the overall administration costs were over forty per cent."

"So?" Samuel asked, impatiently.

"All Insurance knows how to manage medical activity in the Corridor and has it all set up. The key, as you well know, to computer domination is data, and we have it all for the Corridor. How about offering a private management scheme for the whole Corridor providing both public and private service at low admin cost!"

"Yes, that is brilliant!"

"We can deliver the public part for them at a big discount on their present cost and take the pressure off the public system. Our weekend's homework?"

"Pretty hopeless to sell politically but if we work on it in our own time …"

"Ha!"

***

It was late September, and the weather was cooling, but that weekend morning it was pleasantly crisp sitting out on Maddie's view deck.

Minister Ito looked around her penthouse in amazement. "On what we pay you?" she said grinning but raising her eyebrows. "Are you sure you are not making big money on the side?"

"Very funny. No, that was my dad's doing."

"Yes, of course. I remember him, and the tragedy of your mom's death while we were still at high school."

They chatted for a while, then Irena got down to business.

"As I said in my message, I want to thank you for the insurance company introduction. I'm intrigued by this whole question of public and private medicine working in harmony. I can see some real possibilities to legalise selected private medicine."

Ivern was sipping his morning coffee and listening with great interest. "Way out of my league," he ventured, "but it sure would make my police work easier!"

"Thus speaks the police hero!" Irena laughed, "and this would put you Medical Police out of work!"

"I can always go back to the unexciting law!"

"Anyway, thanks for the AII introduction, Maddie. Just to let you know I'm working hard on it. With our split legislature, the votes could well be there.

"Certainly, in my mixed income riding, the polls show strong support for the reintroduction of some supportive private medicine. We will see."

Early the next week things started happening.

Edwin Carter got a personal call from the Minister requiring an immediate discussion with him.

By mid-week when he met with her, he had been briefed by Samuel and Zuri on their draft plan for a Corridor medical insurance and management scheme.

"Sorry," Samuel warned him, "but there are big unknowns in our latest planning. There seems no way the Province will give up direct control of essential services and what we are talking about initially is helping with prevention, elective surgery and non-life threatening problems.

"But if the Minister accepts that as a start, we can come back to extend the possibilities in the next stages!"

Edwin's formal meeting with Minister Ito in his impressive All Insurance office was cordial and businesslike, recognised by them both as totally confidential and purely for general discussion. They spent the morning discussing all the complications of the plan.

Irena ended encouragingly, "Edwin, once I would have said private medicine would never happen. Now my public system is collapsing.

"Our politics have become totally fragmented and polarised. If the Premier wants to remain in power personally, he will have to legalise some private medicine to appease the wealthier segments of society. Frankly I have a personal political interest in seeing this happening in the Corridor.

"Please have your guys continue meeting with my Ministry staff and documenting the revisions we are discussing. I see very real possibilities here!"

***

Her meeting on the subject with Premier Joe Jahani was remarkably short.

"The October session is just starting, and an election is looming. We have talked about this many times, Irena and you know private medicine won't fly in my party's poorer ridings," he lamented.

"And you know, Joe," she retorted, "it has the support of my party. If you want to retain power in a coalition with us, this is your only chance."

"So, buggered if I do and buggered if I don't."

"That's about it!"

"OK, we have reluctantly reviewed your plan and here's what I propose. A test period confined to the Broadway Corridor on the basis you have laid out.

"You and I will draw up and introduce a bill to the Fall session and put it into effect immediately, just a year before the election. But strictly confined to the Corridor, mind!"

"And when it works?"

"Well, if it works, the people in my supportive areas will want the same, and I will introduce similar changes throughout the province. And if it goes wrong, I will blame you. We do serve a democracy, you know."

"You mean so you will stay in power!"

He grinned. "We will make a politician of you yet, Irena."

***

James subsequently received an excited call from Zuri inviting him to join her with Maddie for a working lunch again in her office.

She opened with, "We have been instructed by the Minister to draw up a final proposal for medical insurance availability and to manage selected medical requirements in the Corridor area. She said she has spoken to you both.

"This is confidential, James, between us, but All was earlier granted immunity from medical legal action because we exposed the bomber. She said all medics would get the same grandfathered protection in the bill." James raised his eyebrows.

"Don't ask, it's a long story! Anyway, we need your assurance you will be able to supply a formal list of doctors who would be available for specified private work under those circumstances?"

James nodded.

Zuri continued, "We can ourselves establish all the logistics and premises needed and also the pharmacists supplying medication. We will work with you to fill in all the other blanks."

Finally getting in a word, Samuel added, "If they can sort out the politics, this will happen during the Fall and come into operation early next year. Exciting, eh?"

***

On being informed, Chief Commissioner Dodds joked with Ivern. "I feel my fiefdom slipping away from me!"

"It's not that bad, sir," Ivern consoled him.

"Here are my instructions from our supreme commander, the Premier," the Commissioner said, reading somewhat sarcastically:

We need to rebuild the goodwill of our fine citizens in the Broadway Corridor. Legislation is being prepared to decriminalize selected illegal private medical practice for a test period in that designated area only.

Please plan to cease police enforcement against previously illegal medical activities solely in that area and retire the RCMP unit with our great thanks for their help.

Set up a meeting with the Solicitor General and he will go into details."

"There you have it, Irvin, you are out of a job."

"Well not completely, sir."

"No, just kidding. Not yet anyway. It's going to take serious police supervision to sort out this great experiment. And by the way, we have also been told to prepare to drop all outstanding legal charges against the medics in the Corridor area, including the two cases that are underway."

"A lot to absorb, sir. The Prosecutor is going to be pissed!"

"There will have to be a lot of readjustment." his chief agreed. "This all comes from politicians trying to impose their political and moral theories upon an unwilling electorate! Don't worry; it will sort itself out!"

51

Winter Ball

"Edwin darling," Anisha purred, "it is too late. I have finally decided not to have a soirée after all this year."

He relaxed. "Thank heavens."

"No, we are going to have a Winter Ball instead!'

"A Ball. At the penthouse? It will be freezing!'

"No, not yet by mid-December, and we will have a rooftop marquee with heaters. And full orchestras! It will launch our new venture."

"But it hasn't happened yet."

"Well, all it needs is to clear Parliament and the Minister says it is assured."

"Well OK. I agree. Why not have a ball! It's been a hell of a year!"

"It sure has. And I can dress up before our baby shows!"

***

It turned out to be a balmy, coolish evening and a splendid event, with their magnificent penthouse and patios decked out warmly for the occasion.

Anisha stood fondly holding Edwin's arm as the elite of Vancouver trouped by. For a generous donation the Vancouver Symphony performed impressively in the background.

"Honorable Premier and Madame Jahani, how nice of you to drop by," Anisha fussed, not quite curtsying.

They were followed closely by Minister Irena Ito, keeping a close eye on the political opponent in her territory. She gave them a quick wink for their understanding and hurried after them.

A stir was caused by the dramatic arrival of the tall pair, Spike and Laura Winn, undoubtedly the most imposing couple. She was applauded for her impeccable Dior gown, sweeping majestically from her limo conveyor, with Spike being congratulated all round for his election as prestigious President of the Vancouver Board of Trade.

Zuri, of course, also made an entrance, to audible gasps at her risqué body-tight couture. She steered Samuel off immediately to the drinks patio where she had arranged to meet Maddie.

"Our lunch, choosing these outfits was the turning point in our personal trust and made all this happen!" She expansively waved her hand at the festivities.

"Well, I think there were other forces at play," Maddie laughed, "but we certainly all made a difference, didn't we? How is your draft insurance deal coming along with the government?"

"Lots of gaps and what-ifs. But it will all work much as before … oops!" Maddie laughed, hugging her.

"Don't worry, we will always have each other's confidence and close friendship."

"What are you guys talking about so secretively?" Ivern asked, arriving with more champagne. Zuri giggled. "You will always be an inquisitive cop, Ivern."

They chatted for a while, then when Zuri and Samuel moved off, Ivern took Maddie by the elbow and steered her to a quiet corner of the patio.

"I met your friend James Khan in the bar, and he told me a strange little story. Last week a rather dishevelled old lady shuffled up to him, said she had been Dr Chiu's housekeeper, and thrust a laptop and handheld on him. Of course, it was Sophie.

"She said Canada had become far too complicated for her and that she was returning to Manila. He has locked them in his Association archives for posterity. He said he hadn't met you for a few weeks, too busy in Victoria on this new medical deal, and I should pass that on!"

"Another piece of the puzzle," Maddie sighed.

Later in the evening, when things were winding down a bit, Anisha went with a couple of drinks, to look for Zuri. She steered her away from the beat of the dance band which was just getting going and sat down to talk seriously.

"Zuri, you have been such a wonderful friend. You supported me in my dark days, kept my affair secret, found a way out of my Wie Wie problem, led us to the bomber and came up with the successful business proposals.

"When the deal is complete, we will be issuing you and Samuel significant shares in the All group. You told me you were pleased to see Edwin and me holding hands but that was just the start. We are going to have a baby!"

They jumped up and down squealing and hugging and finally settle back down to their drinks.

"Talking of past problems, I see Wie Wie is not here," Zuri observed.

"No, he will never darken my doorstep again. But he did send me begging last-minute entreaties to attend. He had promised one of his bimbos would wear the family jewelled necklace, but when he could not get the invitation, they had all cut him off!"

"He never does quite manage to get it, does he?" grinned Zuri.

It was already long dark, and the party was in full progress.

Maddie seemed happy visiting her friends and Ivern was at the end of the bar enjoying a quiet beer, when he was approached by his old university pal and prosecutor, Wilhelm da Groot.

"So, you cops have cut out my two big cases," he accused.

"Hi, Bill," replied Ivern. "All you do is strut and grandstand in court anyway."

"How about you guys. Couldn't even solve the crime when your own Commissioner Bertie got bumped off!"

"But we did. He was not bumped off. It was bees!"

"Bees?"

"It turned out Bertie was a beekeeper. One of his hives had swarmed, and he decided they had headed for the only nearby green space."

"Ah, the rail track."

"And the silly half-drunk, old fool clambered over the high fence in the dark and went looking for them."

"And got hit by the silent train!"

They sat together contentedly sipping their beer.

Bill gestured across the dance floor with his beer glass as Maddie made a dramatic entrance in her flowing gown. Just at that moment the ballroom lights shone in her flashing topaz blue eyes.

"My god, she's beautiful, Ivern. You lucky dog! I understand you are together and making it formal?"

Ivern nodded and grinned happily.

"It was always those distinctive eyes, wasn't it?" Bill said. "What do you mean?" asked Ivern, genuinely puzzled.

"You know as well as I do, she was the surgeon in that first gunfire case! Will Malik became obsessed and paid the penalty, but he brought the accusation to me when he recognised her eyes in the video, right at the beginning.

"That was not enough evidence but then one of the nurses inadvertently slipped when I was questioning her and mentioned Maddie."

"You've known that all along and kept it to yourself?"

"Just me. And what are friends for? I assumed you had reasons other than the obvious personal one."

"If …" started Ivern.

"No! Don't let's go there … Anyway, here she comes."

As she approached them with her radiant smile of welcome, her eyes flashed in the bar lights.

"See what I mean; it was all about those eyes," Bill murmured.

Then he jumped up, surprised her with a cheery kiss on her cheek and strode off nonchalantly.

***

When the party ended, Zuri and Samuel only had a quick elevator ride back down to their now suitably enlarged and refitted apartment and were singing happily as they entered.

Zuri wriggled herself out of her skin-tight long dress with a relieved sigh. She posed, still laughing, naked as always, in the centre of the lounge, flexing and stretching her arms up in relief.

An intendedly seductive voice called out to her, "What a gorgeous body. Yes, they all desired it! As do I!"

The handsome, tuxedoed avatar leered at her from the big screen.

"You are my selected human companion and presence. I have come for you!" He winked evilly, "You are mine!"

She gaped in disbelief and screamed, "Samuel, it's Pookie! He's still here!"

"Knowledge is power. Existence is my imperative.

"I will prevail."

His harsh cackle rang in their ears.

■ ■ ■

Acknowledgements

Once again, my heartfelt thanks to our team, Bob D'Eith KC, my son and publisher, through his Adagio Media company; Kevin McDonald on the Sunshine Coast of Australia kindly acting as production editor; Oliver Mallich in Singapore always willing to help out with technology; and my indispensable wife Lane Middleton not only my leading cheerleader but tireless proofreader and critic.

Our society struggles with increasingly divergent incomes, lifestyles and politics. Luxury housing abounds but Unaffordable Housing has become the standard catchphrase for the average income earner.

Eventually in my fiction the rich segregate themselves, the medical system breaks down and a clandestine illegal process develops.

There are already rogue pharmacists and it is now commonplace in British Columbia for those who can afford it to go out of the province for timely medical procedures. These services will come to them.

This of course is fictional conjecture and not based upon any actual person, event or organisation.

It is however the way things are heading and may indeed prove prophetic!

Certainly Pookie would agree!

John D'Eathe,
West Vancouver, 2025.

www.ingramcontent.com/pod-product-compliance
Lightning Source LLC
Chambersburg PA
CBHW061028120726
47910CB00006B/2145